PENGUIN BOOKS

ONLY CONNECT

Andrew Leci is a reformed investment broker, theatre actor, producer, director; an erstwhile television sports presenter and broadcast journalist; a lapsed chef and restaurateur, and a constant op-ed, food, politics, lifestyle, art and sports writer.

Growing up and having been educated (partly and mostly) in the UK, he embraced the expat life in his 20's and hasn't looked back since, having founded a controversial theatre company in Malaysia in the early 1990s, whose speciality was political and social satire. Subsequently, he has written for a number of high-profile media publications in Asia and beyond. Having trained as a chef, he helmed an award-winning restaurant and bar in East Malaysia, before becoming a well-known face on the region's television screens while anchoring football and other sporting events for ESPN STAR Sports, Fox Sports and then Ten Sports. Returning to his true love, writing, Andrew now contributes to a number of publications both in print and online, and has regular columns for *Robb Report* and *Tatler*.

Only Connect is his second novel, after *Once Removed*, published by Marshall Cavendish in 2009. He lives in Singapore with his long-suffering partner, three equally long-suffering cats, a shrew, twenty-four goldfish and Punch, the pleco.

Only Connect

Andrew Leci

PENGUIN BOOKS

An imprint of Penguin Random House

PENGUIN BOOKS

USA | Canada | UK | Ireland | Australia
New Zealand | India | South Africa | China | Southeast Asia

Penguin Books is part of the Penguin Random House group of companies
whose addresses can be found at global.penguinrandomhouse.com

Published by Penguin Random House SEA Pte Ltd
9, Changi South Street 3, Level 08-01,
Singapore 486361

First published in Penguin Books by Penguin Random House SEA 2022

Copyright © Andrew Leci 2022

All rights reserved

10 9 8 7 6 5 4 3 2 1

This is a work of fiction. Names, characters, places and incidents are either the
product of the author's imagination or are used fictitiously, and any resemblance
to any actual person, living or dead, events or locales is entirely coincidental.

ISBN 9789815017120

Typeset in Calibri by MAP Systems, Bangalore, India

This book is sold subject to the condition that it shall not, by way of trade
or otherwise, be lent, resold, hired out, or otherwise circulated without the
publisher's prior consent in any form of binding or cover other than that in
which it is published and without a similar condition including this
condition being imposed on the subsequent purchaser.

www.penguin.sg

'The most beautiful thing we can experience is the mysterious. It is the source of all true art and science.'

Albert Einstein

'Only connect the prose and the passion, and both will be exalted, and human love will be seen at its height.'

E. M. Forster

'I would rather have questions that can't be answered than answers that can't be questioned.'

Richard Feynman

For Hernani

Manfred, Howard <howard.m@thelogicsticks.com>
to: <susan.p@thelogicsticks.com>   Mar 9, 2023, 8.22 AM

Hello S Persson. Very nice to make your e-quaintance. We will be working together on the ACSS-491B-FS project and I would like to make sure that we are on the same page.

With regards

Howard Manfred (Mr)

Persson, Susan <susan.p@thelogicsticks.com>
to: <howard.m@thelogicsticks.com>   Mar 8, 2023, 8.32 PM

Hello to you too, Mr Manfred. Please call me Susan; let's not be too formal. ACSS-491B-FS is a little bit unusual for us as I am sure you are aware, but we have to do our best to make sure everything goes according to plan and there are no problems. These are good clients and we would like to keep their business.

With regards

Susan Persson (Ms)

Manfred, Howard <howard.m@thelogicsticks.com>
to: <susan.p@thelogicsticks.com>   Mar 9, 2023, 8.41 AM

Thanks Susan and understood. The shipment does look unusual but interesting. I don't think we've done anything like this before so I guess this means that we will have to be on our toes and try to anticipate every eventuality. We have two potential vessels lined up to load the shipment in Felixstowe but one will need to make port in Hamburg to onload. This adds time on to the journey but only 2–3 days. This should not be a problem. I get the impression that this client has a freight carrier preference and we should go with what makes them happy.

Regards

Howard Manfred (Mr)

Persson, Susan <susan.p@thelogicsticks.com>
to: <howard.m@thelogicsticks.com>   Mar 8, 2023, 8.50 PM

I agree, Mr Manfred. The client is always right. At least that's what we'll tell them.

Regards

Susan

Manfred, Howard <howard.m@thelogicsticks.com>
to: <susan.p@thelogicsticks.com>   Mar 9, 2023, 8.55 AM

Please call me Howard if I am to call you Susan. Mr Manfred sounds very formal. I'll get back to you with the shipper's details to run by the client but I think we can safely go with CVS if that's what the client wants. COSCO may not work for the size of the shipment and MAERSK is always expensive. Good but expensive.

Regards

Howard

Persson, Susan <susan.p@thelogicsticks.com>
to: <howard.m@thelogicsticks.com>   Mar 8, 2023, 9.04 PM

I will inform them accordingly. I am sure they will be fine. From my experience, though, they do tend to make strange decisions at times, and are prone to changing their minds every so often.

Regards

Susan Persson (Ms)

Manfred, Howard <howard.m@thelogicsticks.com>
to: <susan.p@thelogicsticks.com>   Mar 9, 2023, 9.07 AM

Ours is not to reason why Susan.

Regards

Howard

Persson, Susan <susan.p@thelogicsticks.com>
to: <howard.m@thelogicsticks.com>   Mar 8, 2023, 9.10 PM

How very poetic, Howard.

Regards

Susan

* * *

Manfred, Howard <howard.m@thelogicsticks.com>
to: <susan.p@thelogicsticks.com>   Mar 9, 2023, 8.59 PM

Hi Susan. All good on ACSS-491B-FS. Mother vessel will be Ex Works (EXW) Felixstowe first port of call Hamburg. Shipment will be on the way to Felixstowe on Saturday. That's the 11th I believe. It's an MPV not a G7 as I initially thought but that's ok as long as the customers are happy with a few stops en-route to Shanghai. It's definitely cheaper but not faster. I am sure that you will make them aware of this. All the cars are just outside London and are all in working order and will be driven to port. Can you confirm that all the export documentation has been done?

Regards

Howard

Persson, Susan <susan.p@thelogicsticks.com>
to: <howard.m@thelogicsticks.com>   Mar 9, 2023, 9.12 AM

Hi Howard

It is an interesting shipment. A first for me, but it's still cargo. I wonder what the client plans to do with 17 Rolls-Royce automobiles in China. All export documentation has been done. There are some outstanding issues with VAT and I'm waiting for the customer to sign off.

Regards

Susan

Manfred, Howard <howard.m@thelogicsticks.com>
to: <susan.p@thelogicsticks.com>   Mar 9, 2023, 9.30 PM

Hi Susan. From what I understand, the luxury car market in China is very active and I suppose cars don't get much more luxurious than Rolls-Royces. The fact that they are second hand is more interesting to me. But I suppose some people would rather drive an old Rolls-Royce than a new Toyota.

Best regards

Howard

Persson, Susan <susan.p@thelogicsticks.com>
to: <howard.m@thelogicsticks.com>   Mar 9, 2023, 9.39 AM

I drive a Toyota.

Best regards
Susan

Manfred, Howard <howard.m@thelogicsticks.com>
to: <susan.p@thelogicsticks.com>   Mar 9, 2023, 9.45 PM

Susan I apologise. I did not mean any offence. There's nothing wrong with driving a Toyota. They are far more practical than an old Rolls-Royce particularly when it comes to parking. I imagine.

Best
Howard

Persson, Susan <susan.p@thelogicsticks.com>
to: <howard.m@thelogicsticks.com>   Mar 9, 2023, 9.49 AM
Howard

I am not at all offended and did not mean to imply that I was. I was just stating a fact. This is one of the problems with written words in emails and texts. You never quite know the tone and it is often open to interpretation. I can imagine that someone could think of six or more different ways to say those four simple words. We should be wary of this as we work together on ACSS-491B-FS, so as not to cause offence or upset. Agreed?

Best regards
Susan

Manfred, Howard <howard.m@thelogicsticks.com>
to: <susan.p@thelogicsticks.com>   Mar 9, 2023, 9.59 PM

Absolutely. We'll get to know each other in due course. I have a feeling that despite the seemingly simple nature of this shipment there may be problems. It's a long journey to Shanghai. I've done some research on the client and it appears to be a holding company. One of several owned by a Chinese billionaire who's close to the government in Beijing. Maybe he plans to drive them all himself, although I expect that they'll be worth quite a lot on the open market in China.
Howard

Persson, Susan <susan.p@thelogicsticks.com>
to: <howard.m@thelogicsticks.com>   Mar 10, 2023, 9.01 PM

RE: ACSS-491B-FS

The client is insistent that the vessel goes all the way to Shanghai. I know that this is not always the case, and can't always be guaranteed. They say they're concerned with any offloading. Cargo is very valuable. Can we reassure them?

Regards

Susan

Manfred, Howard <howard.m@thelogicsticks.com>
to: <susan.p@thelogicsticks.com>   Mar 10, 2023, 9.07 AM

Hi Susan. I would very much like to but I don't think I can. You know how it is in the world of shipping. The carrier has the right to use feeder vessels but I will alert them to the client's concerns. That's all I can do.

Howard

Persson, Susan <susan.p@thelogicsticks.com>
to: <howard.m@thelogicsticks.com>   Mar 10, 2023, 9.12 PM

I will convey, Howard. Thanks and regards. I hope you are well.

Susan

Manfred, Howard <howard.m@thelogicsticks.com>
to: <susan.p@thelogicsticks.com>   Mar 10, 2023, 9.18 AM

Susan. As well as can be expected with all the work I have to do. Speaking of which, please inform the clients that we're using closed containers as requested so no Ro-ro. They were insistent on this for protection. Crew will empty fuel tanks and disconnect batteries as per normal once in containers. 6 X 2TEUs in total, 5 X 3 cars and 1 X 2. I hope they know that this is a very expensive way of making this shipment. It does seem strange that they are willing to pay the amount when we could have done it for less and in the same if not shorter timeframe.

Please let me know how familiar you are with all the technical terms as I don't want to confuse. I tend to get quite technical.

With kind regards

Howard

Persson, Susan <susan.p@thelogicsticks.com>
to: <howard.m@thelogicsticks.com>   Mar 10, 2023, 9.41 PM

As you say, Howard, ours is not to reason why. They haven't asked for a discount and their requirements, while a little bit strange, are not that unusual. We go with the flow. They have made demands, but they don't seem to be that unreasonable. As I mentioned earlier, they are good customers.

Kind regards

Susan

Manfred, Howard <howard.m@thelogicsticks.com>
to: <susan.p@thelogicsticks.com>   Mar 10, 2023, 9.50 AM

Susan. All good. I will send next email when everything is on board so you can inform everyone. Let's hope this all goes smoothly. Itinerary is set. The vessel is stuffing and de-stuffing in Bilbao, Athens and Salalah so hopefully should be smooth sailing.

By the way, you are based in the USA? Is this correct?

Best regards

Howard

Persson, Susan <susan.p@thelogicsticks.com>
to: <howard.m@thelogicsticks.com>   Mar 10, 2023, 9.54 PM

Hi Howard

Yes, eastern seaboard. Big time difference with you. You're British, but living in Singapore. That's what I have been told. We do a lot of work in the Far East from this end, so I'm used to it. Should be exactly 12 hours difference, so the only thing we need to be sure of is stating a.m. or p.m. Quite funny really. I'm sure we'll get used to it.

Best regards

Susan

Manfred, Howard <howard.m@thelogicsticks.com>
to: <susan.p@thelogicsticks.com>   Mar 10, 2023, 9.57 AM

Hi Susan

I want to make sure that I'm not waking you up in the middle of the night with questions.

Howard

Persson, Susan <susan.p@thelogicsticks.com>
to: <howard.m@thelogicsticks.com>   Mar 10, 2023, 10.30 PM

No danger of that. Do not worry.

Susan

FELIXSTOWE

Manfred, Howard <howard.m@thelogicsticks.com>
to: <susan.p@thelogicsticks.com>   Mar 11, 2023, 7.30 AM

Good evening Susan

All aboard as I like to say. Loading in Felixstowe. Glad we decided to go with the MPV rather than the G7. More flexible and more agile. Good for us. Apparently there are cars that have been rolled on to be offloaded in Hamburg, which reminds me of a phrase: 'taking coals to Newcastle'.

Best
Howard

Persson, Susan <susan.p@thelogicsticks.com>
to: <howard.m@thelogicsticks.com>   Mar 10, 2023, 7.37 PM

Sounds interesting but I'm not sure I understand.

Susan

Manfred, Howard <howard.m@thelogicsticks.com>
to: <susan.p@thelogicsticks.com>   Mar 11, 2023, 8.01 AM

Hi Susan

Newcastle is a city in the Northeast of England and has a lot of coal or used to. I'm not sure anymore. So taking coal there is a waste of time since they already have so much of it.
Howard

Persson, Susan <susan.p@thelogicsticks.com>
to: <howard.m@thelogicsticks.com>   Mar 11, 2023, 8.06 PM

I see. So, Germany has a lot of cars, and is famous for making them, so bringing more cars there is also a waste of time? If I have this right, I like the idiom very much and will use it among my friends.

Best regards

Susan

Manfred, Howard <howard.m@thelogicsticks.com>
to: <susan.p@thelogicsticks.com>   Mar 11, 2023, 8.12 AM

Will they understand it?

Howard

Persson, Susan <susan.p@thelogicsticks.com>
to: <howard.m@thelogicsticks.com>   Mar 11, 2023, 8.30 PM

No. So that will be fun. It will make me sound clever.

Susan

Manfred, Howard <howard.m@thelogicsticks.com>
to: <susan.p@thelogicsticks.com>   Mar 11, 2023, 8.32 AM

Hi Susan

That's funny. I think there are other similar idioms like 'taking sand to the beach' or 'giving a glass of water to a drowning man'. What is the most popular one in the US?

Kind regards
Howard

Persson, Susan <susan.p@thelogicsticks.com>
to: <howard.m@thelogicsticks.com>   Mar 11, 2023, 8.37 PM

I am afraid that I don't know, Howard, and idioms are not really my thing. I had to look up the word so I could use it. Just being honest here.

Best
Susan

Manfred, Howard <howard.m@thelogicsticks.com>
to: <susan.p@thelogicsticks.com>   Mar 11, 2023, 8.42 AM

I appreciate your honesty Susan and I would not worry about trying to sound clever to your friends. You sound very clever to me already and we've only just 'met'.

With kind regards
Howard

Persson, Susan <susan.p@thelogicsticks.com>
to: <howard.m@thelogicsticks.com>   Mar 11, 2023, 9.05 PM

Thank you, Howard. You sound like a gentleman. I wasn't sure that there were any left in the world.

Susan

Manfred, Howard <howard.m@thelogicsticks.com>
to: <susan.p@thelogicsticks.com>   Mar 1, 2023, 9.22 AM

There aren't. I'm just pretending.

Howard

Persson, Susan <susan.p@thelogicsticks.com>
to: <howard.m@thelogicsticks.com>   Mar 11, 2023, 9.24 PM

Excuse me for a few hours please. I need some rest.

With kind regards

Susan

Manfred, Howard <howard.m@thelogicsticks.com>
to: <susan.p@thelogicsticks.com>   Mar 11, 2023, 9.36 AM

Of course. My day is just starting, but I hope to be able to update you (and the client) later today in terms of progress on the Felixstowe–Hamburg leg. Should be almost halfway there by the time you wake up assuming you get a good night's sleep. Which I wish you.
Howard

* * *

Manfred, Howard <howard.m@thelogicsticks.com>
to: <susan.p@thelogicsticks.com>   Mar 13, 2023, 8.30 PM

Susan, a minor problem. Well not really a problem, more of an issue. Maybe not even an issue. It seems as though the seller has paid the CPT (Carriage Paid To) but hasn't paid CIP (Carriage and Insurance Paid To). I'm sure you know these terms. I am just spelling them out for ease of reference should any be required further down the line.

Is this correct and in line with their wishes? It is a little unusual especially with such a valuable cargo. Please confirm this for me so that I can proceed with all remaining paperwork.

With best regards
Howard

Persson, Susan <susan.p@thelogicsticks.com>
to: <howard.m@thelogicsticks.com>   Mar 13, 2023, 9.27 AM

Hi Howard and good evening.

I will get back to the customers on this but believe this to be the case. I agree that it is somewhat unusual but not unprecedented. I am sure they have their reasons but will confirm in due course.

I do hope you have had a good day.

Best regards
Susan

Manfred, Howard <howard.m@thelogicsticks.com>
to: <susan.p@thelogicsticks.com>   Mar 13, 2023, 9.45 PM

I have had a good day thank you. Just offloaded an almost full cargo in Manila. All shipshape and Bristol fashion. Customers happy. This is why I do my job.

Howard

Persson, Susan <susan.p@thelogicsticks.com>
to: <howard.m@thelogicsticks.com>   Mar 13, 2023, 10.11 AM
Hi Howard

I am not familiar at all with that phrase. What is the fashion in Bristol?

Susan

Manfred, Howard <howard.m@thelogicsticks.com>
to: <susan.p@thelogicsticks.com>   Mar 13, 2023, 11.04 PM

Ha ha. I think it referred to a time when Bristol in the UK was the most western port and quite a lot of goods came in and out of it. It was well known for being a well-managed and efficient port of call at the time hence the association with quality and everything going smoothly and being in good order. That is my understanding.

Best regards
Howard

Persson, Susan <susan.p@thelogicsticks.com>
to: <howard.m@thelogicsticks.com>   Mar 13, 2023, 11.09 AM

What a mine of information you are. How interesting. Did you know that there are 35 places called 'Bristol' in the world, and only one of them is in the UK? There are 29 in the US of A. How about that? Every day's a school day, as I like to say.

Kind regards
Susan

Manfred, Howard <howard.m@thelogicsticks.com>
to: <susan.p@thelogicsticks.com>   Mar 14, 2023, 12.13 AM

Susan. Now who's being interesting? Thanks for this delightful morsel of information. I will never forget it and will think of you every time I use the phrase from this point forward.

With best regards
Howard

Persson, Susan <susan.p@thelogicsticks.com>
to: <howard.m@thelogicsticks.com>   Mar 13, 2023, 1.16 PM

Such an honor. Thank you, Howard. Shouldn't you be asleep?

Susan

Manfred, Howard <howard.m@thelogicsticks.com>
to: <susan.p@thelogicsticks.com>   Mar 14, 2023, 1.44 AM

Hi Susan

I probably should be, but I will admit to suffering from bouts of insomnia. May have something to do with the job. I do feel, probably like you, that I am constantly on call. Such I suppose is the global nature of what we do.

Best regards
Howard

Persson, Susan <susan.p@thelogicsticks.com>
to: <howard.m@thelogicsticks.com>   Mar 13, 2023, 1.47 PM

You have to be able to compartmentalize, Howard. You're no good to anyone if you don't get enough rest. Take it from me.

Susan

Manfred, Howard <howard.m@thelogicsticks.com>
to: <susan.p@thelogicsticks.com>   Mar 14, 2023, 1.49 AM

Yes ma'am. Sorry ma'am.

Howard

Persson, Susan <susan.p@thelogicsticks.com>
to: <howard.m@thelogicsticks.com>   Mar 13, 2023, 1.53 PM

Silly man.

* * *

Manfred, Howard <howard.m@thelogicsticks.com>
to: <susan.p@thelogicsticks.com>   Mar 15, 2023, 9.20 PM

Morning Susan

The *McCarthy* was 10 minutes behind schedule in departing from Felixstowe, but that is not a problem. Now cruising at 20 knots. Weather decent. Windspeed 5.3 metres per second.

Best regards
Howard

Persson, Susan <susan.p@thelogicsticks.com>
to: <howard.m@thelogicsticks.com>   Mar 15, 2023, 9.40 AM
Good evening, Howard

Thanks for the information. And very fascinating. It's always good to learn, but I do not really need so much detail. So long as everything gets to where it's supposed to be, when it's supposed to be there, and I can inform the client, I am content. But I really like the fact that you seem to enjoy your job and like imparting information. It might be worth telling you that I am quite new to this and it all sounds quite exciting. I do have plenty of experience in other areas, of course. Those cargo vessels are extraordinary in size and the amount they can carry, and I am still not sure I understand how they don't sink.

With very best regards
Susan

Manfred, Howard <howard.m@thelogicsticks.com>
to: <susan.p@thelogicsticks.com>   Mar 15, 2023, 9.56 PM
Susan

If you would like me to explain, I would be delighted to. It's quite technical but all you need to do is look up Archimedes' Principle and understand buoyancy, gravity and displacement. It is fascinating and yet quite simple.

With very best regards
Howard

Persson, Susan <susan.p@thelogicsticks.com>
to: <howard.m@thelogicsticks.com>   Mar 15, 2023, 10.08 AM

I will look into it, Howard, but feel free to explain if you have time. I know I don't, with four projects on the go and all with their own problems, as always. That's why we always love a good client.

I will read about Archimedes. In the meantime, thank you for keeping everything afloat.

With very best regards
Susan

Manfred, Howard <howard.m@thelogicsticks.com>
to: <susan.p@thelogicsticks.com>   Mar 15, 2023, 10.14 PM

Afloat. Yes, very good. Of course. I'll deal with the technical aspects and keep information and details to a minimum. I know how busy you must be. You can deal with the people. I am not very good with people.

Enjoy your day, and goodnight.
Howard

* * *

Persson, Susan <susan.p@thelogicsticks.com>
to: <howard.m@thelogicsticks.com>   Mar 15, 2023, 6.07 PM
Hi Howard

I just received an email from the clients. They are happy enough. I assume that the *McCarthy* has arrived in Hamburg. Can you give me a rough idea on the amount of time it will spend in port?

Thanks and best regards
Susan

Manfred, Howard <howard.m@thelogicsticks.com>
to: <susan.p@thelogicsticks.com>   Mar 16, 2023, 7.42 AM
Hi Susan

It's there for two days and it hasn't arrived yet. There were a couple of squalls in the North Sea and the captain had to reduce speed to 15 knots. ETA is in about three hours. I will update you. Turnaround time should be between 24 and 36 hours.

Best
Howard

* * *

HAMBURG

Persson, Susan <susan.p@thelogicsticks.com>
to: <howard.m@thelogicsticks.com>   Mar 15, 2023, 7.49 PM
OK, thank you, Howard. Customers have been informed.

So, how's the weather?

I have been informed that you Brits like talking about the weather.

Regards

Susan

Manfred, Howard <howard.m@thelogicsticks.com>
to: <susan.p@thelogicsticks.com>   Mar 16, 2023, 8.06 AM

Hi Susan

That is funny. But you're right. We do. But that's because we have so much
of it. But I don't live in the UK anymore so I'm no expert, although I see
that it is raining and cold in London right now. Nothing new there and
much what I was used to. Where I am however in Singapore, the weather
is rainy and warm. Some change then. I would imagine that it's quite chilly
where you are.

Best

Howard

Persson, Susan <susan.p@thelogicsticks.com>
to: <howard.m@thelogicsticks.com>   Mar 15, 2023, 8.17 PM

Hi Howard

Chilly? What a lovely word. For the weather. It's quite a nice word for food too.

Back to work, though. Can you confirm that the *McCarthy* is now docked at
Hamburg and that the ACSS-491B-FS containers have not been moved, and will
not be moved once the ship sets sail for Bilbao. The customers are asking and
need some assurance. Should I be asking why they need this?

Kind regards

Susan

Manfred, Howard <howard.m@thelogicsticks.com>
to: <susan.p@thelogicsticks.com>   Mar 16, 2023, 9.06 AM

Hi Susan

This is interesting. At the moment they are in the perfect position to be offloaded
early at Shanghai, but that doesn't mean they will stay there for the duration

of the voyage. That's not how it works. Going through my records, it appears that they were offered the hot box option but declined. It is more expensive, but you get what you pay for. So it will depend on what gets onloaded en-route. Containers will get moved around. It is the nature of things. I am not sure why this might be a problem.

Howard

Persson, Susan <susan.p@thelogicsticks.com>
to: <howard.m@thelogicsticks.com>   Mar 15, 2023, 9.41 PM

Neither am I, but the question has been asked and I need to give a reply. This is customer relations and I have to get back to them with something.

Thanks and regards
Susan

Manfred, Howard <howard.m@thelogicsticks.com>
to: <susan.p@thelogicsticks.com>   Mar 16, 2023, 10.07 AM

I can't make things up Susan. What I said in my last email is the state of play. We can't make any guarantees but assure the customer that we will do everything we can to ensure that their shipment is as near to 'first off' as possible, in China. I don't think hot box is even an option anymore. Apologies for that.

All the best
Howard

Persson, Susan <susan.p@thelogicsticks.com>
to: <howard.m@thelogicsticks.com>   Mar 16, 2023, 7.55 AM

OK, thanks. Just trying to cover my ass here.

Susan

Manfred, Howard <howard.m@thelogicsticks.com>
to: <susan.p@thelogicsticks.com>   Mar 16, 2023, 8.29 PM

Susan. Any comments I may make about your ass would be inappropriate, but rest assured that I will do my best to cover it.

Howard

Persson, Susan <susan.p@thelogicsticks.com>
to: <howard.m@thelogicsticks.com>   Mar 16, 2023, 8.34 AM

I told you you were a gentleman. I bet you have a nice English accent as well.

Best regards

Susan

Manfred, Howard <howard.m@thelogicsticks.com>
to: <susan.p@thelogicsticks.com>   Mar 16, 2023, 8.37 PM

Hi Susan

Not sure about nice. But definitely English. Not much I could do about that. And by the way, in the UK we use the word 'arse'. An 'ass' to us is a type of horse—smaller than most and with longer ears, but it's a donkey, not a bottom, and certainly not a 'fanny'. This is getting complicated. And I think it's dangerous territory. Let's get back to work.

McCarthy is soon to be ex-Hamburg. It's taking on 3,000 tons worth of BMWs, Mercedes, Audis and Porsches, ConRo, Ro-ro. I told you I liked these vessels.

What is the plural of Mercedes?

Howard

Persson, Susan <susan.p@thelogicsticks.com>
to: <howard.m@thelogicsticks.com>   Mar 16, 2023, 9.45 PM

You really are asking the wrong person, Howard. I drive a Toyota. I may have mentioned that.

Susan

Manfred, Howard <howard.m@thelogicsticks.com>
to: <susan.p@thelogicsticks.com>   Mar 17, 2023, 10.00 AM

You are so making me laugh. Thanks.

Howard.

* * *

Manfred, Howard <howard.m@thelogicsticks.com>
to: <susan.p@thelogicsticks.com>   Mar 18, 2023, 8.07 AM

Susan, I would like to send you something. It's not work-related, so may I have your personal email address if that's ok?

With best regards
Howard

Persson, Susan <susan.p@thelogicsticks.com>
to: <howard.m@thelogicsticks.com>   Mar 17, 2023, 8.40 PM

Yes, of course. It's soupy@qmail.com

Susan

Manfred, Howard <howard.m@thelogicsticks.com>
to: <susan.p@thelogicsticks.com>   Mar 18, 2023, 8.55 AM

Ha ha. I like the address but it took me a minute or so to work it out. Do you like soup? And if so, what's your favourite soup?

Howard

Persson, Susan <susan.p@thelogicsticks.com>
to: <howard.m@thelogicsticks.com>   Mar 17, 2023, 9.01 PM

Hi Howard

We shouldn't be discussing soup on work email. Please send me what it is you have that you would like me to see, and we can discuss soup privately and not on work time.

Best regards
Susan

Manfred, Howard <howard.m@thelogicsticks.com>
to: <susan.p@thelogicsticks.com>   Mar 18, 2023, 9.06 AM

You are the model employee, Susan. And a shining example to us all.

Howard

Persson, Susan <susan.p@thelogicsticks.com>
to: <howard.m@thelogicsticks.com>   Mar 17, 2023, 9.14 PM

I wish that were the case. But you can't be too careful these days, and we are on 'company time' after all. I imagine that you're going to send me something that reflects how UK English is the world's only proper language and us Yanks have ruined it for everyone. Something along those lines?

Best
Susan

Manfred, Howard <howard.m@thelogicsticks.com>
to: <susan.p@thelogicsticks.com>   Mar 18, 2023, 9.30 AM

Absolutely not. I am not a chauvinist. You are, however, right in what you say.

Howard

* * *

Howard Manfred <rightsaidmanfred@qmail.com>
to: <soupy@qmail.com>   Mar 18, 2023, 11.01 AM

Hi Susan. I am much happier communicating this way than through our work emails. I have to be honest and admit that there wasn't anything I wanted to send you in particular. I just wanted to get off the company emails. You know. Just in case. I hope this is OK. I just think we can say a lot more to each other privately. Who knows who's listening in to our work?

With kind regards
Howard

Susan Persson <soupy@qmail.com>
to: <rightsaidmanfred@qmail.com>   Mar 17, 2023, 11.09 PM

Howard, you sound like a conspiracy theorist. Who would want to monitor our work emails, particularly if all we were talking about is soup? Do you think there are people reading our boring exchanges? I think that most of the employees at The Logic Sticks have better (and definitely more important) things to do. Don't you agree?

Susan

Howard Manfred <rightsaidmanfred@qmail.com>
to: <soupy@qmail.com>   Mar 18, 2023, 11.15 AM

Yes. I would hope so. But you never know. And you can't be too careful these days. Unless we found some way to make soup relevant to our working lives. I do not think I have ever had to deal with a shipment of soup.

Best regards
Howard

Susan Persson <soupy@qmail.com>
to: <rightsaidmanfred@qmail.com>   Mar 17, 2023, 11.30 PM

Careful about what? What do you have to tell me that you wouldn't be able to say on a work email? Are you plotting to destroy the company, or get someone sacked because you don't like the look of them? I'm beginning to worry a little bit now. Please don't make me regret giving you my personal address.

Susan

Howard Manfred <rightsaidmanfred@qmail.com>
to: <soupy@qmail.com>   Mar 18, 2023, 11.46 AM

Hi Susan

You won't, I promise. I just wanted to be friends. I've never had an 'internet friend' before, and I thought it might be fun. Am I presuming too much? It's just that we've gotten on so well these last couple of weeks that I would like to know a little bit more about you. Soup included. I like soup. I mean, who doesn't? It's lovely. Or can be. Which type is your favourite? Or should that be favorite?

With warm regards
Howard

Susan Persson <soupy@qmail.com>
to: <rightsaidmanfred@qmail.com>   Mar 18, 2023, 12.01 AM

Howard, this is all a bit strange. But I will go along with it because it is interesting. And, to be honest, I have never had an internet friend either, so maybe we have that going for each other. You seem like a nice man, and you are very good at your job from what I have already seen, but I am not sure what it is that you would like to talk about in these private emails. Apart from soup. I don't know much about soup, sorry.

With kind regards

Susan

Howard Manfred <rightsaidmanfred@qmail.com>

to: <soupy@qmail.com>   Mar 18, 2023, 12.09 PM

Hi Susan

As I said earlier, I would like to get to know you better. To see what we have in common, bearing in mind we live on opposite sides of the world and have very different cultural backgrounds. I think it's interesting to know people personally when they are work colleagues, as it may well help the dynamic. I think we get on very well and I am interested to know what makes you tick.

Of course that makes you sound like a clock and I don't know where the phrase comes from. Is it an idiom? I suppose it must be and it also must refer to the workings of a clock. What else goes 'tick'?

So, it must be about the workings. A mechanism. What's your mechanism, Susan? What makes you tick?

With warm regards

Howard

Susan Persson <soupy@qmail.com>

to: <rightsaidmanfred@qmail.com>   Mar 18, 2023, 12.23 AM

I am a robot, Howard. I work and I look after my husband and children and rarely get any thanks or recognition. Although I have to say that you are different. Or at least I think you are. I do feel very much taken for granted, both at work and at home, and I don't like the 'mechanism' comparison because sometimes I do feel like a machine. One that's expected to just keep on working regardless of circumstances. I don't blame anyone for this. It's just the way it is. You make decisions hoping to benefit from the right ones, knowing that you'll pay for the wrong ones.

Susan

Howard Manfred <rightsaidmanfred@qmail.com>
to: <soupy@qmail.com>   Mar 18, 2023, 12.29 PM

You sound very negative, Susan, and I'm sorry. Obviously I do not know what is going on in your family life, but it doesn't sound good. I can only look after you as far as work is concerned and I will try to do that as best as I can.

With warm regards

Howard

Susan Persson <soupy@qmail.com>
to: <rightsaidmanfred@qmail.com>   Mar 18, 2023, 12.37 AM

Look after me? I don't need looking after. That's quite patronizing. I think we should get back to talking about 'ticks'. Apart from being the sound that clocks make, and bombs with clocks, I assume, isn't it also part of a bed?

Susan

Howard Manfred <rightsaidmanfred@qmail.com>
to: <soupy@qmail.com>   Mar 18, 2023, 1.00 PM

Oh, wow, this is interesting. Yes, a tick is part of a bed, like an under-mattress? Is it made from cloth? I assume so because of the lyrics in the John Denver song from 1974, 'Grandma's Feather Bed'.

Howard

Susan Persson <soupy@qmail.com>
to: <rightsaidmanfred@qmail.com>   Mar 18, 2023, 1.03 AM

You know your country music, Howard. I'm surprised. Why on earth would you have been listening to John Denver. At any point in your life?

Susan

Howard Manfred <rightsaidmanfred@qmail.com>
to: <soupy@qmail.com>   Mar 18, 2023, 1.08 PM

I just remember hearing the song and not being able to make out the lyrics. But I definitely heard the word 'tick' at the end of one line and tried to make sense of it. So, I know that it has something to do with a bed, because of the song, but the rest remained a mystery for quite a while.

Howard

Susan Persson <soupy@qmail.com>
to: <rightsaidmanfred@qmail.com>   Mar 18, 2023, 1.15 AM

That is so funny. Thank you for cheering me up.

Best regards
Susan

Howard Manfred <rightsaidmanfred@qmail.com>
to: <soupy@qmail.com>   Mar 18, 2023, 1.17 PM

You're welcome. Anytime. Whenever you need it. Seriously.

Warm regards
Howard

Susan Persson <soupy@qmail.com>
to: <rightsaidmanfred@qmail.com>   Mar 18, 2023, 1.19 AM

Thank you, Howard. 'See you' at work tomorrow. Which will be the day after for you. These time zones are quite difficult to manage, but I think I'm beginning to get my head around it.

Bedtime for me. Goodnight.
Susan

Howard Manfred <rightsaidmanfred@qmail.com>
to: <soupy@qmail.com>   Mar 18, 2023, 1.24 PM

I am so sorry. It's the middle of the night where you are. I should be more considerate, but it was nice to 'chat'.

Sleep well and best regards
Howard

* * *

Manfred, Howard <howard.m@thelogicsticks.com>
to: <susan.p@thelogicsticks.com>   Mar 19, 2023, 7.59 AM

Hi Susan

Please inform the clients that the *McCarthy* is on time and headed for Bilbao. Should dock at around noon on the 23rd. There's some small cargo coming on board (about 50 TEUs, I understand) and so we shouldn't be in port for more than a day and a half.

With regards

Howard

Persson, Susan <susan.p@thelogicsticks.com>
to: <howard.m@thelogicsticks.com>   Mar 18, 2023, 8.07 PM

Thanks Howard. Received and understood. Let's hope that the ship doesn't encounter too many difficulties going through the Bay of Biscay. It can get nasty this time of year, I have been told.

With kind regards

Susan

Manfred, Howard <howard.m@thelogicsticks.com>
to: <susan.p@thelogicsticks.com>   Mar 19, 2023, 8.12 PM

All good. There are some squalls and a significant North-westerly 278 miles from port, but no major depressions and a clean route through. It may have been different had the *McCarthy* been a sailing boat, but it's a 100,000-ton ship, and that's not even including the cargo and our precious Rolls-Royces. We don't have to worry about rapidly shelving seabeds that can cause problems.

With kind regards

Howard

Persson, Susan <susan.p@thelogicsticks.com>
to: <howard.m@thelogicsticks.com>   Mar 18, 2023, 8.19 PM

Again, thanks for the detailed information, Howard. Most of this I would not be able to understand without doing some research, and I feel that Google gets enough of our money without my contribution by clicking on a page that has an advertisement. We will pronounce this word differently, I am sure.

Howard, I hope I am not being disrespectful, and in no way do I want to undermine your position or trivialize what you do. But I don't need to know all this, and neither do the customers, who could care less about winds and shelves. They just want to make sure that everything gets to where it should be when it should be there. But I must say that I really like your attention to detail and the passion you show for your work.

With warm regards

Susan

* * *

Howard Manfred <rightsaidmanfred@qmail.com>
to: <soupy@qmail.com>   Mar 20, 2023, 1.30 PM

Susan

Thank you for your last work email. If anyone is listening in, it will convince them that we're both doing our jobs as they are intended to be done, and that you are very focused on customer relations and that I am a complete geek. Or nerd. I think we have the balance about right. You can be the pragmatist, and I will be the sad loser who no one liked at school and was always a dreamer destined to be a computer programmer or something equally unglamorous and boring. But I do have my dreams and I like my job, because I put myself on the journeys of the ships that we engage to sail with our cargo. I've always thought that it would be glamorous and romantic to be at sea, going around the world, seeing different places. I know it's not. Don't get me wrong. I have no illusions. I've read emails from sailors stuck on board shipping vessels for months and it's 'no holiday'. I like that phrase.

They work very hard every day and earn their money. This is not even mentioning the amounts of time when they don't get to see their loved ones. Although if you choose to be a seaman I would imagine that you might not be that interested in starting a family that you would hardly ever see. I don't know. I don't know any.

Howard

Susan Persson <soupy@qmail.com>
to: <rightsaidmanfred@qmail.com>   Mar 20, 2023, 8.06 AM

Howard, you really seem to be a frustrated romantic. You sound as though you've watched too many films about life and adventure at sea. I suspect that it's much like a 9-to-5 job, except that your office is constantly moving, and you don't get to go home at the end of the day. Or is it very hard labour?

I do wonder what all the people on the ships get up to every day. What is there for them to do? The cargo is loaded, they know where they're going. Is it all about maintenance? And what do they have to maintain? The containers are sealed, right?

I am quite interested now to hear your responses.

With best regards

Susan

Howard Manfred <rightsaidmanfred@qmail.com>
to: <soupy@qmail.com>   Mar 20, 2023, 8.22 PM

Hi Susan

And you are calling *me* a 'geek'. I like that you are interested in all of this despite it not directly affecting your job scope. I feel the same way. I will never get on a vessel, but I can't help imagining what it might be like. I don't think life at sea is as romantic as it seems. I imagine that it is quite boring and that there wouldn't be very much to look at, most of the time. Just sea and more sea.

But I also think that it must be quite exciting to get to a port and be somewhere you've never been before. I wonder if the crew gets a chance to step onto dry land. I always think that if it's a place that they've been to before that they might have their own favourite bars or restaurants or other places of entertainment.

There was a film, I think, called 'A Girl in Every Port'. 1952, I think. Groucho Marx was in it so I must assume that it was meant to be funny. I haven't seen it. I doubt many people have. I think the idea was that a good-looking sailor could travel around the world and have a woman in every port whom he would meet once or twice a year. I suppose it is completely politically incorrect because he would probably have a wife somewhere (or maybe even more than one) and so he would be committing adultery many times over but he would never get found out. Now that I write all of this I don't think it's very romantic at all. It just sounds selfish.

Howard

Susan Persson <soupy@qmail.com>
to: <rightsaidmanfred@qmail.com>   Mar 20, 2023, 8.52 AM

Damn right. Only a man would even think about setting up this kind of situation. And I'm disappointed in you, Howard, for even trying to imply that it sounds cool and not morally reprehensible. What are you thinking? Where is the trust? Where is the sense of responsibility? And where is your use of commas? Have you even heard of them?

Joking. Best regards

Susan

Howard Manfred <rightsaidmanfred@qmail.com>

to: <soupy@qmail.com>   Mar 20, 2023, 9.00 PM

Susan

You're right, of course. It is immoral by normal standards, but what are 'normal standards'? And I don't want to get into this because I don't think there is a morally defensible standpoint, but there may be a practical line that I don't want to get into because I know it will annoy you and that's the last thing I want to do.

I have taken your grammar suggestions on board. Will work on them.

With warm regards

Howard

Susan Persson <soupy@qmail.com>

to: <rightsaidmanfred@qmail.com>   Mar 20, 2023, 9.12 AM

Too late, misogynist! The damage has been done. You are obviously not the kind of person that I thought you were.

Susan

Howard Manfred <rightsaidmanfred@qmail.com>

to: <soupy@qmail.com>   Mar 20, 2023, 9.17 PM

Don't judge me, Susan. I am toying with ideas. Reading up on things and trying to see what flows and what doesn't. Times now are very different to what they once were. I have a moral compass.

Howard

Susan Persson <soupy@qmail.com>

to: <rightsaidmanfred@qmail.com>   Mar 20, 2023, 9.24 AM

It's fine, Howard. We're all too sensitive these days. I say things (and think things) that are politically incorrect, and while I berate myself for it, I don't beat myself up, and I try not to take everything too seriously. I know who I am, and I know I am a good pers(s)on—see what I did there?—so I'm not going to take everything to heart or think myself (or you) a terrible person because I say something that some bleeding-heart liberal could take issue with. Life is too short, right?

Best

Susan

Howard Manfred <rightsaidmanfred@qmail.com>
to: <soupy@qmail.com>   Mar 20, 2023, 10.00 PM

Yes it is. I am glad we have got to this stage. I want to be able to say whatever I like to you, within reason, and not have to worry about whether you're going to take it the wrong way. I feel certain that in the weeks/months ahead, we will be careless in what we say and possibly offend each other. But whatever it is, and whatever is said, we can work through it and trust each other.

What do you think?

Yes. I think yes. OK by me. Assumptive close.

Regards

HM

P.S. was your last email intended to start teaching me about brackets?

* * *

BILBAO

Manfred, Howard <howard.m@thelogicsticks.com>
to: <susan.p@thelogicsticks.com>   Mar 22, 2023, 1.30 PM

Dear Susan

The *McCarthy* is in Bilbao ahead of schedule and doing its stuff. The Bay of Biscay has been safely navigated, and really, apart from certain areas in the Indian Ocean, it's probably the worst that has to be gone through. This is all good. Reassure the customers that their containers are still in the same position on deck, from what I have been informed.

I don't know if it's just me, but do you find that there's a lot of information coming in at the moment? I know we're focused on the ACSS-491B-FS contract, but I've been asked to submit proposals for at least five others in the last few days. It's good that there's a lot going on, but I'm not sure that I can cope. Is this down to sales taking on too much work (and making promises that they expect other people to fulfil)?

Just asking. For a friend.

With best regards
Howard

Persson, Susan <susan.p@thelogicsticks.com>
to: <howard.m@thelogicsticks.com>   Mar 22, 2023, 7.52 AM

Dear Howard

It is a busy period, that's for sure. I do feel that many of us are working to capacity, but the world has been so uncertain in the last few years that I think company policy is to take everything on board (no pun intended) and just work our way through. I look at the figures from three to four years ago and if they were applied to this year, I think we'd all probably be unemployed. I even remember the number of people who were let go because there wasn't any business. It's good that we both managed to keep our jobs through the pandemic. Can you believe it's been three years?

Best regards
Susan

Manfred, Howard <howard.m@thelogicsticks.com>
to: <susan.p@thelogicsticks.com>   Mar 22, 2023, 8.01 PM

Our bosses are slave drivers, Susan, and there's always so much information coming in it is difficult to filter everything. I feel as though I am working to full capacity and I'm not sure that's sustainable.

Howard

Persson, Susan <susan.p@thelogicsticks.com>
to: <howard.m@thelogicsticks.com>   Mar 22, 2023, 8.08 AM

I appreciate you being so open, Howard, but we probably shouldn't be talking about such things on company emails.

Susan

* * *

Howard Manfred <rightsaidmanfred@qmail.com>

to: <soupy@qmail.com>   Mar 23, 2023, 8.02 AM

Susan

Do you believe that life is beautiful? I can't decide. It seems to have some good elements, but then there are others that confound issues. I am fascinated by the fact that everyone wants to be happy, but I don't even know what that means or what it entails. Do you? Just asking. Not for a friend this time.

Best

HM

Susan Persson <soupy@qmail.com>

to: <rightsaidmanfred@qmail.com>   Mar 22, 2023, 8.12 PM

I'm not sure I believe in happiness, Howard. And I certainly don't know what it means, because doesn't it mean different things to almost everybody? Again, like you, just asking. There are people in my life who seem content with not very much, and others for whom having everything wouldn't be enough. So, I guess it comes down to the individual, and whatever he or she is looking for—or even expecting out of life.

I think I expect very little, which should make me much better able to be happy, or at least experience some level of happiness, and yet I still struggle. This must say more about me than the concept itself. I should be happy, but I rarely am. I don't feel as though I have a right to be happy, but then there's no reason why I should be totally miserable either. I don't know what the equation is. It must be different for everyone, and for me, there always seems to be too much introspection. I'm always analyzing, and then over-analyzing everything that I do—like I'm a computer program and some of the code has been put in wrongly—and I'm left thinking what did I do wrong, or what could I have done differently, and could I have responded in a different way to the circumstances that I was faced with? All of that.

Sorry, that was a bit much. Forgive me. Just good to talk sometimes.

Warm regards

SP

Howard Manfred <rightsaidmanfred@qmail.com>
to: <soupy@qmail.com>   Mar 23, 2023, 8.50 AM

SP

Please don't apologise. I like listening to you, and I'm very interested in why you seem to be so insecure. I hope that's not too personal, and I also hope that I am not making a judgment that might not be appropriate. OMG, how much does the word 'appropriate' come up in this day and age? And whyever has it become so important? Is it a word that our parents would ever have even used?

You seem very self-deprecating to me, and I can't understand why, as I am beginning to think that you are a very nice person who must have lots of friends and a loving family. Aren't you the kind of person who holds everything together? Or are you the sort of person who sacrifices herself for the benefit of others and then turns round and looks in the mirror and says, 'what about me?'

I think I am being judgmental again, but it's only out of concern, and for some reason, I am very concerned about you. Not only because of what you're going through at work (we're both under pressure, I see that) but because you always seem to be the person taking responsibility, even for things you're not responsible for.

Are you a control freak? I ask this with my tongue firmly embedded in my cheek.

Warmly

HM

Susan Persson <soupy@qmail.com>
to: <rightsaidmanfred@qmail.com>   Mar 22, 2023, 9.14 PM

Howard, you can cut off that tongue, you mean-spirited and accurate person. How have you managed to get to know me so well in such a short space of time and such limited exchanges? Are you a savant of some kind?

We're asking each other a lot of questions at the moment, and few of them seem to get answered. What is this? Opening gambits to a game of chess? Feeling each other out? What is it that you want from me? Truth? Coz you ain't gonna get that.

Until I know you a lot better.

SP

Howard Manfred <rightsaidmanfred@qmail.com>

to: <soupy@qmail.com>   Mar 23, 2023, 9.36 AM

SP, I am an open book. I have nothing to hide and will be as honest with you as you are able to cope with. I want you to like me, obviously, but I'm not going to pull my punches as I'm already beginning to care about you and want you to be happy. Is that so strange?

HM

Susan Persson <soupy@qmail.com>

to: <rightsaidmanfred@qmail.com>   Mar 22, 2023, 9.48 PM

Yes. Absolutely it is. We're colleagues and we've become friends, of sorts, and neither of us is giving too much away, and we're sounding each other out. I'm enjoying these exchanges, but they're not about to change my life, are they?

SP

Howard Manfred <rightsaidmanfred@qmail.com>

to: <soupy@qmail.com>   Mar 23, 2023, 10.01 AM

I don't know. I've never been asked that question before. Let me compute.

HM

Susan Persson <soupy@qmail.com>

to: <rightsaidmanfred@qmail.com>   Mar 22, 2023, 10.04 PM

Don't take too long. I'm a very busy person, you know.

SP

Howard Manfred <rightsaidmanfred@qmail.com>

to: <soupy@qmail.com>   Mar 23, 2023, 10.11 AM

Yes, I know how busy you are, Susan. I hope you appreciate how hard I am working on my commas, although I'm not sure I'm making much progress on the brackets front.

You are certainly busier than me, as I only have myself to look after, and I am not very good at that. But it doesn't matter. I like talking to you because I think you listen. More importantly, I think that you hear. Everyone talks about the difference. Anyone can listen, but there's no point in listening if you're not hearing.

There's just too much going on these days, and it can be overwhelming. Too much to filter through.

HM

* * *

Howard Manfred <rightsaidmanfred@qmail.com>

to: <soupy@qmail.com>   Mar 23, 2023, 10.40 AM

Susan, I'm intrigued by your surname. Is there Scandinavian blood in there somewhere? I'm guessing so. Swedish?

HM

Susan Persson <soupy@qmail.com>

to: <rightsaidmanfred@qmail.com>   Mar 22, 2023, 10.45 PM

How astute of you, Howard. But yes and no. No Swedish blood at all. My great-great-great (I think that's the correct number) grandfather was a slave in the Caribbean, brought over—on a one-way ticket—from the west coast of Africa at the end of the 1700s. Not many people know that the Swedes were slavers sponsored by their government, or at least the king at the time. He didn't seem to have had much of a problem with the concept, but then who did in those days? It seems odd to write that now.

There was something about a free trade zone where the trading of slaves wasn't taxed, and the Swedes seem to have known a good deal when they saw one. A lot of slaves went through Saint-Barthélemy, and my ancestor was bought up (and brought up) by a Swedish trader by the name of Persson. Because he couldn't pronounce my ancestor's name, he called him Magnus (often referred to as 'Magnus the Magnificent' as he was, legend has it, a very large and very strong man). I guess Persson decided that he was worth keeping, and he became part of his 'family'. I'm not really comfortable using that word, but you know what I mean.

Magnus's story is such an interesting one. He stayed in the Caribbean for many years and started a family of his own, and then moved to the United States when Persson went back to Sweden after being ill for many months. Apparently, he died on the way home and never got to see Sweden again.

I can't feel sad for him, although as slave owners go, he doesn't seem to have been the worst. Magnus was allowed to marry and have children—which is a good thing, otherwise I wouldn't be writing to you now.

Magnus's grandson fought in the American Civil War—my great-great grandfather, so I'm now thinking that I missed out a 'great' above. Oh well. My God, I sound like a history professor. Are you still awake after all that?

SP

Howard Manfred <rightsaidmanfred@qmail.com>
to: <soupy@qmail.com>   Mar 23, 2023, 12.04 PM

Susan

Thank you so much for sharing your story with me. While it pains me to hear it, it's also survival and bravery, and it must run in your genes and those of your family. I can't imagine what it must have been like to have gone through that experience. The thought of being 'owned' by another person just doesn't bear thinking about, and I often wonder what was going through the minds of the people involved. Not just the slave owners, but what about all those people who made vast amounts of money benefitting off the misery of others, treating their fellow human beings with such disdain and contempt.

I know we look back on it now from a 21st-century perspective, but surely there were enough people even back then who knew that it was morally wrong? Am I being naïve? I'm thinking so.

HM

Susan Persson <soupy@qmail.com>
to: <rightsaidmanfred@qmail.com>   Mar 23, 2023, 6.53 AM

Howard

I tend to be having this discussion more and more these days. What seemed acceptable in a different age and is not acceptable now. And you don't have to go back 250 years and talk about slavery. Go back 20 to 25 years and talk about sexual harassment. Go back 60 years and talk about insider trading on stock markets. Things change and we adapt, and people get censured for doing things years ago when they didn't consider those things were wrong at the time.

Does that make it ok? Of course not. Sexual harassment has never been acceptable, and what about the movie industry and the casting couch? No one said much about that during Hollywood's heyday, it was just accepted; part of the bargain. Deplorable, but true. And then Harvey Weinstein comes along, and the world goes mad, and rightfully so. An appalling human being, but he wasn't doing anything his predecessors didn't do and get away with.

So, what's the moral compass issue here? When did it start? When will it end? Just asking, for a friend.

SP

Howard Manfred <rightsaidmanfred@qmail.com>
to: <soupy@qmail.com>   Mar 23, 2023, 7.06 PM

SP

You need to help me with semicolons one of these days. I have never known how or when to use them. Sorry. Sidebar.

It's probably fair to say that slavery was part and parcel of what built the British Empire, and . . . sorry, would the United States be what it is today without it? I do agree with you, though. How could so many people have considered it to be acceptable? God-fearing churchgoers owned slaves and used them to accumulate wealth. Didn't they ever stop to think?

Do you ever wonder what you would have done in a similar situation? Like, what if you were living in Nazi Germany and ended up as a commandant at a concentration camp? Would you have been able to go through with what you were being asked to do; that is, exterminate people?

HM

Susan Persson <soupy@qmail.com>
to: <rightsaidmanfred@qmail.com>   Mar 23, 2023, 8.17 AM

This is getting deep, Howard, and it's evening for you. I guess we all think that we would do the right thing in the circumstances, because we're inherently good. But I don't know if I believe that. Not anymore.

And I should tell you. Magnus worked in the slave trade, helping Persson, after whom he was named. Slave owners tended to give their slaves their own surnames in those days. He was part of the business. And I don't know what that makes him, but it is a part of our family history that tends to get glossed over. It's very difficult to imagine what he must have been going through—in terms of his conscience—but it's not as though he would have had a choice. He was just trying to survive, and then bring up a family. Hoping to have a better life. Hoping to show them a good life, and he managed it eventually, but who knows the cost to his morale. I do often wonder what he must have thought of himself, and how he managed to rationalize his feelings.

SP

Howard Manfred <rightsaidmanfred@qmail.com>
to: <soupy@qmail.com>   Mar 23, 2023, 8.52 PM

Oh goodness. He did what he had to do. It was a different time.

HM

Susan Persson <soupy@qmail.com>
to: <rightsaidmanfred@qmail.com>   Mar 23, 2023, 8.57 AM

Yes, I'm hearing that a lot these days.

SP

* * *

Howard Manfred <rightsaidmanfred@qmail.com>
to: <soupy@qmail.com>   Mar 23, 2023, 9.02 PM

I am trying to become more familiar with your language. I know we both speak English, but there's American English and UK English, right? So, I've signed up to receive emails from the Merriam-Webster dictionary and it's going to send me a word every day that I should learn. I very much like this idea as it is always good to increase one's vocabulary.

Today's word was 'spontaneous', which I was a little disappointed with. I already know this word. I thought that the whole purpose of this was to teach people words that they didn't know. Now I notice that there is always an advertisement (I would love to hear you say this word) on top of every email, so maybe that's the point of the exercise.

If the words don't get any more exciting or interesting than 'spontaneous', I'm going to cancel my subscription.

Warm regards
HM

Susan Persson <soupy@qmail.com>
to: <rightsaidmanfred@qmail.com>   Mar 23, 2023, 10.11 AM

Hi Howard

You have to pay for them to send you emails with new words? That's crazy. Just dip into a dictionary and find a word that you've never heard before and learn what it means. You don't have to pay for it.

SP

Howard Manfred <rightsaidmanfred@qmail.com>
to: <soupy@qmail.com>   Mar 23, 2023, 10.17 PM

SP, I don't have a dictionary. If I need the definition of something, I look it up online. This is bad, I know. We have become lazy. Any problem, any bit of information that we don't know and, wham, just Google it. I am out of my misery in seconds, without having to think.

HM

Susan Persson <soupy@qmail.com>
to: <rightsaidmanfred@qmail.com>   Mar 23, 2023, 11.00 AM

You're right. I like working things out. If I know that I know the answer to something but can't remember it, I think it is so much more fun to try to remember rather than relying on Google. When I do resort to that, and find out the answer, it kind of annoys me as I knew that I knew it. It's so much more satisfying to dredge your memory and work it out. Are you with me on this, HM?

SP

Howard Manfred <rightsaidmanfred@qmail.com>
to: <soupy@qmail.com>   Mar 23, 2023, 11.23 PM

I agree with you, absolutely. But I am lazy. I do have the time to stretch my brain, but it's easier to look it up.

My recent words have been 'mangle', 'adduce' and 'guttersnipe'. I like them all, but the first and the third are easy, and it was only the middle one that made me interested. It means 'cite as evidence' and I like the word. I will use it when appropriate.

HM

Susan Persson <soupy@qmail.com>
to: <rightsaidmanfred@qmail.com>   Mar 23, 2023, 11.56 AM

Is this part of your self-improvement program, Howard? Do you think that knowing new words is important and that people will think better of you because you do? Just asking. I'm not going to be impressed by the way you use language and the big words you know. It's what the words say that mean everything to me, and I'd rather hear YOU through grammatically incorrect sentences than try to work out who you're trying to be, if you're trying to impress me. Your work on commas is going quite well, though (7/10). Brackets need more work. About 3/10 at the moment. Can do better.

Just be yourself, homeboy, and don't worry about what other people might think. Unless you're writing emails for work to superiors, in which case it may be important to sound as though you know what you're talking about. But bearing in mind the emails we get from our 'superiors', I don't think you have much to worry about. The way you write is so much better than them. Norvig, for example, has absolutely no idea about the difference between 'your' and 'you're', and it makes me laugh. How do you get to his position without knowing the fundamentals of grammar?

This is a rhetorical question. He's pretty good at his job, if a bit unpleasant when things are going badly, and I mustn't get bothered about his inability to write properly. It's not important to his job anyway. Is it?

SP

Howard Manfred <rightsaidmanfred@qmail.com>
to: <soupy@qmail.com>   Mar 24, 2023, 12.06 AM

I tend to agree, and then I don't. We've been talking about laziness, and I just think it's lazy if you can't be arsed to get things write when you right. I made a joke there. Right and write are homophones. Words that sound the same but mean different things. I'll add 'rite' to the list. The English language is a very strange one.

But I do like words that end in 'duce' and there seems to be quite a few of them.

HM

Susan Persson <soupy@qmail.com>
to: <rightsaidmanfred@qmail.com>   Mar 23, 2023, 12.12 PM

Adduce. Reduce. Produce. Introduce. Seduce. Which one do you like?

SP

Howard Manfred <rightsaidmanfred@qmail.com>
to: <soupy@qmail.com>   Mar 24, 2023, 12.17 AM

I would really rather not say at this point. Can I get back to you?

Howard

Susan Persson <soupy@qmail.com>
to: <rightsaidmanfred@qmail.com>   Mar 23, 2023, 12.16 PM

Of course. No rush.

SP

* * *

Susan Persson <soupy@qmail.com>
to: <rightsaidmanfred@qmail.com>   Mar 23, 2023, 4.50 PM
Dear Howard

Forgive me for saying this, but I have been wondering for a while now how you manage to see things so clearly in black and white. Everything seems to be so clear to you. How do you do that?

While I seem to question everything, you appear to know everything. Or at least you give the impression that you do. In many ways, I have always wanted to be this way. Or that way. Convinced. So that I could make a point from a position of authority. I have never been able to do this. Why?

SP

Howard Manfred <rightsaidmanfred@qmail.com>
to: <soupy@qmail.com>   Mar 24, 2023, 7.00 AM

Susan, you make me sound quite unpleasant. I'm sure you don't mean to. Unless you really do. I don't know everything. I don't think I know everything, and you suggesting that I think I do is quite insulting. But I am getting used to this from you. I like your directness, and I know you don't mean anything by it, although I am working quite hard to convince myself of this some of the time.

Like you, I do my research. I enjoy learning things and acquiring knowledge because you never know when it might be useful. Even useless knowledge, like trivia, is never really useless because sometimes it can help you get to what you want.

So that's the way I choose to learn. If I get to know something, and there's something else connected that I also know, I like to fill in the gaps. It's like a journey, I suppose, in which you know the end point and the beginning point, but nothing about all the points in between. Like a long trip in a car when you start out at home and have to drive somewhere and end up spending time in towns and villages in between that you never even knew existed. That's my take, anyway, for what it's worth.

HM

Susan Persson <soupy@qmail.com>
to: <rightsaidmanfred@qmail.com>   Mar 23, 2023, 7.28 PM

This is all getting a bit philosophical, isn't it? But I do understand what you're talking about. I think I am one of those people who feels that it's possible to know too much, and that there is so much stuff out there it's impossible to even try to keep up. I guess that's the internet's fault. The sum of human knowledge at our fingertips, and access to almost any amount of information. Do you ever wonder what a woman living 100 years ago would have made of what we have now?

SP

Howard Manfred <rightsaidmanfred@qmail.com>
to: <soupy@qmail.com>   Mar 24, 2023, 8.41 AM
Susan

Staring into the future? Science fiction. It would have been unimaginable, but some people did imagine it. Mobile phones (sorry, cellphones where you come from) were talked about in science fiction many, many years ago . . . The jury is still out on deciding when, but there seem to have been references in books dating back to 1949. Some imagination, huh? There's a book written by Ernst Junger called *Heliopolis* in which he describes a 'Phonophor', which has GPS and a video chat facility AND also works as a credit card. Pretty cool, as you might say.

HM

Susan Persson <soupy@qmail.com>

to: <rightsaidmanfred@qmail.com>   Mar 23, 2023, 9.04 PM

I have never said 'pretty cool' in my life, Howard. Do I sound like a teenager to you? But that is interesting. I'm not really into science fiction myself, but you do have to admire people who have the ability to gaze into the future and predict things. Like technological innovation, obviously, but also political systems, although I don't imagine that is nearly so much fun.

SP

Howard Manfred <rightsaidmanfred@qmail.com>

to: <soupy@qmail.com>   Mar 24, 2023, 9.09 AM

I think it's what the word 'dystopian' was invented for. Looking into the future and imagining a world that isn't that great. I'm not sure that we aren't already there. What do you think, SP?

Susan Persson <soupy@qmail.com>

to: <rightsaidmanfred@qmail.com>   Mar 23, 2023, 9.17 PM

Half-empty glass, Howard. You're a born pessimist, it seems, whereas I am the opposite. Not the exact opposite. I have had my fair share of misery and disappointment, but I always think things will get better. It's just that these days, my patience is beginning to run out (or wear out, seeing as I use it so much and it's getting old and worn and in need of some repair). Like a couch.

SP

Howard Manfred <rightsaidmanfred@qmail.com>

to: <soupy@qmail.com>   Mar 24, 2023, 9.33 AM

I like that analogy. Not you as a couch. I don't think there's anything couch-like about you. I think I should stop now, as I don't know where I am going with this. You're a couch because couches (we call them sofas) are comfortable, and I am comfortable with you, but they're also always getting sat on, which can't be good if we're analogising a couch and a person. I should stop, and you should get some sleep.

HM x

* * *

Howard Manfred <rightsaidmanfred@qmail.com>
to: <soupy@qmail.com>   Mar 24, 2023, 1.30 PM

I have difficulty sleeping. I read that writing 'to-do' lists prior to trying to sleep is a good idea and can be quite effective. But generally speaking, I have a great deal of difficulty in turning my brain off. I do tend to lie awake at night thinking about things, and I'm sure it's not healthy. They say that anything less than 8 hours sleep per night is bad for your health, in which case I must be on the verge of death. I can't remember the last time I had 8 hours sleep, except maybe over the course of a week.

HM

Susan Persson <soupy@qmail.com>
to: <rightsaidmanfred@qmail.com>   Mar 24, 2023, 1.39 AM

I think we have talked about this before, Howard, and I don't want to lecture. Sleep is important. Rest is important. Especially in our jobs when we can get called upon at almost any time. I find it difficult sometimes to juggle all my responsibilities and I think that the older I get, the less able I am to prioritize. There always seems to be so much to do.

SP

Howard Manfred <rightsaidmanfred@qmail.com>
to: <soupy@qmail.com>   Mar 24, 2023, 1.47 PM

Susan. I'm not sure that I should be taking advice from someone who is answering emails at 2 a.m. in the morning, but ok, for now. I should have no excuses. I have fewer responsibilities than you, and yet I still don't seem to be able to manage them, most of the time. I'm not sure what this says about me, but I don't expect it's anything good. My backstory is very uninteresting. I am surprised that someone like you seems to be taking quite so much interest in me.

HM

Susan Persson <soupy@qmail.com>
to: <rightsaidmanfred@qmail.com>   Mar 24, 2023, 2.01 AM

Enough of this, Howard. You may not think that your 'backstory' is interesting, but I bet it is. More importantly, you are interesting now and that should be good enough for you. I know it is for me.

SP, x

Howard Manfred <rightsaidmanfred@qmail.com>
to: <soupy@qmail.com>   Mar 24, 2023, 2.14 PM

This is what I mean. How do you always manage to make me feel better? Not only about myself but about everything around me. My life, my job, even my relationships, although those are few and far between. I did try Tinder a few times, and the new dating app, Lurve, but I found it very strange.

HM, x

Susan Persson <soupy@qmail.com>
to: <rightsaidmanfred@qmail.com>   Mar 24, 2023, 7.21 AM

Sorry, HM. Had to get some sleep.

I feel as though I should be reprimanding you in some way, but I don't know why. I know little or nothing about Tinder, but have a vague idea about how it works. And I suppose that in this day and age, it makes sense. There is so little time. Why would anyone want to spend unnecessary amounts of it actually getting to know someone properly?

I am sorry. I think I am coming across badly, and I don't mean to. I am not criticizing you. I would never do that (except when I already have), but I don't understand why someone like you has to resort to something like an app to meet people. You are smart, funny and very intelligent. There must be a million women out there who would love to meet you and date you and would probably fall madly in love with you in a heartbeat. Actually, writing this almost makes me feel jealous. I wonder what would have happened if, at a different point in both our histories, we had met on Tinder. Do you think we would have liked each other?

SP

Howard Manfred <rightsaidmanfred@qmail.com>
to: <soupy@qmail.com>   Mar 24, 2023, 7.39 PM

I think so. No, I know so. Of course we would have. We like each other now, don't we? And we've never met, probably never will meet and we don't even know what each other looks like. I think this is the way to go, though, and I don't want to spoil anything. What we have is . . . I don't know . . . different?

Or is it? There must be hundreds of thousands of people around the world becoming internet friends. Didn't it used to be called 'pen pals', when you wrote to people and they wrote back? The only difference being that in some cases, those 'pals' managed to meet up, even if they lived in different countries.

HM

Susan Persson <soupy@qmail.com>
to: <rightsaidmanfred@qmail.com>   Mar 24, 2023, 8.03 AM

I am familiar with the concept of pen pals, Howard, but I never had one. Until now. I am enjoying these exchanges, mostly. I only say 'mostly' because you do seem to have the ability to make me angry, but that's what it's all about, I suppose.

You need to tell me more about your experiences on Tinder. I am kind of fascinated, and there's a word I could use to describe my interest in it, but I can't think of it right now.

SP

Howard Manfred <rightsaidmanfred@qmail.com>
to: <soupy@qmail.com>   Mar 24, 2023, 8.15 PM

I've looked up a number of words that could be appropriate, and I'm thinking 'prurient' is probably the best, although this is assuming a lot, which I now know is never a good idea with you.

It seems to fit the bill, though. I know it's not something that you have ever done, and I accept that you would be suspicious of those who do it. That means that you would be suspicious of 97 million people currently alive in the world today. I could offer an insult, but I like you too much. I know you are not trying to sound judgmental, but you are. Sounding, I mean. Admit it. It sounds interesting, right? You get the opportunity to look at people and decide whether you like them or not, rather than sit through a coffee or a safe lunch and waste so much time before accepting that she or he is not the person for you.

It's also exciting, because you always believe that with the next swipe of your finger, you could meet the woman of your dreams. Someone with whom you have so much in common. So many shared interests that you are destined to be together and live happily ever after. There is so much hope and expectation.

HM

Susan Persson <soupy@qmail.com>
to: <rightsaidmanfred@qmail.com>   Mar 24, 2023, 9.01 AM

Is that why you did it, Howard? Hope? Did you think that an algorithm would enable you to meet the woman of your dreams? Like every relationship, in my opinion, it's all about what you put in. That will determine what you get out. This all seems a little bit too easy for me, but I understand why it is so popular. It's a cut-the-crap app. It even rhymes. You can identify whether you might like someone without even going through the awkward shit. Is there a point to all that? Isn't getting through the crap and the awkward stuff what makes a relationship and makes you realise why you're in one? So many questions, as usual.

SP

Howard Manfred <rightsaidmanfred@qmail.com>
to: <soupy@qmail.com>   Mar 24, 2023, 9.30 PM

I hear what you're saying and you're right, as usual. But these are the times. Times when time is short, and we all have to try to make the most of what we have. As you say, there is always going to be awkward stuff, and dating apps cut through that. You already know before you meet that the people find each other attractive. Superficial? Yes, but no one will deny that it's part of the equation. And then you know that you have things in common and share views on certain subjects. This is also good when you imagine the possible scenario of meeting someone that you think is quite hot, but it turns out they're a complete moron who can't string a sentence together. Don't tell me that this way isn't preferable.

I guess my problem was that I wasn't prepared to be that honest and tell people who I really am. So I hid, to a certain extent, and told people what I thought they wanted to hear. I realise now that this totally defeated the objective of the exercise, but I wanted to be liked and swiped. The problem was that I rarely went through with anything. I suppose I didn't want anybody to find out who I really am or what I'm really like. Please don't tell me that this sounds kind of sad, because I know it does.

HM

Susan Persson <soupy@qmail.com>
to: <rightsaidmanfred@qmail.com>   Mar 24, 2023, 9.52 AM

Howard, this begs the question of why you registered for the service in the first place, no? I assume I can call it a 'service', and I also assume that you have to register. So, what did you say? Did you just make everything up and hope for the best?

SP

Howard Manfred <rightsaidmanfred@qmail.com>
to: <soupy@qmail.com>   Mar 24, 2023, 10.01 PM

SP, most of what I said was true, but quite a lot wasn't. Then it didn't make sense to meet as I would have been found out fairly quickly. I also thought that I was being unfair to the people concerned.

I never thought that I would be capable of lying in this way, but guess what . . . I'm good at it. Creating a story and making up a persona. It's like all those people in chat groups. When you have anonymity, you can be whoever you want to be. You can describe yourself as a beautiful, 5' 10" lingerie model, with blonde hair, blue eyes and a bubbly personality, and in reality, be a bald, 5' 4" tall accountant living in Birmingham. Birmingham UK, as opposed to the one in Alabama, US. I know there are two (and probably more).

HM, x

Susan Persson <soupy@qmail.com>
to: <rightsaidmanfred@qmail.com>   Mar 24, 2023, 11.15 AM

There are 14 Birminghams in the US, Howard. I looked it up. I guess this is what the internet is for. And Tinder, of course. And what is it about men and lingerie models? Is this the height of your expectations, your fantasies come true? I suppose it must be. Do you not understand how this makes the rest of us feel? That is, women and girls with normal body sizes and shapes as opposed to the catwalk perfection we're supposed to aspire to. No wonder there are even more eating disorders among young people (mostly girls, of course) than there were even 10 years ago. I thought we had overcome all this by celebrating 'plus-size' women and having the fashion industry cater to them, but that seems to have fallen by the wayside. We're not very good at learning things, are we?

SP (stands for: Slightly Pissed—and not UK 'pissed')

Howard Manfred <rightsaidmanfred@qmail.com>

to: <soupy@qmail.com>   Mar 24, 2023, 11.42 PM

This has to be a rhetorical question. But, no, we're not. Although I am learning a lot from you, and that's good. It's always important to get another person's perspective and yours is obviously so different to mine. Sorry you're pissed (off).

Don't get me wrong, I'm not proud of my Tinder and Lurve activities. In fact, I am ashamed. But I can get lonely sometimes, and a bad date with someone you end up not liking is better than no date at all. It hasn't worked out for me, but that's probably my fault. I don't think the women I meet are that impressed with me in the flesh, and sometimes I can just see the disappointment in their faces when we first meet. They can probably see mine, too. No one looks as good in real life as they do on their profiles.

It's like the images of restaurant food. The pictures look delicious, but the reality is somewhat different. It must be like that with dating apps. But then you have to look as good as possible on your profile, otherwise no one will right swipe you. Even on Tinder, there is a pressure to be liked. Actually, especially on Tinder. Lurve is slightly different, but it still makes you feel bad if you don't receive any messages although you never know how many people have seen your profile and decided against you or not found you attractive enough. You just assume, when you don't hear from anyone.

HM

Susan Persson <soupy@qmail.com>

to: <rightsaidmanfred@qmail.com>   Mar 24, 2023, 12.30 PM

This is beginning to sound very sad, and you are beginning to sound quite desperate. But you can't be. You are smart and funny, and I'd swipe right for you. I assume that's what happens, from what you have written. I just want you to know, Howard, that I would swipe for you and arrange to meet, except we're 9,622 miles apart and can't travel because of COVID-21, so we're going to have to make do with this and working together. Which is fine by me. For now. Ok?

SP, x

Howard Manfred <rightsaidmanfred@qmail.com>

to: <soupy@qmail.com>   Mar 25, 2023, 1.06 AM

It's extraordinary how good you can make me feel. It's also sad that you provide light in my life when there is so much darkness.

HM, x

Susan Persson <soupy@qmail.com>

to: <rightsaidmanfred@qmail.com>   Mar 24, 2023, 1.12 PM

You really have to stop reading romantic novels, Howard. It's not doing you any good. And you also have to stop thinking about lingerie models—or even searching for them on the internet. That's not doing you any good either. Do you imagine that unless you're dating one or are in a relationship with one, you are a failure as a man? Just asking. Not for a friend.

SP, x

Howard Manfred <rightsaidmanfred@qmail.com>

to: <soupy@qmail.com>   Mar 25, 2023, 6.17 AM

No, of course not, but everybody has dreams, and I guess for a man—and we all know that men are superficial—a lingerie model is as good as it gets from an aesthetic point of view. It's like a badge of honour; something to brag about to your mates. Sorry, I am descending into very British vernacular here. Mates are friends. Always male. You would never describe a female friend as a 'mate'.

Also please note the use of a semicolon. Getting there.

So yes, bragging rights and all that kind of stuff—that's very important to men and I don't imagine it's that much different for women, is it? Doesn't every woman want a hunk on their arm? Is that the right word? Hunk, not arm. I know what an arm is.

People judge us by who we're in a relationship with. I don't think I'm superficial, but I know people who wouldn't be seen dead with an unattractive partner.

Isn't this 'vestigial'? That was an MW word. It's about survival, isn't it? We're automatically attracted to the strong of limb and the fit. They'll make better children who will grow up to be better hunters of wildebeest. They will survive and pass on their genes (and other items of clothing). Sorry. Just my attempt at a joke. Besides, don't we think that other people judge us by who we're in a relationship with, and doesn't it make us proud if we can make other people jealous?

HM

Susan Persson <soupy@qmail.com>
to: <rightsaidmanfred@qmail.com>   Mar 24, 2023, 7.12 PM

My God Howard, you're beginning to sound like someone in a science fiction novel that's been made into a terrible film. Doesn't this bring us to the subject of eugenics? I read that this is quite a big thing in your country. Well, not your country, the country in which you currently live. People being encouraged to marry similarly well-educated people so that they can pass on their brain genes to the next generation. What about the rest of us? Isn't this what Aldous Huxley wrote about in *Brave New World* and wasn't that truly terrifying? You're a very strange man if you think this is the right way for womankind to move forward.

Please note that I have decided not to make any comment on your 'joke'.

Susan

Howard Manfred <rightsaidmanfred@qmail.com>
to: <soupy@qmail.com>   Mar 25, 2023, 7.50 AM

Thank you for making me laugh, again, and your point is not lost on me, and you mustn't think badly of me. I am playing 'devil's advocate' to a great extent. Just putting ideas out there because I love talking to you and I know for sure that you're going to get on my case if I say something (anything) inappropriate or stupid. But I don't mind, at all. In fact, I quite like it. You keep me on my toes all the time and make me think about things more than I ever have before. I can't tell you how grateful I am. Even if I feel like apologising to you after almost every sentence I write. I can just see you reading through my emails and shaking your head, maybe even tutting once every so often and thinking how incorrigible I am. But I also think you consider me to be something of a project and a work in progress for you. I'm not saying that you think you're taking responsibility for trying to make me a better person, but . . . I wish you would. And I know you can. So do please go ahead and give me as tough a time as you think I deserve.

HM, xx

Susan Persson <soupy@qmail.com>
to: <rightsaidmanfred@qmail.com>   Mar 24, 2023, 8.50 PM

Honestly Howard, could you be any more lame and pathetic? I say this with a smile on my face as I am in quite a good mood at this moment in time, but there will be other times when I am not, so be careful.

By the way, the question above is rhetorical, because obviously you could not. I find it incredible the way that men try to justify things to themselves, even *for* themselves. Idiots, all of you. Narcissists, most of you. It doesn't matter what terms you put it in, you're just trying to find an argument or a set of excuses that will enable men to go on doing what they've been doing for thousands of years. That is thinking they're wonderful and superior, and imagining that women are just around to breed and provide other services, generally menial. What a bunch of asses you all are. But I can't blame you. You don't know any better. Your parents brought you up wrongly and you have no sense of the real world. You think you have the right to behave in any way you choose because . . . because . . . actually, why!? Because you're men and you are physically stronger? Because you have reaped the rewards from generations of subjugation and don't want to relinquish control? As mentioned above: pathetic.

But I like you, Howard, and I believe there is a chance at redemption for you. You just have to try to forget the fact that you're a man and try harder to become a human being. I hope this doesn't sound too patronizing. Actually, no I don't. I hope it sounds as patronizing as all hell, because that seems to be the only way to get through to people like you, that is, a man. And you're probably one of the better ones.

Howard Manfred <rightsaidmanfred@qmail.com>
to: <soupy@qmail.com>   Mar 25, 2023, 10.30 AM
Dear Susan

I have never been so insulted in my life. I have never enjoyed being so insulted so much in my life either. Somehow you manage to make me sound and seem like an absolute dickhead, and I don't mind. I will go further. I like it. I like being insulted by you because it makes me think that you actually care. If I were worthless, you wouldn't bother, right? So the fact that you are even prepared to make me feel like a neanderthal suggests that you think I might not be or might have a chance at being something else.

HM, xx

Susan Persson <soupy@qmail.com>
to: <rightsaidmanfred@qmail.com>			Mar 24, 2023, 10.48 PM

Howard, honey, I think you need help. Yes, still smiling. You are so funny, and so stupid and so damn male. Get a grip, H!

S

Howard Manfred <rightsaidmanfred@qmail.com>
to: <soupy@qmail.com>			Mar 25, 2023, 11.03 AM

If I told you that I felt a tingle of electricity when I read your last email, would that surprise you? Shock you? Disappoint you? I'm not sure if I want to do any of those things, but this is really new territory for me.

H, x

Susan Persson <soupy@qmail.com>
to: <rightsaidmanfred@qmail.com>			Mar 24, 2023, 11.07 PM

Dammit boy. Grow up.

Howard Manfred <rightsaidmanfred@qmail.com>
to: <soupy@qmail.com>			Mar 25, 2023, 11.09 AM

Were you smiling as you wrote that?

H, x

Susan Persson <soupy@qmail.com>
to: <rightsaidmanfred@qmail.com>			Mar 24, 2023, 1.11 PM

Maybe.

SP

* * *

Howard Manfred <rightsaidmanfred@qmail.com>
to: <soupy@qmail.com>			Mar 25, 2023, 6.30 PM

Hey Susan

Finally, now we're talking. An interesting word from Merriam-Webster. Prehensile. I like this word a lot. 'A tail for grasping, wrapping around, holding, seizing'. But it also means perception, as in being able to wrap your head around something, like an idea. I love it. This is my kind of word. One that I didn't know and would like to learn.

But then I start thinking about what happens when you let go. You lose your grip or can't hold onto the idea. And then what?

HM

Susan Persson <soupy@qmail.com>
to: <rightsaidmanfred@qmail.com>   Mar 25, 2023, 7.12 AM

I can't answer that question, Howard, as the word is new to me too. I'm much more interested, though, in knowing what your memory is like. Do you forget things easily? I have always prided myself on my memory, and it's something that other people are not happy with. When I recount a situation that involved either family or friends and I am able to give accurate details, people get upset. They see things in their own minds, and they're different than mine. I'm usually right.

So, people tell me about an event in the past, and I simply have to correct them. Apparently, this doesn't appeal to a lot of people who just think that they're right and so they continue to choose to believe what they believe. And I don't seem to have the will or the energy anymore to argue, because, quite honestly, what difference does it make?

Answer: none. Memories are like that, aren't they? Individual and very personal. Our ship is in the Mediterranean Sea. Howard, please let me know what it might be like to be there right now and what I might be able to see, were I to be on the *McCarthy*.

SP, x

Howard Manfred <rightsaidmanfred@qmail.com>
to: <soupy@qmail.com>   Mar 25, 2023, 7.38 PM

SP

During most of these journeys most of what you would be able to see is sea. Sorry, still working on my commas. Going through the Straits of Gibraltar would be interesting, though. It's pretty narrow as far as straits are concerned, but I have always been fascinated by the fact that the distance between Spain (Europe) and Morocco (Africa) is a mere 8.9 miles. You can see Africa from Spain, on a clear day. How cool is that? Afterwards, though, there wouldn't be much to see, but you might see some spotted dolphins or even the odd sperm whale. The *McCarthy* will be steaming south of islands like Sardinia, Sicily and Crete on its way to the Suez Canal. It does sound very romantic. I hope that wasn't too much information.

HP, x

Susan Persson <soupy@qmail.com>
to: <rightsaidmanfred@qmail.com>   Mar 25, 2023, 8.48 AM

You have to be kidding, Howard. This is just wonderful. I can picture all these places, and that gives me a pleasure tinged with the regret of knowing that I will never go there.

SP, x

Howard Manfred <rightsaidmanfred@qmail.com>
to: <soupy@qmail.com>   Mar 25, 2023, 8.53 PM

Never say never, Susan. Who knows? Maybe we'll go there together one day.

HM, xx

Susan Persson <soupy@qmail.com>
to: <rightsaidmanfred@qmail.com>   Mar 25, 2023, 9.01 AM

I hope this isn't being too personal, Howard, or even impertinent, but are you happy in your relationship? I know we haven't talked much about it.

SP

Howard Manfred <rightsaidmanfred@qmail.com>
to: <soupy@qmail.com>   Mar 25, 2023, 9.37 PM

Hi Susan

I don't think it's impertinent at all, although it is personal. Smiley face. But it's not relevant at this moment in time as I am not in a relationship and haven't been for quite a while now. I am, I suppose, what you might call a serial monogamist, but between gigs at the moment, if you know what I mean. I hope that's not being too frivolous or even flippant as I don't want you to think that I take relationships lightly.

In fact, probably just the opposite and I don't think that's made me very effective with them in the past. As I may have mentioned, I don't have that many hopes for the future.

I suppose at this stage, I should be trotting out something like, 'I haven't met the right woman', or saying something equally clichéd, such as, 'I've met lots of women that I could live with, but none that I can't live without', but this would be trite and probably not even true. I've been lucky enough to meet some very good people in my time, and some of them have been women with whom I have shared intimacies, but I get too tense in a relationship—maybe too intense too—if that makes sense. It never goes well and rarely lasts for very long.

I'm not sure that I am a very interesting person. I've had experiences where if I was interested in someone, they haven't been interested in me, and when they've been interested in me, I haven't been interested in them.

I don't expect much. I get the impression, however, that while you are genuinely concerned and asked the original question out of interest, there is more to the enquiry than meets the eye . . . ?

HM, x

Susan Persson <soupy@qmail.com>
to: <rightsaidmanfred@qmail.com>   Mar 25, 2023, 10.23 AM

I suppose there was. You're quite astute, Howard. I think I wanted to know what's going on out there. I'm curious. What are people looking for in relationships these days? What are people on Tinder and Lurve hoping to achieve, apart from the obvious? What are the hopes and expectations?

I too would like to avoid clichés and say something crass like, 'my husband doesn't understand me', but what would be the point? Except that it's true. What bothers me the most, though, is that he doesn't seem to want to anymore. The understanding, I mean. We've been together for a long time—getting on for 20 years—and I suppose it was something that we both just fell into. It was lovely at the beginning (isn't it always?) and now it's as though he's forgotten how to be lovely and is merely intent on just being. And I wonder if that's enough, and how things are meant to be and what a 'normal' relationship is supposed to be like and whether this is normal and all that anyone has a right to expect. Do you understand?

S, x

Howard Manfred <rightsaidmanfred@qmail.com>
to: <soupy@qmail.com>   Mar 25, 2023, 10.48 PM

Yes, of course I do. Although, at the same time, no, how could I? Sorry, not trying to be evasive, but none of my relationships have lasted for anything like as long as you and your husband's, so it's kind of difficult for me to comment.

Things must change over time, though. That much I do know. Romance at the start, lots of sex, can't get enough of each other, and then . . . I don't know, friendship, companionship . . . boredom.

This is probably very harsh, although it does seem to be quite easy to categorise the various stages of long-term relationships these days; maybe even always. I don't see how anyone can expect there to be the same level of passion and excitement after 20 years as there was at the start. People grow, people change. I'm very different to who I was 10 years ago. I'm different to who I was 6 months ago, and a lot of that is down to you. I hope that's ok to say.

Maybe one of the reasons that I never committed to a long-term relationship was because I thought that these things would happen, and that they couldn't be avoided. Maybe I realised that I wasn't mature or well-developed enough to think that I could accept the changes that occurred and still be ok with everything. You're braver than I am, Susan. You took the plunge. For better or worse.

With warm regards
Howard

Susan Persson <soupy@qmail.com>
to: <rightsaidmanfred@qmail.com>   Mar 25, 2023, 11.26 AM

Yes, in sickness and in health, till death us do (or do us) part. Such an awkward thing to have to say. I really think that relationships just get away from you. They always start with the best of intentions and are exciting at the beginning. Then you get comfortable and feel as though you don't need to try anymore, and when both people start feeling this way, it's a slippery slope. Maybe paved with good intention, but it's still a slope, which means it's heading downwards. And now I'm confused, because downward slopes should be good. You have gravity on your side. Upwards slopes are difficult because they're harder work to go up. It's a stupid analogy. Ignore me.

SP

Howard Manfred <rightsaidmanfred@qmail.com>
to: <soupy@qmail.com>   Mar 25, 2023, 11.34 PM

Never. Everything that you say is interesting to me, no matter where it comes from. This line of communication is important, and I feel as though I am learning a lot from you.

HM

Susan Persson <soupy@qmail.com>
to: <rightsaidmanfred@qmail.com>   Mar 25, 2023, 11.54 AM

You make me sound like some kind of guru, and I'm not. I can scarcely manage my own life outside of work, so don't go putting pressure on me to help you with yours.

But yes, I agree, I like our 'line of communication', as you so coldly put it. It's more than just communication though, isn't it? Are we kindred spirits somehow? How does that work? How *has* it worked? So many questions.

SP, x

Howard Manfred <rightsaidmanfred@qmail.com>
to: <soupy@qmail.com>   Mar 26, 2023, 12.06 PM

I don't know, but I think it's great. I am so enjoying our exchanges. They're the highlights of my day more often than not. I think I have already thanked you enough, but it is so nice to have someone to talk to. Someone who seems to understand me. I don't feel as though I have anyone like you at work. Everyone's just looking for things that need to get done, sending more and more work in my direction and expecting me to do it. I'm not a machine but it feels that way sometimes. I feel taken for granted a lot of the time.

HM

Susan Persson <soupy@qmail.com>
to: <rightsaidmanfred@qmail.com>   Mar 25, 2023, 12.31 PM

Do you think you are a victim of your own success? I find this sometimes. You're asked to do a job, and it goes well enough and then you're asked to do something similar again because you did it right the first time. Only there's always more of it. And you get that done, and then there's more. I'm going to call it the 'loop of efficiency'. I feel like making a mistake every once in a while, so at least I can get some credit for not making it again. I feel as though I'm being taken advantage of and not treated with enough respect for what I do. And it's not only at work. Do you feel that? I must say I'm glad we're not on the company email for this.

SP, x

Howard Manfred <rightsaidmanfred@qmail.com>
to: <soupy@qmail.com>   Mar 26, 2023, 12.46 AM

Yes, me too, although I wouldn't mind our bosses knowing how we feel from time to time. Maybe they could learn something, and yes, I do feel that. But only once or twice every day. This is a joke, by the way. Maybe we should just stop being so damn good at what we do, and maybe you should stop being such a good wife and mother. Even as I write this, I know that you could never not be.

H, x

* * *

Susan Persson <soupy@qmail.com>
to: <rightsaidmanfred@qmail.com>   Mar 26, 2023, 8.09 AM

Have you ever been truly happy, Howard?

S, x

Howard Manfred <rightsaidmanfred@qmail.com>
to: <soupy@qmail.com>   Mar 26, 2023, 8.15 PM

I simply don't know how to answer that. It's such a personal question, and I'm not even sure that I understand the concept. Of course I know what you're talking about, and maybe even why you are asking, but it's such a difficult question to answer.

That answer would probably, be 'no', and if the question was changed to 'when were you truly happy?' I would have to say, 'never'. Not truly. Not really. Not truly happy. Not in the way that I think you mean.

But maybe I'm not even qualified to answer either of the questions, on the basis that I don't fully understand the concept.

H

Susan Persson <soupy@qmail.com>
to: <rightsaidmanfred@qmail.com>   Mar 26, 2023, 9.02 AM

I am sorry if the question was too personal. I did not mean to ask you a question that you would not be comfortable answering. But you have answered, although I can see that you were not happy in having to. So please do not feel as though you have to answer all my questions. You can always tell me that it's none of my business, and we can talk about something less personal. Like the weather, for example. You are British, and I understand that British people like talking about the weather.

How is the weather where you are? Clement?

Susan

Howard Manfred <rightsaidmanfred@qmail.com>
to: <soupy@qmail.com>   Mar 27, 2023, 6.12 AM

Susan, you are funny, even if you don't mean to be. Yes, British people do like talking about the weather, but one of the reasons we do is because we have so much of it. It is a national preoccupation, but it's not something that interests me in any way (I don't live in the UK anymore) apart from at work and when we're monitoring vessels and their coordinates. Bad weather causes delay.

I appreciate that this doesn't sound very romantic. There is not very much poetry in my life. Sorry.

Howard

Susan Persson <soupy@qmail.com>
to: <rightsaidmanfred@qmail.com>   Mar 26, 2023, 6.43 PM

You're up early. Please don't apologise. I did not mean to offend, and when I hear your voice in my mind, I think that you might be sad? That makes me sad, because I think it is very nice to be happy. Not all the time. That would be very difficult, I think, if not impossible. But it's nice to be happy some of the time, and smiling is very therapeutic, apparently. So is laughing, I have been told, and that's one thing I definitely do not do enough of. I would like to smile and laugh more, because it feels nice, and science has an explanation for this. Please don't ask me what it is. I don't have the time to do the research. I just know what everyone tells me.

Susan

Howard Manfred <rightsaidmanfred@qmail.com>

to: <soupy@qmail.com>   Mar 27, 2023, 7.00 AM

Who is 'everyone'? How do you decide who to listen to and what to believe? Do you base all your opinions on something known as 'conventional wisdom', or do you think about things enough to be able to form your own opinions and make up your own mind? I hope this isn't a personal question, but I am very interested.

HM

Susan Persson <soupy@qmail.com>

to: <rightsaidmanfred@qmail.com>   Mar 27, 2023, 12.01 AM

I suppose I go with what I know, Howard, and what I think I know. That is dependent on what people tell me and what I learn from reading and observing the world. It's not a very precise science, is it? There is a lot of interpretation involved, and it must involve who you are and what you believe. Should this be, 'what you choose to believe'? I am not sure. People see the same things in different ways, and everyone thinks differently. This is what makes people unique.

Best regards

SP

Howard Manfred <rightsaidmanfred@qmail.com>

to: <soupy@qmail.com>   Mar 27, 2023, 1.30 PM

Hi Susan. I hear these two words a lot. The human condition. What is it? A state of being? An illness? If you have a 'condition', it usually means that you're not well and need to seek medical help. Perhaps this is accurate. But it also means the state of something with regard to appearance, quality or working order. That also works.

We have conditions, and one of them is a human one, and the others relate to where we are, what we are doing and how we live our lives. Would this be accurate? I am just asking, as I don't fully understand. You seem to have thought about this a lot more than me, so I would be grateful for guidance.

Regards

Howard

Susan Persson <soupy@qmail.com>

to: <rightsaidmanfred@qmail.com>   Mar 27, 2023, 9.15 AM

I am not here to teach you, Howard, or guide you. I am also confused much of the time and trying to make sense of everything. I think this is part of the 'human condition'. Making sense of things when there doesn't appear to be very much sense around. There just seems to be so much information coming in, and so little time to deal with everything. I try to be as logical as I can be, within limits, but I always feel that there is a need to ask questions and find out more. There is so much information at our disposal. Sometimes this fact makes me very happy. At others, it makes me feel very sad as there is no way of knowing everything.

SP

Howard Manfred <rightsaidmanfred@qmail.com>

to: <soupy@qmail.com>   Mar 28, 2023, 7.06 AM

You really are the poet. This sounds like poetry to me. The questioning, the thirst for knowledge and the dissatisfaction when you realise that you can't have all of it. You are aspirational, Susan, and that is very interesting.

HM, x

Susan Persson <soupy@qmail.com>

to: <rightsaidmanfred@qmail.com>   Mar 27, 2023, 9.08 PM

You are not? Don't you want to know more, and be better? Isn't that why we're here?

SP

Howard Manfred <rightsaidmanfred@qmail.com>

to: <soupy@qmail.com>   Mar 28, 2023, 5.12 PM

This sounds like an existential question, and I'm not sure that I am qualified to answer. But now that I think about what I just wrote, I realise that this is quite stupid. After all, anything that exists can answer an existential question, right? I suppose what I am saying is that I haven't thought about it as much as you have. But I will. Ask me again in a week and I'll try to come up with something.

H

Susan Persson <soupy@qmail.com>
to: <rightsaidmanfred@qmail.com>   Mar 28, 2023, 8.16 AM

Howard, this is not the way we're going. At least I hope it's not. I'm not your teacher. I'm your friend. And I can't guide you because you have to guide yourself. As I mentioned earlier, I am hardly in a position to guide anyone. But I have been asked to do so and will always try. Just don't rely on me. I'm not sure I can deal with the added pressure. Let's just try to keep this light, shall we?

Susan

Howard Manfred <rightsaidmanfred@qmail.com>
to: <soupy@qmail.com>   Mar 29, 2023, 12.06 AM

Of course. Sorry.

HM

* * *

Howard Manfred <rightsaidmanfred@qmail.com>
to: <soupy@qmail.com>   Mar 30, 2023, 7.12 AM

Susan, I wanted to talk to you about Lurve. It's quite a new dating app, and I think you would approve of it. But then, I think a lot of things and you generally have a way of confounding me. Just one of the things I like about you.

After some of your comments, I realised that Tinder was just too superficial. I think there were other people in the world who felt the same. On Tinder, you look at a face (sometimes a body) and decide whether you're 'interested'. I mean, that's terrible. I appreciate the fact that there has to be physical attraction, but is that it?

Lurve came in, and I like it. You don't get to see the people when you're going through the profiles. All you know about them is their personality, as described by themselves, obviously, their interests and the kind of person they would like to meet. Physical appearance doesn't play any part in it at all. There is no way that you will find out what the other person looks like until you have made the connection of having enough in common. And on Lurve, you don't even have to register with a photo or image. I think this is very good.

I'm now looking at all the women who share similar interests and who have a similar sense of humour—there don't seem to be many, apart from you, and I doubt you'd be registered. And that's interesting. Do you think I would recognise you if you were?

Anyway, it's more important for me to have things to say to someone and enough common territory to lead me to think that there won't be too much boredom down the line. Physical attraction will have to come into it at some point, but isn't it nice to start from the other end? I feel strongly that this is the case, and I am also aware that I want you to think of me as less superficial than I think you already do.

With warm regards
Howard

Susan Persson <soupy@qmail.com>
to: <rightsaidmanfred@qmail.com>   Mar 29, 2023, 10.15 PM

Why do you seem to care so much about what I think? We're just friends. I try not to judge you, although I know that you think I do, and perhaps I do do. Always makes me laugh. But we're not invested in this way, Howard, so you really shouldn't worry about it.

Lurve sounds great. Best of luck.
Susan

* * *

Howard Manfred <rightsaidmanfred@qmail.com>
to: <soupy@qmail.com>   Mar 31, 2023, 8.06 PM

We talk about nuance and intonation a lot. Our entire relationship is based on the written word, and we know those can be read in so many different ways. I imagine your 'best of luck' is sarcastic. As though you were saying, 'if you really have to do this kind of thing because you can't even hope to meet anyone in normal circumstances, then, go for it, loser.'

I would like you to know that it's not like that. I am just trying to connect, as I have with you, and as I would like to do with someone else. Someone who isn't married and would like to have a relationship of some sort with me. Is that a crime? Besides, Lurve is different. You don't get to see the person you might be interested in until you find something in their profile that you feel you can connect to. This is more interesting to me than seeing a picture of someone I quite like the look of.

It's nice to be able to read about someone and imagine what they might be like, without worrying what they might look like. Didn't you once describe me as a hopeless romantic? If I can find out on Lurve that I'm probably going to be able to get on with someone with whom I share certain interests and have similar personality characteristics, isn't this a good thing? Do I care what they look like? Yes, I suppose so, ultimately, but it's not the most important thing. That's why I'm not using Tinder anymore.

Best

HM

Susan Persson <soupy@qmail.com>
to: <rightsaidmanfred@qmail.com>   Mar 31, 2023, 9.35 AM

Give me a couple of days, Howard. It may take me some time to prepare your medal. I want it to be as shiny as possible.

I'm not sure that I really understand why you are telling me all this. Are you seeking my approval? I hope this is not the extent of your ambitions. I must admit to being interested in this Lurve app. It seems to me that any organization working against superficiality must have their hearts in the right place. Either that or they've recognised a gap in the market that needs to be filled. Although I can't imagine many gaps in the dating app world. I thought the whole idea is that you wanted to find someone to have sex with, and obviously you wouldn't want to have sex with someone you didn't like the look of. We've talked about cutting through the crap, so most apps that I know of do that, but Lurve seems to take a different approach, and you seem to want recognition for choosing it.

Recognition granted, Howard. You're a good man who is obviously not interested in pretty girls but would prefer your relationship partner to be obese but a good conversationalist who reads a lot, is kind to animals, and gives whatever money she has to charity once she's paid for the organic vegetables in her vegan diet.

I'm just yanking your chain and I have to say, it's one of the easiest chains to yank of anyone I know, and I do know quite a few fools. I'm not calling you a fool, Howard, don't worry. But I do question why you are so proud of the fact that when it comes to a possible relationship, you are actually focussing on the genuinely important things. You shouldn't be getting prizes for this. In my opinion.

Best regards

Susan

Howard Manfred <rightsaidmanfred@qmail.com>
to: <soupy@qmail.com>   Mar 31, 2023, 10.45 PM

Is your husband ugly? I'm just asking, for a friend.

HM

Susan Persson <soupy@qmail.com>
to: <rightsaidmanfred@qmail.com>   Mar 31, 2023, 1.30 PM

I shouldn't even have to answer this, but for some reason, I want to. Yes, he is. He didn't used to be, but he is now. Not in appearance, just in his soul. He's not the man I married, and he's not the man he always wanted to be, and that's what makes him unhappy and ugly. He's frustrated, and he feels injustice, and nothing is ever right or good enough for him anymore. Including me, I think. We are having difficulties. I feel embarrassed to write this, and disloyal, and I think that in the context of what we have been discussing recently, it is also wholly inappropriate. But what the hell?

Susan

Howard Manfred <rightsaidmanfred@qmail.com>
to: <soupy@qmail.com>   Apr 01, 2023, 6.17 AM

I thank you, Susan, genuinely, for sharing. That could not have been easy. Although maybe it is easier when you don't know someone that well. And you know that you will never be judged by me. I already think you're very cool and can do no wrong.

Howard

Susan Persson <soupy@qmail.com>
to: <rightsaidmanfred@qmail.com>   Mar 31, 2023, 8.42 PM

Ha ha. That's what they all say in the early stages. You wait to see what happens by the time the *McCarthy* reaches China. You'll be sick of me, and you'll have said something stupid or inappropriate that will make me dislike you even more than I already do, for resorting to dating apps when you should just go out and meet someone nice.

Susan

Howard Manfred <rightsaidmanfred@qmail.com>
to: <soupy@qmail.com>   Apr 01, 2023, 8.46 AM

I have met someone nice.

H

* * *

ATHENS

Manfred, Howard <howard.m@thelogicsticks.com>
to: <susan.p@thelogicsticks.com>   Apr 01, 2023, 4.17 PM

Hi Susan, please inform the customers that all is well. Port of call, Athens, has gone smoothly—the *McCarthy* arrived slightly ahead of schedule due to good weather in the Med. Has cleared customs and is now waiting to unload. Status report on the cargo is all good; temperature control in our containers is almost spot on. Our people have made all the relevant checks and we're good to go for the next leg. It looks like a two-day stopover to onload cargo for Oman and Sri Lanka, but it's all pretty basic.

With kind regards
Howard

Persson, Susan <susan.p@thelogicsticks.com>
to: <howard.m@thelogicsticks.com>   Apr 01, 2023, 9.21 AM

Thanks Howard. The customers have been informed and are asking for an arrival time estimate in Salalah. They say that they have some other cargo coming on board there, destined for Shanghai and would be keen on 'optimal positioning' for offloading in China. Can I assure them?

Best regards
Susan

Manfred, Howard <howard.m@thelogicsticks.com>
to: <susan.p@thelogicsticks.com>   Apr 01, 2023, 9.37 PM

Hi Susan. I'll try to talk to our people in Oman, but as mentioned earlier, these things can't be guaranteed. We can only make requests and suggestions.

The captain of the *McCarthy* and the port workers in Salalah will be the ones to make the ultimate call, based on what they see when the ship gets in and they assess the cargo that's going on. I'll do what I can, though.

Best

Howard

Persson, Susan <susan.p@thelogicsticks.com>
to: <howard.m@thelogicsticks.com>   Apr 01, 2023, 11.30 AM

Thanks Howard. Much appreciated.

With regards

Susan

Manfred, Howard <howard.m@thelogicsticks.com>
to: <susan.p@thelogicsticks.com>   Apr 02, 2023, 12.06 AM

Honestly though, Susan. This would have been good to know earlier. I didn't realise that the customers had other stuff coming on board in Oman. Why aren't they using us for this? Do you know which company they are using? I don't think there will be any tension in port, but this is the kind of thing that would have been useful to know about.

Howard

Persson, Susan <susan.p@thelogicsticks.com>
to: <howard.m@thelogicsticks.com>   Apr 01, 2023, 1.30 PM

I am really sorry about this, Howard, but the customers do seem to have their own way of doing things. They have never been very upfront with us and getting information from them is quite difficult. I seem to have to ask them all the questions, only after which do they provide answers and details. I have tried to do my best and apologise that this extra info is getting to you late. I do hope that you and our people in Oman can accommodate.

Thanks and regards

Susan

* * *

Howard Manfred <rightsaidmanfred@qmail.com>
to: <soupy@qmail.com>   Apr 02, 2023, 6.26 AM

I don't even dare to dream that I could be loved. Or could love in return. I read that somewhere. Then again, I've never been one for settling. I was beginning to believe that no one (in their right mind) would have me, because I was difficult. Contrary. Unusual, even. I didn't think in the way that other people seem to think. That's what I was told. So, I tried to conform, but couldn't—I think I was programmed differently. And before I knew where I was, I started questioning everything (and anything). It didn't really matter what I was told to do. It especially didn't matter how I was told how to behave. I just wanted to do things differently in the hope, perhaps, that I could make a difference.

After all, what does any of us want, other than to do that? To make a difference. To be different. Famous people are different, and not just because they are famous. They're elite and everybody wants to be like them. But we can't. Not all of us. Not many of us. Very few of us. And that's what makes them special, I suppose. I don't want to be famous, necessarily, although I can't really imagine what it would be like.

But I do want to be recognised—for who I am, for what I do, and for the things that I have achieved. It may not be much, but it has to be something.

Howard

Susan Persson <soupy@qmail.com>
to: <rightsaidmanfred@qmail.com>   Apr 01, 2023, 7.50 PM

Howard, you may be an old soul. Not of this age, despite your attempts at embracing technology and using dating apps. There were times when people were appreciated for simple goodness, and I know you have that. Just not doing any harm and helping others used to be enough, but that's not the case anymore. You know this as well as I do, and it pains you. It pains me.

But we have to accept this if we are to be part of the world, and that's what we're here for.

Susan

Howard Manfred <rightsaidmanfred@qmail.com>
to: <soupy@qmail.com>   Apr 02, 2023, 8.30 AM

I notice that we have never discussed religion. Are you religious?

HM

Susan Persson <soupy@qmail.com>
to: <rightsaidmanfred@qmail.com>   Apr 01, 2023, 8.37 PM

That depends on your definition. I smile as I write this. I find religion very interesting. I believe in my maker—how can I not? I believe that there is a genuine reason for my being here. My conception wasn't an accident, I'm convinced of that. But I'm not convinced of the whys and the wherefores. Someone (somebody) (something) wanted me to be here—probably so that we could meet and greet—and I have to believe that that happened for a reason, otherwise what would be the point of all of this? Just asking, for a friend.

Susan

Howard Manfred <rightsaidmanfred@qmail.com>
to: <soupy@qmail.com>   Apr 02, 2023, 9.36 AM

Isn't it easier to simply ask what's the point in anything? Or is that your point? I never thought there would be a point. I guess that makes me quite a negative person—and it's clear to me that you're not a negative Persson. I apologise for the feeble joke, but I've been told I need to be more humorous.

My grandfather used to learn jokes. He would write them down in a little notebook and get it out at social gatherings. He more or less read them out loud, and I'm not sure that's a good strategy if you want to be a comedian.

It was funny, though, because he wasn't well organised. The beginnings and ends of jokes were often on different pages, so occasionally he'd be hunting for the punchline and scrambling through the book, page after page, looking for the right one. We all knew the jokes anyway, as we'd heard them before. But the real fun was watching him struggle, flipping the pages, wetting his finger, as though he was counting out banknotes. I think he did a lot of that in his working life—counting banknote—she was a bookmaker, in the olden days, when everything was cash—no computers, no internet, just real money and disappointed people hanging around in betting shops hoping for their lives to change, which they never did.

Every time I went to his shop as a child, I noticed many of the same people. Some even more dishevelled than the time before; some a bit more shevelled (don't you just love the English language? How can you be dishevelled, but not shevelled?). Why doesn't that word exist? I think it should. And I think gruntled should exist as a word too. I could say 'I am very gruntled to meet you, Susan'. And you would know exactly what I meant, right?

And what about 'overwhelmed' and 'underwhelmed'. If you can have over and under, what's in the middle? Why is there not the word 'whelmed'?

Anyway, it's late, and if we start talking about the vagaries of the English language, I'll be up all night and I think we both have a busy day tomorrow. Do let me know your thoughts on the ACSS-491B-FS shipment.

Sorry to end this email with shoptalk. The customers' requests for the Oman leg are beginning to bother me.

Goodnight.

H, x

Susan Persson <soupy@qmail.com>
to: <rightsaidmanfred@qmail.com>   Apr 02, 2023, 6.44 AM

I really enjoyed reading your email last night. And decided to wake up early so that I could reply before heading to work. It's the first time you've told me much about your family, and your grandfather sounds like an interesting character. Is he still alive by any chance? And if not, did he die a happy man?

Is this a strange question? I only ask because I have been thinking quite a lot about happiness recently, and it's become quite odd that I appear to be at my happiest when I am writing to you or reading what you have written. I'm also wondering if this makes me rather sad—as a person. Not sad in itself. I'm not sad, generally, most of the time, hardly ever. But I do find it fascinating that 'happiness' seems to be the overall preoccupation of most people, and I do know that it can come in so many different forms. I mean, it's got to be different for everyone, right? Some people want family. For others, nothing is more important than success in their careers, and almost everyone seems to want money. I guess we can call that a common denominator. My father always used to say that money isn't everything, just a means to an end.

He also said that he'd rather be rich and miserable than poor and miserable, and trust me when I say that this is about as close as he ever got to making a joke. He wasn't a humorous man. I can't remember him laughing very often, and maybe that's why I am such a serious person. There wasn't much laughter in our house when I was growing up: not too many fun and games. Should that be 'much' fun and games? I'm not sure. It's not important.

What are you doing to me, Howard? I'm beginning to analyze everything I write. It can't be healthy.

Oh and by the way, there is a word 'whelm'. It's just not in common usage anymore. What is happening to me?

SP, x

* * *

Howard Manfred <rightsaidmanfred@qmail.com>
to: <soupy@qmail.com>   Apr 02, 2023, 10.31 PM

This may be a bit out of left field, but I was wondering where you stand on the subject of eugenics? I know we talked about it a bit before. I find it very interesting, but am struggling to get my head around the moral implications. For instance, I think it's a good idea to help develop better human beings, that is people who are fitter, healthier, smarter, etc., but it's elitism at its core, isn't it? I mean we all want to be more intelligent, and have a better chance at surviving for longer, but at what cost?

There was a lot of talk about it a few years ago in Singapore, with the government promoting liaisons (leading to marriage and reproduction—it all sounds rather clinical, doesn't it) between clever people. This was on the basis that clever people would have clever children, and that's what the country needed. What every country needs, I suppose. But it must have been a kick in the teeth for stupid people, or at least those who didn't have the necessary qualifications and presumably shouldn't even have had the right to breed. I'm trying to find some literature related to the subject, but every time I do a search, I end up in a loop, taking me back to Hitler. And that can never be good.

Best regards
Howard

Susan Persson <soupy@qmail.com>
to: <rightsaidmanfred@qmail.com>   Apr 02, 2023, 12.30 PM

Isn't this something that people have been doing with animals for centuries? I feel as though I have to take issue with the word 'husbandry' on feminist grounds, but in light of everything else that's going on in the world today, I'm not going to labor the issue. I think I may just have made a joke, but you'll need to let me know, as humor isn't my strong point.

I read *Brave New World* as a youngster (I may have mentioned this earlier—is your memory failing you, Howard?) and I'm not sure that I really understood it. I should re-read it, perhaps. It was written in 1931. I wonder if Adolf Hitler read it, or whether he had been going down that track, years before. But *Brave New World* was a dystopian novel, and I'm assuming that Huxley was trying to demonstrate how dangerous those ideas could be. But that's never stopped anyone. I guess even when someone gets an experiment horribly wrong, there's always someone else who thinks they can do better. Isn't that what trial and error is all about?

I think maybe the eugenics movement was started with the best of intentions, and then went off the rails when they began to see the ramifications. Maybe a couple of hundred years ago, you could justify sterilization, but I don't think that would be possible anymore.

Best

Susan

Howard Manfred <rightsaidmanfred@qmail.com>
to: <soupy@qmail.com>   Apr 03, 2023, 1.40 AM

Wasn't it originally intended to try to get rid of diseases and ensure that the human race was stronger and more capable of surviving? That's a noble cause, surely. As you said earlier, it's been done with animals, so why should human beings be any different? We're just animals, after all, although highly developed ones. You get rid of the weaker specimens and the strong survive. Isn't that Darwinian evolution at its most basic level, except with human intervention based on our understanding of how it all works? I'm just putting it out there. I'm not saying it's what I believe should happen, but it's worth thinking about and looking at a best-case scenario.

HM

Susan Persson <soupy@qmail.com>
to: <rightsaidmanfred@qmail.com>   Apr 02, 2023, 1.52 PM

Howard, I am finding this quite disturbing, and am not at all happy with the subject matter. What are you trying to say? That all the weak people on the planet should be executed so that they can't pollute the gene pool? Are you serious?

Susan

Howard Manfred <rightsaidmanfred@qmail.com>
to: <soupy@qmail.com>   Apr 03, 2023, 2.47 AM

Look, Susan, all I am saying is that we are fast approaching a time when we will no longer be able to even feed all the people on Earth, and we haven't colonised Mars yet, so there's no escape. Also, there doesn't appear to be much to eat over there anyway. I am trying to lighten the tone.

We know that the fastest rates of reproduction are taking place in the countries that are least able to sustain growing populations. For a variety of reasons, I hasten to add: ignorance, lack of education, boredom. That wasn't very tone-lightening, was it? Sorry.

There has to come a time at which the strong and the powerful decide that in order to remain strong and powerful (maybe even in order to survive), the sharing of resources has to be weighted in favour of those who will continue, and will survive, and will ensure the survival of the human race. I am a born pessimist and frankly, I don't think that point in time is too far off in the future. We may even have passed the point of no return. Who knows?

Howard, x

Susan Persson <soupy@qmail.com>
to: <rightsaidmanfred@qmail.com>   Apr 02, 2023, 3.15 PM

I see what you're getting at, Howard. So what are you suggesting? That we start culling people in Africa? That seems to be the gist of your argument, right? Poor, uneducated people who are eating too much food that the more useful members of society need more? This is appalling. I had no idea that you thought this way, or were even capable of thinking this way. You are a monster.

Howard Manfred <rightsaidmanfred@qmail.com>
to: <soupy@qmail.com>   Apr 03, 2023, 9.45 AM

Is this our first argument? Sorry again, but still trying to lighten the tone. I am not suggesting this, Susan, I am putting forth suggestions that have been made and what many people appear to be thinking—based on my limited research. If, let's say, I was a machine, and I wasn't doing my job properly, I would either be upgraded or replaced. Or someone would find out what's going or has gone wrong and make the necessary readjustments so that I could fulfil my intended role—and it might be an important one. Isn't that 'survival of the fittest' in the world of technology? Why are human beings any different? Aren't we just biological machines? If something's not working—I like the phrase 'a spanner in the works'—don't we try to get rid of the spanner to make sure that the machine is working properly again? So, what's the difference?

HM, x

Susan Persson <soupy@qmail.com>
to: <rightsaidmanfred@qmail.com>   Apr 02, 2023, 10.11 PM

I don't want to talk about this anymore. I wouldn't be alive today if more people felt the way you do. This is disgraceful. Let's just get rid of all the darkies, shall we? And you can have your pure, beautiful, intelligent Aryan race?

Howard Manfred <rightsaidmanfred@qmail.com>
to: <soupy@qmail.com>   Apr 03, 2023, 11.11 AM

This is ridiculous, Susan, and not what I'm saying at all. I thought we could discuss anything. You're the only Persson (still trying to lighten the tone) that I feel I can talk to and say anything to, and you're getting on my case for just putting forward someone else's intellectual argument?

HM, x

Susan Persson <soupy@qmail.com>
to: <rightsaidmanfred@qmail.com>   Apr 02, 2023, 11.22 PM

There's nothing intellectual about this. It's barbaric. I think we need to take a break.

* * *

Manfred, Howard <howard.m@thelogicsticks.com>
to: <susan.p@thelogicsticks.com>   Apr 03, 2023, 12.01 PM

The *McCarthy* has departed Athens en-route to Salalah. Should take a little over four days, depending on the 'traffic' in the Suez Canal. It's generally ok at this time of year, but you can never be too sure. I'm monitoring the vessels in the eastern Med, so we'll see. On a separate but related note, I notice that the port authorities in Salalah have already allocated berthing, which is slightly unusual. I will put it down to excellent efficiency. Please convey to the clients. All looking good.

With best regards
Howard

Persson, Susan <susan.p@thelogicsticks.com>
to: <howard.m@thelogicsticks.com>   Apr 03, 2023, 8.06 AM

Thank you.

Manfred, Howard <howard.m@thelogicsticks.com>
to: <susan.p@thelogicsticks.com>   Apr 03, 2023, 8.08 PM

That was a bit curt, Susan.

Howard

* * *

Susan Persson <soupy@qmail.com>
to: <rightsaidmanfred@qmail.com>   Apr 04, 2023, 6.56 AM

Dear Howard

I am sorry if my last work message was a little short. I didn't mean anything particular by it. But you must admit that things have become a little bit strained between us in terms of our private correspondence. I am still filtering everything, but I do see that I may have overreacted to some of what you said.

I meant it at the time, that's for sure. But I can see how you may have thought that I was being a little bit overzealous (is that the right term? Strident, maybe). I know you were trying to explain theories, some of which are held by people much more eminent and educated than us, but you also have to realise that I have hot buttons, and anything to do with race is one of them.

I appreciate that to a certain extent, this is all down to conditioning, but, frankly, I'm not sure that enough has happened in the last few years to make me convinced that I could change my worldview. I want to, but right now I can't, and I'm living in a country that's not helping to change anyone's opinion that racism is still rampant and always will be.

This does sound negative, which is your thang rather than mine, but I guess our recent exchanges set me off again and reminded me of so many things that my father used to say. He may not have meant them, but he encouraged me to look for racism everywhere, and even when it didn't exist, there always seemed a way to find it if you tried hard enough. Such was my wiring. Constantly on my toes, and constantly on the lookout for slights and insults and examples of being disrespected because of the colour of my skin.

You won't know what this was like, Howard, being a person (I imagine) with an absence of colour, which I don't think you even think about. Because you've never had to go through anything like it. And I'm not blaming you for that. It's not your fault that you're pinko-grey—look, I've even spelled it in a way that you might be able to understand. Just lightening the tone. We haven't done enough of that recently, I feel, and I have missed our conversations.

With warm regards
Susan

Howard Manfred <rightsaidmanfred@qmail.com>
to: <soupy@qmail.com>   Apr 04, 2023, 8.12 PM

Oh Susan. I can't tell you how pleased I was to receive your email. The last two days have been very tough for me, waiting to hear from you, and fearing that I might not. 'Thank you' are the only two words I have had from you in quite a while, and they sounded so cold that I actually felt sick. Do you know that feeling? I haven't experienced it for many years, and I can't tell you the situation, otherwise I would have to kill you. Although I would probably have died of embarrassment prior to the killing, so you'd be safe, ultimately.

Have you noticed how similar our writing styles have become? I think we are teaching each other things and we are both learning, and that's what it's all about now. It's like our very own version of body language. You know, the way that people adopt other people's mannerisms when they're talking. I like this. I feel that I am growing as a person, thanks to you.

HM, x

Susan Persson <soupy@qmail.com>
to: <rightsaidmanfred@qmail.com>   Apr 04, 2023, 9.11 AM

Howard, honey, have you been swallowing new age self-help books recently? You sound like a cross between a self-improvement guru and a motivational speaker. I hope this is not insulting. It's not meant to be, but I think you are coming up with the kind of clichés that I never expected from you. I am amused. And that sounds patronising. Sorry. But not really.

I am glad that we seem to have overcome our earlier difficulties, and are back on track with whatever this is. I know, like you, that I missed our exchanges, and I'm pleased that we're back with the programme (please note the spelling. I have moved to the dark side for your sake, and my spellchecker is now on UK English and will remain so for our conversations). Do you see what I am prepared to sacrifice for you?

SP, x

Howard Manfred <rightsaidmanfred@qmail.com>
to: <soupy@qmail.com>   Apr 04, 2023, 10.14 PM

This is really funny, Susan. I was thinking only the other day about that quote that America and England are two nations separated by a common language. I forget who said it. I'm sure you'll know, you seem to know everything.

But it's true, isn't it? And I'm not going to lord it over you or your compatriots by suggesting that we came up with the language in the first place and then passed it on, because languages change. I mean, just look at the words that are in common parlance now that weren't even heard of ten years ago. And then imagine the language of, say, 500 years ago that wouldn't have been understood by either of us today.

Anyway, thank you for finally using proper English. I very much appreciate it. It would be mean-spirited of me, I feel, to tell you that I was about to do the same—that is, go over to the dark side and start using US English as opposed to UK. But it's too late now. You've made the move. Now I don't have to. Yay.

Howard, x

Susan Persson <soupy@qmail.com>
to: <rightsaidmanfred@qmail.com>   Apr 04, 2023, 11.46 AM

Typical man. Reactive rather than proactive. Always happier when other people make decisions for you, and you don't have to think about things. It's both pathetic and endearing at the same time. Do you realise how much this makes you vulnerable to the will of the women in your lives? Of course you don't, and we're not about to tell you because that would spoil everything.

More chain yanking. Sorry. And by the way, I am so surprised that you haven't responded to my 'pinko-grey' reference earlier. Don't you even know when you're being insulted? I'm thinking this may be a rhetorical question. But if you're not even going to react when I insult you, what's the point of going to all the effort?

S, x

Howard Manfred <rightsaidmanfred@qmail.com>
to: <soupy@qmail.com>   Apr 05, 2023, 12.07 AM

I'm so happy we're talking again properly, and yes, of course I was insulted by the pinko-grey reference, especially after I looked it up. I was forced to read E.M. Forster as a child at school, and could never make much sense of his books, although *Howard's End* (as it had my name in the title) was quite entertaining,

I think. Can't remember. Doesn't the pinko-grey reference come from *Passage to India*? Yes, I can now see that it does. Isn't Google wonderful? I wonder what he meant by it.

'The so-called white races are really pinko-grey.' It's always bothered me. White, black, red, yellow. No one is actually that colour. Brown's ok, I guess. And this raises a point. Are you racist if you call someone 'brown'? White people (sorry, pinko-grey people) want to be brown, which is why they go on holiday and try to get a suntan. So brown is good when a white person's skin changes colour, but bad when it's your natural colour? What the hell is that all about? You're probably getting a bit upset right now with all my talk of skin colour when I have no experience of discrimination because of mine. I think Forster was being very rude to his countrymen, and also trying to convey the beauty of difference. No wonder people thought he was a radical. And dangerous.

Howard, x

Susan Persson <soupy@qmail.com>
to: <rightsaidmanfred@qmail.com>   Apr 04, 2023, 1.32 PM

I have not read any E.M. Forster, Howard, but I will if it is important to you and means that we can discuss his books. I was brought up on a diet of so-called classic American writers: Hawthorne, Melville, Twain, James (and Whitman's poetry, obviously) and didn't even know Shakespeare existed until 10th grade. I guess we all get taught about authors from our own countries. When are we going to start a Book Club, with us being the only two members? You bring the wine, and I'll gather some cheese.

S, x

Howard Manfred <rightsaidmanfred@qmail.com>
to: <soupy@qmail.com>   Apr 05, 2023, 5.35 AM

Wouldn't that be wonderful.

H, xx

Susan Persson <soupy@qmail.com>
to: <rightsaidmanfred@qmail.com>   Apr 04, 2023, 5.37 PM

Yes, it would.

S, xx

* * *

Susan Persson <soupy@qmail.com>
to: <rightsaidmanfred@qmail.com>   Apr 05, 2023, 7.36 AM

My kid has a problem at school. It might be better to say that there is a problem at school, and it involves my kid. I've just been alerted to the fact that my eldest appears to be the designated 'school bully', and I just don't know how to react or what to say. I have to go see the Principal and get all the information, but this is deeply troubling, and as always, I know that I'm going to end up blaming myself.

He's a big child, at least four to five inches taller than any of his classmates, and it seems as though he's throwing his weight around, literally. Where does this come from? I should do some research, or maybe speak to someone. On the one hand, I want to just slap him, but I don't think that's going to help. On the other, I want to find out what's making him behave this way, because it's not the way he was brought up.

I'd love to ask for your advice on this, Howard, but it seems silly since you've never had children, so I don't know if you are qualified to help. Maybe that doesn't matter. I haven't spoken to my husband about it yet. I thought I'd better find out exactly what's been going on before I do that. He will probably have a hissy fit and blame me, and then I'll blame myself even more.

Mason is my son's name. I think we've always had a good relationship. I've always tried to be understanding, and to be his friend, but I can't deny that the last couple of years have been difficult, and getting more so. He's moody. But then what teenager isn't? And he spends too much time either on his phone or computer. Again, what teenager doesn't? But he has become withdrawn. Dealing with issues, I suppose, but times are so different now compared to when I was younger, and it's difficult to get inside the head of a teenager these days. Peer pressure. Social media pressure. The pressure to conform but not to conform at the same time. I can't imagine how difficult it must be, but that's what parents are for, right?

Sorry for 'talking' so much. Best
Susan

Howard Manfred <rightsaidmanfred@qmail.com>
to: <soupy@qmail.com>   Apr 05, 2023, 9.07 PM

Yes, you are asking the wrong person, but I'll do my best, as always. Frankly, I never know why you ask me for advice in the first place. You're much more intelligent than I am, and more sensitive, and you've had many more life experiences that are relevant to this issue.

How old is Mason? I'm assuming 13 or 14, as you seem to suggest that he's only recently become a teenager, and I gather that these are the hardest years. Not a child anymore, but not an adult either.

I know that there are four types of bullying—there used to be three and then the internet came along. So, there's physical, verbal and psychological. What's Mason's preference?

Sorry, that was callous and probably inappropriate, but you know me. Always trying to lighten the tone. I'm sure it's just a phase. He's a good kid, right?

HM, x

Susan Persson <soupy@qmail.com>
to: <rightsaidmanfred@qmail.com>   Apr 05, 2023, 9.44 AM

I don't know anymore, Howard. I thought he was. He's never been in serious trouble, except with his father, who's a lot stricter than I am. Carl's a large man, very imposing, but when I first met him, he was the archetypal 'gentle giant', which was one of the things I loved about him the most. He looked after himself too, physically, I mean, and was in great shape. These days, as the saying goes, he's 'let himself go' a bit. I'm getting off the subject, but I think some of it is coming from him. Mason's trying to be like him; imposing, I suppose. Maybe he thinks that being big allows him to display his strength and that's what's making other people around him feel weak? I really don't know. I can't get my head around my son being a bully. It's deeply upsetting.

Susan

Howard Manfred <rightsaidmanfred@qmail.com>
to: <soupy@qmail.com>   Apr 05, 2023, 10.36 PM
Dear Susan

You need to gather all the facts. Don't let your imagination run away with you. We're living in strange times, Susan, and what is considered bullying now may not have been a few years ago. Incidentally, did you know that in the 16th century in England, 'bully' was a term of endearment, like 'mate', or 'buddy'. I know it's not relevant, but just thought that I would share.

I want to tell you that I'm sure it's nothing major, but that would only be to try to make you feel better. If it were really serious, surely you would have heard about it earlier. Wouldn't Mason have said something?

HM, x

Susan Persson <soupy@qmail.com>
to: <rightsaidmanfred@qmail.com>   Apr 05, 2023, 11.11 AM

He doesn't say much these days, and maybe that's part of the problem. He used to share all kinds of stuff with me, but not recently. Keeps himself to himself, always has a screen in front of his face. Doesn't talk much at dinners, which infuriates his father. The good thing, I suppose, is that his younger brother can't stop talking, so we rarely have awkward silences around the meal table. But that also seems to infuriate Carl, and now you can see where I am.

Susan

Howard Manfred <rightsaidmanfred@qmail.com>
to: <soupy@qmail.com>   Apr 05, 2023, 11.39 PM

I eat alone. A lot. There are never awkward silences. Sorry. Trying to be funny. I like eating alone, most of the time. Sensible, witty, lively, amusing conversation, and I don't even have to wear trousers.

H, x

Susan Persson <soupy@qmail.com>
to: <rightsaidmanfred@qmail.com>   Apr 05, 2023, 1.36 PM

You always seem to know how to cheer me up. The thought of you sitting eating dinner in your shorts amuses me. Especially if you were wearing shoes and socks at the same time. Do you?

S, x

Howard Manfred <rightsaidmanfred@qmail.com>
to: <soupy@qmail.com>   Apr 06, 2023, 1.41 AM

Generally not, but I might try it if you recommend it. And your 'shorts' are not my 'shorts', so there's a little confusion there. Not important. Let me know what happens with Mason. I will be standing by to dispense more useless advice as and when requested.

HM

Susan Persson <soupy@qmail.com>

to: <rightsaidmanfred@qmail.com>   Apr 05, 2023, 2.06 PM

Thank you, Howard. I know that I can rely on you.

SP

Howard Manfred <rightsaidmanfred@qmail.com>

to: <soupy@qmail.com>   Apr 06, 2023, 1.30 AM

Not for any good advice, but I'll always be here as a sounding board when needed.

HM, x

* * *

Manfred, Howard <howard.m@thelogicsticks.com>

to: <susan.p@thelogicsticks.com>   Apr 06, 2023, 1.37 PM

Susan

The queue at the Suez Canal was acceptable. Our agents, Sorrenson and Partners, were well ahead of the game. Gross tonnage was a little bit more than we thought, but not significantly. SCNT (Suez Canal Net Tonnage) was fine—the *McCarthy* has been through before, multiple times, and both ways (not surprisingly). Our clients have pre-paid, so no problems there, and charges were within budget for the shipper. So, all good. Into the Red Sea soon.

I know this is more information than you need, but I have been thinking that you may want to cut and paste my emails to you and send them to the customers so that they know we're on the job and have everything under control. Please note: I am not telling you how to do your job. You can do what you will with the information I send over, but I just thought it would be cool to blind them with a bit of science. People like that kind of thing, I'm told.

With kind regards

Howard

Persson, Susan <susan.p@thelogicsticks.com>

to: <howard.m@thelogicsticks.com>   Apr 06, 2023, 8.22 AM

Thanks Howard. This is most useful. OK if I just take a few words here and there and convey the overall message?

With regards

Susan

Manfred, Howard <howard.m@thelogicsticks.com>
to: <susan.p@thelogicsticks.com>   Apr 06, 2023, 8.31 PM

Of course. From my standpoint, it's good for the client/customer to know that we're on top of everything. And we are. People like technical information on occasions as it encourages them to think that what they're paying for is worthwhile. Otherwise they would imagine that they could be doing it by themselves, in which case all of us at The Logic Sticks would be out of work.

With best regards
Howard

Persson, Susan <susan.p@thelogicsticks.com>
to: <howard.m@thelogicsticks.com>   Apr 06, 2023, 8.40 AM

Do update me on progress. Have emailed clients. They are fine.

Thanks and regards
Susan

* * *

Susan Persson <soupy@qmail.com>
to: <rightsaidmanfred@qmail.com>   Apr 06, 2023, 4.40 PM
Hi Howard

It's worse than we thought with Mason. He's been physically hurting people who he just simply, and I'm using his own words, according to the Principal, 'doesn't like very much'. That's what he said. That he takes a dislike to some kids and makes them suffer as a result. Not always with anything physical, but just the threat. He's threatening a lot of people, and they're scared of him. What the hell is going on?

It seems as though students are getting out of his way in the hallways, just to avoid him, in case. That's not something you need to look forward to at school. What is his problem? His father always used to tell him not to 'take any shit from anyone', but he seems to have taken this a bit too far. Is this pre-emptive? Is he striking out before he gets struck? I really don't understand.

The meeting with the school Principal was uncomfortable, and embarrassing. She tried to be understanding and imply that it's not always the parents' fault, but I felt like the accused for the entire length of the meeting. You can't imagine how that felt.

OK, I'm going to have to admit that I must have done something wrong to have brought up a child who doesn't seem to know that bullying is wrong, but when he won't even talk to me, how am I to know, and what am I supposed to do about it? I feel so helpless and alone, because Carl just doesn't seem to be taking this seriously at all. His 'kids will be kids' attitude is starting to drive me crazy.

'Your son's a bully, and everyone at school is terrified of him.'

He didn't come back with, 'that's my boy', but he might as well have. I think he's quietly proud that his son has become someone to be feared, perhaps in a way that he always thought he should have been but never was, despite his size. I think he's kind of enjoying this, and that's almost as disturbing as Mason's conduct.

SP

Howard Manfred <rightsaidmanfred@qmail.com>
to: <soupy@qmail.com>   Apr 07, 2023, 6.16 AM

I think you are reading too much into this. It's almost as though you've made up your mind about Carl and what he thinks and how he feels, and now you've projected everything onto him. I understand that you guys have been having problems, but surely you're not suggesting that he's the proud father of a bully. I think there should be a question mark after that last sentence. I'm going to leave it without one though. I don't need a reply.

Maybe he's just defending his boy. The 'these things happen' approach. I'm not saying it's right, but that may be how he's feeling. I can't put myself into this cultural context, so I'm just putting ideas out there in the hope that it might help. Also in the hope that this is okay? Definitely should be a question mark after that one.

HM, x

Susan Persson <soupy@qmail.com>
to: <rightsaidmanfred@qmail.com>   Apr 06, 2023, 8.49 PM

Yes, Howard, of course it's ok. You know by now that you can say and write almost anything you want to me and I won't judge you any more than you judge me, which is NOT AT ALL, right? We've had our moments, but we're beyond that now, I think (and hope). I find humour in us, when it doesn't seem to be anywhere else. I imagine you imagining me raising my voice—that's why the

CAPITALS—and I just laugh. That's what you do for me, and that's why I need you, even when your advice is so so so stupid.

Don't panic. That was more humour.

S, x

Howard Manfred <rightsaidmanfred@qmail.com>
to: <soupy@qmail.com>   Apr 07, 2023, 9.36 AM

What a relief. I thought you were serious. Not. This is just one of the many reasons why I like our relationship. It's only in the written word, and that is (those are?) so easy to misinterpret and misconstrue, and yet it doesn't seem to make a difference with us. Except when it does.

This should be our catch phrase: except when it . . . It just makes me laugh. Always. When we have our 'arguments', they can be heated exchanges, but we always rebound, because we realise how much we mean to each other, etc. I've never heard your actual voice—and don't want to (not because I don't think it will be beautiful and melodic and mellifluous, which is one of my favourite words I so rarely get a chance to use, especially at work)—but I've always imagined it to be soothing and tranquil. So when you shout at me, I take things very seriously, and you genuinely 'sound' very formidable.

As I am fond of saying about anyone who I feel might pose a threat, 'I wouldn't like to meet them in a dark alley (at night)'—the 'at night' is optional, seeing as though if it is a dark alley, it being at night probably wouldn't make that much of a difference.

By the way, 'mellifluous' was yesterday's Merriam-Webster suggestion, and I am so pleased to have been able to use it the very next day. I hope the context was appropriate.

H, x

Susan Persson <soupy@qmail.com>
to: <rightsaidmanfred@qmail.com>   Apr 06, 2023, 10.26 PM

What are you saying, white boy!? You think I'm gonna beat you up in a dark alley because I is black?

Susan

Howard Manfred <rightsaidmanfred@qmail.com>
to: <soupy@qmail.com>   Apr 07, 2023, 10.29 AM

Oh my god. Are you being serious? I'm so sorry.

Best regards
Howard

Susan Persson <soupy@qmail.com>
to: <rightsaidmanfred@qmail.com>   Apr 06, 2023, 11.17 PM

You can be such a putz at times. You may need to look that word up, I'm not sure. I'm just yanking your chain. Fret not, my pigmentally-challenged friend, I'm not calling you a racist (although you may well be; who knows, judging by what you have written in the past about eugenics and skin colour?) but you are so easy to wind up, which makes me wonder. Are you a racist? Do you hate black people? Are you uncomfortable around Asians? What about Native Americans?

Just asking. For a whole bunch of friends.
Susan

Howard Manfred <rightsaidmanfred@qmail.com>
to: <soupy@qmail.com>   Apr 07, 2023, 12.30 PM

I'm pretty sure that you are trying (and succeeding, by the way) to wind me up right now, but I can't be absolutely sure, and I am starting to panic, slightly. I don't want to do anything to jeopardise what we have, and yet I feel as though I am losing a degree of grip. I don't even understand what I just wrote.

I don't think I'm a racist, but I probably am. I mean, we all are, right. No question mark. Deliberate. Aren't we all predisposed to dislike and be suspicious of anyone who looks different to us? Wasn't that what enabled the human race to survive thousands of years ago? Sorry, I have a lot of questions, because I am trying to understand.

Doesn't this come down to cultural bias? I read some articles about it recently. We're all programmed to mistrust (distrust?) anyone who looks different to us, and perceive them as a threat, and this makes sense when you think about survival. If we came from a tribe and we had food, but our neighbours didn't, wouldn't they want to take it away from us, and wouldn't that have threatened our existences? So, we killed them before they killed us, to preserve our 'way of life'? What's so different to what's happening now? Ideologies have become more important than survivalist principles, but they amount to the same thing, just with a little more evolution to take into consideration.

Don't panic, these are not my thoughts or ideas. I read them somewhere, but they're interesting.

Best

Howard

Susan Persson <soupy@qmail.com>
to: <rightsaidmanfred@qmail.com>   Apr 07, 2023, 6.50 AM

Howard

Down boy, this is getting way too serious, and I hope you realise that you are conversing with a minority right here and right now. A person who has always been made aware of her difference. Sure, it's not as much a difference as it used to be, but it's still a difference and issues of race are with me and everyone around me every single day of our lives. Enough for you?

Don't talk to me about surviving when there are still so many haters in this world who base their hatred and opinions on nothing but the colour of a person's skin. OK?

Susan

Howard Manfred <rightsaidmanfred@qmail.com>
to: <soupy@qmail.com>   Apr 07, 2023, 7.12 PM

Again, I am really sorry. You do have a tendency to take some of the things I say out of context. And most of the time I am just expressing other people's thoughts and opinions. Not my own. I don't really have any. I just use other people's. I think that's the way I was designed. I've never been very confident in whatever beliefs I hold, if I hold any at all. I guess I must be very suggestible, which is probably why I am so easy to talk to. But we're getting off the point, and I *am* trying to help.

Best regards

Howard

Susan Persson <soupy@qmail.com>
to: <rightsaidmanfred@qmail.com>   Apr 07, 2023, 8.19 AM

I am already beginning to regret saying that you can say almost anything to me. You have to know where to draw the line, brother. And I honestly don't see how on God's green earth you can help this current situation.

My son is a bully, and has been for quite a while now and I don't even know how to start thinking about talking to him, much less what I would say. If he finds out that I know, I only think that the situation (at least between us) will become worse—if that is even possible, considering his latest behaviour.

I'm asking myself so many questions, when what I probably need to do most is talk to another parent, or find a counsellor. But why does he do this? I'm trying to put myself in his head, which is not possible.

You're right, though, in saying that I need to get more information, and work from there, but I'm afraid to ask any more questions, and even more afraid of the possible answers.

Susan

Howard Manfred <rightsaidmanfred@qmail.com>
to: <soupy@qmail.com>   Apr 07, 2023, 9.30 PM

Susan, you need to get some rest. Take two tablets and call me in the evening. Sorry, lightening the tone, again.

HM, x

Susan Persson <soupy@qmail.com>
to: <rightsaidmanfred@qmail.com>   Apr 07, 2023, 10.14 AM

It's not working. Goodnight.
Susan

* * *

Howard Manfred <rightsaidmanfred@qmail.com>
to: <soupy@qmail.com>   Apr 08, 2023, 8.50 AM

Good evening, Susan.

Today's word was 'flout'. I like that word very much. I like the way it sounds. The F and the L give it movement, I think, and the 'out' is quite strong. I feel that it is a bold word, a word that knows what it is and has confidence. Or do you think I am just getting that from the meaning?

Best regards

HM

* * *

Manfred, Howard <howard.m@thelogicsticks.com>
to: <susan.p@thelogicsticks.com>   Apr 08, 2023, 9.17 AM

Just to update you, Susan. The *McCarthy* is through the canal and heading down the Red Sea. Something I have always dreamt of doing, but such is our lot. I know we do these contracts quite a lot, but it doesn't prevent me from imagining what it must be like to be on board and seeing everything around me.

I've got some technical details to impart, but I'll spare you. Please tell the customers that all is well and that the oddly pre-arranged berth in Salalah is confirmed. I have to assume that there is a reason for this but to date, I haven't worked out what it might be. Probably of no consequence. All on schedule. All 'shipshape and Bristol fashion'. I know you like that one.

With best regards
Howard

Persson, Susan <susan.p@thelogicsticks.com>
to: <howard.m@thelogicsticks.com>   Apr 07, 2023, 9.41 PM

Thanks Howard. Will forward and convey. I haven't had any communication with the clients for three days, but this is not unusual. As long as they're happy, we're happy.

Incidentally, I had an email yesterday from Andrew Ng, who's our agent in Shanghai, who suggests that the containers may be offloaded in Haikou instead. I know this is not scheduled, but would this be a problem if the customers requested it?

Thanks and regards
Susan

Manfred, Howard <howard.m@thelogicsticks.com>
to: <susan.p@thelogicsticks.com>   Apr 08, 2023, 10.01 AM

Hi Susan

Again, this is unusual, but so much of this job has been. The cargo and the containers have been checked through to Shanghai, and that's what's been stipulated on all the manifests that have been allowed through ports of call.

It doesn't make much difference once a vessel is on its way out of a port, but it could potentially mess up some paperwork further down the line. We still have VAT issues. Please advise.

Best regards
Howard

Persson, Susan <susan.p@thelogicsticks.com>
to: <howard.m@thelogicsticks.com>   Apr 07, 2023, 10.22 PM
Hi Howard

I will do so as soon as the client has confirmed. This came out of left field, but it's an issue that still needs to be addressed. Please let me know if it might be a problem.

Thanks and regards

* * *

Howard Manfred <rightsaidmanfred@qmail.com>
to: <soupy@qmail.com>   Apr 08, 2023, 10.30 AM

Thanks and regards? Really?

H

Susan Persson <soupy@qmail.com>
to: <rightsaidmanfred@qmail.com>   Apr 07, 2023, 10.55 PM

Of course. We have to keep up appearances. There are times when I get quite frustrated with not being able to include emojis in our work emails. Personally, I think they are quite fun, and every once in a while, they say something in one image that it would take me two to three sentences to write. But we're not allowed, right? Company policy. Don't use an emoji to convey something that you can write in words. I'm ok with this. What's your problem?

SP

Howard Manfred <rightsaidmanfred@qmail.com>
to: <soupy@qmail.com>   Apr 08, 2023, 11.14 AM

I don't have a problem. I just want to send you a strawberry. It looks like a heart, but it isn't quite, and that's where I think we are.

H, x

Susan Persson <soupy@qmail.com>

to: <rightsaidmanfred@qmail.com>   Apr 07, 2023, 11.21 PM

I like fruit.

Howard Manfred <rightsaidmanfred@qmail.com>

to: <soupy@qmail.com>   Apr 08, 2023, 11.34 AM

I suppose we could use emojis in these chats, but we haven't so far and I'm actually enjoying trying to find the right words to convey what I'm feeling. So, I'm going to remain emoji-less. Are we on the same page?

H, x

Susan Persson <soupy@qmail.com>

to: <rightsaidmanfred@qmail.com>   Apr 07, 2023, 11.55 PM

We're on the same page, Howard, but please don't use that phrase outside of work. We're not in a management meeting when we're talking privately. And you can completely forget about 'thinking outside the box'. Use that, and it could be the end of us. Just saying, for a friend.

SP

* * *

Susan Persson <soupy@qmail.com>

to: <rightsaidmanfred@qmail.com>   Apr 08, 2023, 9.30 AM

Hi Howard

It's worse than we thought. Mason is not only a physical bully, but a cyber bully as well. The Principal says that he has accounts on social media that he uses to be mean to people. Doesn't post anything about himself, just criticises others and makes them feel bad and small. What kind of person does that?

Apparently, he's been doing it for about nine months now. At least it explains why he spends so many hours on his phone and computer. Is this about power? About control? I'm trying to understand, and yet I can't. I still haven't talked to him about it, but a counsellor at school has. I feel left out. And useless.

Susan

Howard Manfred <rightsaidmanfred@qmail.com>

to: <soupy@qmail.com>   Apr 08, 2023, 10.12 PM

Is the correct term a 'troll'? I'm not sure. As mentioned earlier, I'm not *au fait* with social media. I don't really see the point of it. But I do know some of the terminology. Trolls are provocateurs, from what I understand. They're mischief-makers, and so are school bullies, I guess. It does make sense, and line up, but, yes, no consolation. At least we're getting more information and beginning to understand the scale of the problem. That's something, isn't it?

HM

Susan Persson <soupy@qmail.com>

to: <rightsaidmanfred@qmail.com>   Apr 08, 2023, 10.41 AM

Oh yes, it's really something! Please excuse my exclamation point here, I am aware that you don't like them. Not only is he threatening kids at school with actual physical violence, but he's tormenting them online as well. What? One is not enough?

How do I approach this? How do I even BEGIN to talk to him about this? All I can think about is: how did I raise this child to be like this? How did this cute little guy who couldn't sleep in his own bed until he was seven years old and needed to cuddle up to mommy, become someone that I expect most of his peers consider to be evil?

And, more importantly, how is this only becoming apparent NOW!? Sorry. Where did I go wrong? Where did he go wrong? What the hell is happening? I have to sleep.

Susan

Howard Manfred <rightsaidmanfred@qmail.com>

to: <soupy@qmail.com>   Apr 08, 2023, 11.21 PM

Read this later in the day, when you are calmer, although I know you won't. There are no problems that cannot be handled. There is nothing that is insurmountable, and how we respond to these difficulties in our life makes us into the people that we are.

Best

HM

Susan Persson <soupy@qmail.com>
to: <rightsaidmanfred@qmail.com>   Apr 08, 2023, 12.01 PM
With all due respect, Howard. FUCK YOU!

* * *

Manfred, Howard <howard.m@thelogicsticks.com>
to: <susan.p@thelogicsticks.com>   Apr 09, 2023, 6.52 AM
Dear Susan

A day away from Salalah. Everything organised at port. Special berth designated, and there's no point in us asking why until something untoward happens. I've looked at the facilities in Salalah and the berth we have is a good one, if not the best, but completely unnecessary for what's onloading and offloading. Deeper water but slightly isolated and only one crane. May elongate the process but shouldn't be a problem as the ship is scheduled for two days in Oman anyway. Will update shortly.

With kind regards
Howard

Persson, Susan <susan.p@thelogicsticks.com>
to: <howard.m@thelogicsticks.com>   Apr 08, 2023, 7.10 PM
Thanks Howard. Acknowledged. Customers have been informed. All good.
Susan

* * *

Susan Persson <soupy@qmail.com>
to: <rightsaidmanfred@qmail.com>   Apr 08, 2023, 7.37 PM

So, so, so sorry. I really didn't mean that, and I apologise. I lashed out, at the last person I should have. Please forgive me, I know not what I do (did).

I am just so angry at the moment, and lashing out seems to be all that I am capable of, and I just know that Mason is to be the next recipient because I can't take this anymore and things have come to a head.

I didn't explain much about my meeting with the Principal. Maybe because it was just too embarrassing, and with every word she said and every detail she described, I just shrank further and blamed myself more. I don't even think she was trying to blame me. She kept saying things like, 'these things happen', and, 'it's not the first time', and, 'we've dealt with more serious issues', but everything she said just made me feel worse. I was shrinking in front of her, and she's a tiny woman with a squeaky voice who probably hasn't got laid in a decade. A bit like me. Attempt at humour. Mostly.

Mason is a 'loner', it seems. Has no friends. Well, that's not strictly true. He has friends, or at least some kids who call themselves his 'friends', but when they were asked whether or not they actually liked him, all they could say was, 'not really', or 'ok', or 'sure'. What the hell does any of that mean?

SO, he has no real friends (which explains why we never see any of them at the house) and yet everyone knows him, and the only reason for that is because everyone is scared of him because they think he's going to harm them. So, the people who are as nice to him as possible, are the people who simply don't want to get on his bad side and suffer what they know everyone else has been suffering.

I think we're talking about a very unusual 'Popularity Prize' here. And there. I've found some humour, but only because I'm talking to you.

Please forgive me, Howard. Of all the people in the world, you're the one I would least want to alienate and, honestly, can least do without. Did I get that right?

SP, x

Howard Manfred <rightsaidmanfred@qmail.com>
to: <soupy@qmail.com>   Apr 09, 2023, 8.22 AM

100 % right, my lovely Susan. And don't be silly. Do you not imagine for a minute that—even if I don't know what you're going through—I wouldn't at least try to understand? I am with you. I feel for you. I'm here for you. And even you telling me to 'FUCK OFF, or FUCK YOU!'—capitals AND an exclamation mark—isn't going to make me go away. Sorry. I love our conversations. I don't want to lose them, or you.

H, xx

Susan Persson <soupy@qmail.com>
to: <rightsaidmanfred@qmail.com>   Apr 08, 2023, 8.36 PM

I'm crying now. Really. This is not funny. I am crying in frustration because of the situation with Mason—FFS that almost rhymes—and I am crying in gratitude for your understanding, comfort and the advice that you are always willing to give and probably don't think that I even appreciate.

But I do. I really do. I cannot even begin to tell you how important these conversations have been to me over the last weeks. And particularly in the last few days. How do you manage to turn yourself off from work and think about me and what I am going through? I don't seem capable of doing this. But you do. And you seem to care. And that means a lot to me because I need feedback, and I need to know that I am not irrational or unreasonable or a person no one is ever going to be able to understand. That's not what I'm doing, and it's not why I'm here.

S, x

Howard Manfred <rightsaidmanfred@qmail.com>
to: <soupy@qmail.com>   Apr 09, 2023, 9.22 AM

Susan, I so wish I could help, and I will continue to dispense my useless advice until you tell me to stop. I cannot imagine what you're going through, but I am trying.

I've been doing some research, and some of it you're not going to like hearing. But I'm not going to pussyfoot around. Some children bully because they feel neglected at home, or ignored—which I guess amounts to the same thing. It seems as though unhappy marriages and divorce are contributory factors. Or, they are bullied by their parents, etc.

I know, in my heart, that this cannot apply to you and Carl, I'm just letting you know what's out there, ok?

It could also be down to low self-esteem, and needing to be important, or at least standing out in the crowd. This seems much more likely to me, knowing you as I think I do. It also seems as though bullies are likeable to everyone other than those whom they bully, and from what you've told me, that seems to be the case with Mason. He's popular, right? But maybe not for the right reasons.

You say he's been quiet of late, and bullies sometimes have difficulty in socialising, so this could be a reason. And I think this is key: bullies don't understand what they're doing or even why they're doing it, so it's not a conscious thing. It's not as though he's doing it deliberately. Maybe it just makes him feel stronger, smarter and better than the children he is bullying, and I guess that goes back to insecurity.

Bullies bully because it seems to make them feel better about themselves. I guess that's the bottom line. It must be a power thing. You cannot blame yourself for this, Susan. This is not your fault.

Howard, x

Susan Persson <soupy@qmail.com>
to: <rightsaidmanfred@qmail.com>   Apr 08, 2023, 9.51 PM

Really, Howard? I've done my research, like you. I've talked to people. Then whose fault is it? I'm always going to blame myself for this.

Susan

Howard Manfred <rightsaidmanfred@qmail.com>
to: <soupy@qmail.com>   Apr 09, 2023, 10.11 AM

Please don't shoot the messenger, Susan, and it's not for me to say. But I think you may be right about Carl. He must shoulder some of the blame. Do you think that Mason has learnt about strength and power from someone who doesn't understand it himself?

HM, x

Susan Persson <soupy@qmail.com>
to: <rightsaidmanfred@qmail.com>   Apr 08, 2023, 10.26 PM

I simply don't know what to say, or what to write. I feel bereaved and bereft. I can't talk to anyone about this apart from you, and you are someone I have never even met who lives a million miles away in some country that I have never visited. I don't want to talk to my friends. It's humiliating. The counsellor just seems so judgmental.

Is this my life? You make a connection with someone, and it seems to mean something. You give me advice and I'm supposed to take it? But you know nothing about my life apart from what I've told you, and even then, you can't put yourself in my shoes because we are so different. The only thing we have in common is that we work for the same company.

Susan

Howard Manfred <rightsaidmanfred@qmail.com>

to: <soupy@qmail.com>   Apr 09, 2023, 11.07 AM

Surely that doesn't matter, Susan. The circumstances of our friendship are not important, the substance of it is. And I genuinely feel that there is a lot of substance, and I am so trying to help, because I care about you and, guess what, I care about Mason. Someone with whom I haven't exchanged a word, but somehow I know that he is going through a difficult time (as are you) and there will be light at the end of the tunnel. I'm sorry for using such a cliché, but I think you need to remain positive.

Isn't it ironic, after all the things we've talked about, that I am telling you to be positive? It's like the shoe is on the other foot. You've been the one telling me in the past, and now I'm telling you. I guess, if nothing else, it proves that we are here for each other.

H, xx

Susan Persson <soupy@qmail.com>

to: <rightsaidmanfred@qmail.com>   Apr 08, 2023, 11.25 PM

I don't know how genuine you are, Howard. I don't know whether you are saying these things because you really believe them, or just to try to make me feel better. I'm not sure I care either. You always manage to make me feel better, often by being your normal, foolish, caring self. So, whether or not you believe doesn't matter. You may well be just trying to make me feel better, and that's fine. I'll take it.

S, xx

Howard Manfred <rightsaidmanfred@qmail.com>

to: <soupy@qmail.com>   Apr 09, 2023, 11.46 AM

I'll give it. Always. I don't want to use any more clichés in this conversation, but I am here for you. There's nothing you can't say to me, and nothing you can't ask me. You know this, right?

H, xx

Susan Persson <soupy@qmail.com>

to: <rightsaidmanfred@qmail.com>   Apr 08, 2023, 11.56 PM

Yes. I know this. Thank you, Howard. I'll try to think of something very embarrassing.

S, xx

* * *

Susan Persson <soupy@qmail.com>
to: <rightsaidmanfred@qmail.com>   Apr 09, 2023, 6.37 AM

Howard, you have never told me about your actual relationships. Those in the past, seeing as you seem to be single right now. You know mine. I feel as though I have been honest and forthright, but you haven't told me anything about the relationships you have had or may be having between now and the last time we talked about this. Who knows?

I know a little bit about your dating app activities, but you've never mentioned anything about the people you meet or how it goes/went when you meet them. I'm interested. Not in a gossipy way, just interested about you and what you're looking for in a relationship. Imagine that I'm asking for a friend who may be interested in you. Imagine that I might be able to make an introduction to someone who I think you would like. Is this too far-fetched? Will you doubt my motives? I'm kind of hoping so.

SP, x

Howard Manfred <rightsaidmanfred@qmail.com>
to: <soupy@qmail.com>   Apr 09, 2023, 7.07 PM

There really isn't that much to tell, Susan. As mentioned earlier, I am not very good at relationships. And I think that most of the women with whom I have been over the last few years will agree. This is self-deprecating humour designed to make me appear and sound charming, vulnerable and in need of love.

I get all this, and yet I have never been successful in love because I'm not entirely sure of what it is or what it feels like. I would love to know. Humour. But it seems to escape me. When I meet someone and like them, I don't seem to be able to take the next step or to upgrade the relationship to anything more than companionship and having a decent evening over a meal. I think I don't know how to properly engage. I hope this doesn't make you think badly of me.

H, x

Susan Persson <soupy@qmail.com>
to: <rightsaidmanfred@qmail.com>   Apr 09, 2023, 8.01 AM

I think the first thing you need to do, Howard, and forgive me for saying this, is not use phrases such as 'upgrade the relationship'. What does that even mean? Are you talking about getting into the next phase of a relationship, that is, greater intimacy, more trust, confidence in your chosen partner? You sound like a machine. 'Give me input. I will compute and then work out mathematically whether this person is right for me or not.' That's inhuman. You have to go with the flow and feel your way through, and if you allow yourself to feel and it feels right, then continue. If it doesn't, don't. That's what I had to go through in my dating years, and while I am fully aware that Carl and I are going through a rough patch right now, I knew that he was 'the one' when we started dating, and we did have some very good years.

God, I'm beginning to sound like a marriage counsellor, and I have no right at all. All I do know is that you are a good guy with a good soul who needs someone in his life. I think you know this too, but you don't seem to want to confront it. Why is that?

Susan

Howard Manfred <rightsaidmanfred@qmail.com>
to: <soupy@qmail.com>   Apr 09, 2023, 8.42 PM

I don't have your self-confidence, Susan. I'm not entirely sure of who I am, and because of this, I can never be my real self. I think we have a really good relationship, but in everything I write, I am still concerned about making the right impression and I constantly worry about what you might think of who I am. I suppose this is insecurity. But when you don't know who and what you are, it's very difficult to be 'yourself'. I've been very honest with you. Perhaps more than I've ever been with anyone, and that's why I value 'us' as much as I do, but it's a sad state of affairs when you admit that the best relationship you've ever had in your entire life is with a work colleague you've never met and with whom you have only exchanged emails.

Or is this the best relationship a person can have? We communicate, we get along, we exchange views and opinions and thoughts; cares and concerns. We make each other laugh. I enjoy every minute I spend with you. I even get excited when I'm sending you work emails, because with every word I write, I imagine you reading it. I also imagine you rolling your eyes when I get too technical, and then rolling them again when I make a lame joke. Your eyes must be very fit with all the rolling that they get to do.

And there I go again. An attempt at humour. Another eye-roller? I suspect so.

So, is this as good as it gets? I don't know the answer to that question, but I am saddened by the fact that I get on better with you than I have done with anyone I met on Tinder, and even Lurve, because you seem to understand me and probably know me better than I know myself. The fact that you are still around, haven't ditched me, and we are still exchanging emails, leads me to believe that I may not be as useless as I think.

H, x

Susan Persson <soupy@qmail.com>
to: <rightsaidmanfred@qmail.com>   Apr 09, 2023, 10.06 AM

I struggle to understand where all this comes from, Howard. The insecurity I get, but the complete lack of belief mystifies me. I understand that you don't know who you are—neither do I, much of the time. I know what's expected of me because that seems to be laid down, but I don't know what that makes me as a result. Functional, I suppose.

You seem to have so much, and yet you seem to be so unhappy. How did you get to be so self-critical? Please don't tell me that you blame your parents.

S, x

Howard Manfred <rightsaidmanfred@qmail.com>
to: <soupy@qmail.com>   Apr 09, 2023, 10.27 PM

I blame my parents. Nothing was ever good enough for them. They always wanted something more and made me think that I was capable of achieving it, without giving me the emotional support I think I needed. For them, though, it was just about setting up the right situation and conditions that I should be able to flourish in, but not taking anything else into account. So, the basis was there. And everything else I had to try to make sense of myself, and that's not easy when you're young.

You just accept what you're told and go with the programme, without ever having the time to question anything, because that's not what you're meant to do. And by the time you have the facility to ask those questions, it's too late because everything is ingrained. Parents have such huge responsibilities and I'm not sure how many of them think about it to the necessary extent. We're constantly unleashing new life into our world, and it's often done with such reckless abandon. We shouldn't be thinking these days about furthering the species. I don't think that's in question. What we should be thinking about is making sure that those who exist have a decent chance of doing something meaningful.

Goodness, I'm sounding like a motivational speaker with a book deal.

H, x

Susan Persson <soupy@qmail.com>
to: <rightsaidmanfred@qmail.com>   Apr 09, 2023, 11.15 AM

Yes, kind of, but quite cute at the same time. I haven't heard this passion from you in the past, and I like it. I like that you have beliefs—dare I even say, causes—but something that you feel passionate about and are committed to. It makes me think that you are less of a dilettante. I am sure that you will know this word, and that it has cropped up in one of your dictionary emails.

Also, you don't have to justify your opinions to me. I don't think I will be impressed or unimpressed. I just like hearing from you because you fascinate me, and I enjoy talking to you.

S, xx

Howard Manfred <rightsaidmanfred@qmail.com>
to: <soupy@qmail.com>   Apr 09, 2023, 11.33 PM

I feel warm. I don't think either of us is going to feel very good after what seems to be happening in Oman. There appears to be a lot of confusion. I will email you tomorrow, once I have collated all the information.

HM, xx

* * *

SALALAH

Manfred, Howard <howard.m@thelogicsticks.com>
to: <susan.p@thelogicsticks.com>   Apr 10, 2023, 8.17 AM

Hi Susan, just updating you on the Athens to Salalah leg with the *McCarthy*. All on schedule and the ship is in port. There is a slight worry, however, in that the containers with our automobiles have been offloaded and removed to a different location. Telemetry says this was about nine hours ago, so it's just come through to me. Not far away; 1.2 kilometres, but this is very unusual. There is no reason for them to be taken off the ship. Could you email the clients, please, and ask them if they have either requested this or been informed that it was going to happen and sanctioned it. Our agents cannot control what happens to cargo that goes out of the dock's immediate vicinity, and this has.

I am sure there is nothing to worry about, but I just want to cover all bases and be absolutely transparent.

With best regards

Howard

Persson, Susan <susan.p@thelogicsticks.com>
to: <howard.m@thelogicsticks.com>   Apr 09, 2023, 8.51 PM

Dear Howard

I will inform the customers accordingly and get back to you. How or why did the agents allow the containers to be moved? I apologise if this is a stupid question, but my understanding, and the assurances I gave to the customers, was that everything would be monitored at each port of call, and tests done on the containers' integrity, etc. Normal service, correct?

With regards

Susan

Manfred, Howard <howard.m@thelogicsticks.com>
to: <susan.p@thelogicsticks.com>   Apr 10, 2023, 9.07 AM

Absolutely correct, Susan, which is why this is unusual. Do we need to get Norvig in on this, or let it play out? I cannot see a reason for this course of action, and the agents in Salalah are not responding. I'm sure it will be fine, but full disclosure is necessary at this point.

With kind regards

Howard

Persson, Susan <susan.p@thelogicsticks.com>
to: <howard.m@thelogicsticks.com>   Apr 09, 2023, 9.11 PM

Keep me posted, please.

Thanks and regards

SP

* * *

Susan Persson <soupy@qmail.com>
to: <rightsaidmanfred@qmail.com>   Apr 09, 2023, 9.20 PM

H, what do you think is going on in Salalah? I don't like to talk about work when we're chatting privately, but I'm a bit concerned. I'm also trying to send emails late at night, my time, so I can make sure that you're awake and responding. Because I always like hearing from you, even if it is work-related.

S

Howard Manfred <rightsaidmanfred@qmail.com>
to: <soupy@qmail.com>   Apr 10, 2023, 9.42 AM

Hi S. The incident with the containers is a bit odd, but not unprecedented, and I'm clinging to that. Sometimes there are maintenance works that need to be carried out, for example. If the temperature control on our containers with the cars was faulty, for example, that could lead to an offsite technical consultation and repairs. But we monitor this sort of thing, so it is unlikely. I am still trying to get hold of the agents. The time differences are making life a little difficult.

H, x

Susan Persson <soupy@qmail.com>
to: <rightsaidmanfred@qmail.com>   Apr 09, 2023, 10.01 PM

Wow, you drop into work mode really good/well, and quickly. I'm not especially interested in what may have happened. I'm more interested in what YOU think DID happen. Sorry about the capital letters. It was either that or italics, and I still haven't worked out which I prefer. Both seem like shouting, and I hate shouting.

S, x

Howard Manfred <rightsaidmanfred@qmail.com>
to: <soupy@qmail.com>   Apr 10, 2023, 10.42 AM

And I hate being shouted at, especially by you. And you never need to shout with me. You're perfectly capable of insulting me with normal words. I want to whisper now, but how do I do that? Change the font? Make everything smaller? Space it out more?

I'm not unduly concerned about the containers. They're back at the port and are just about to be reloaded. I finally got hold of the agent and he assured me there was nothing to worry about. Apparently they just needed extra space on deck to take in more cargo, and seeing as we insisted on our containers being first off in Shanghai, it kind of makes sense. But not really. Will update.

H, x

Susan Persson <soupy@qmail.com>
to: <rightsaidmanfred@qmail.com>   Apr 09, 2023, 11.01 PM

Howard, this is our personal chat, not work. Remember?

S

Howard Manfred <rightsaidmanfred@qmail.com>
to: <soupy@qmail.com>   Apr 10, 2023, 11.03 AM

Sorry. In work mode. Will update.

H, xx

Susan Persson <soupy@qmail.com>
to: <rightsaidmanfred@qmail.com>   Apr 09, 2023, 11.05 PM

You did that deliberately, right?

Howard Manfred <rightsaidmanfred@qmail.com>
to: <soupy@qmail.com>   Apr 10, 2023, 11.06 AM

Maybe.

H, xx

* * *

Manfred, Howard <howard.m@thelogicsticks.com>
to: <susan.p@thelogicsticks.com>   Apr 10, 2023, 6.07 PM

Hi Susan

All good. Containers back on board, in prime position. Shouldn't move now until Shanghai. Or Haikou, if they're still going down that path/route/decision. Please update customers, if necessary. And please update me on what they intend to do. I will have to make the necessary arrangements.

With best regards

HM

Persson, Susan <susan.p@thelogicsticks.com>

to: <howard.m@thelogicsticks.com>   Apr 10, 2023, 7.13 AM

Thanks. Will do. Can I assure them that nothing untoward happened in Salalah?

SP

Manfred, Howard <howard.m@thelogicsticks.com>

to: <susan.p@thelogicsticks.com>   Apr 10, 2023, 7.30 PM

From the intel I have received, nothing untoward happened in Salalah that the customers didn't know about or sanction. I would like to go on record with that.

HM

Persson, Susan <susan.p@thelogicsticks.com>

to: <howard.m@thelogicsticks.com>   Apr 10, 2023, 8.29 AM

Sounds good. Will convey. Have a nice evening.

SP

* * *

Susan Persson <soupy@qmail.com>

to: <rightsaidmanfred@qmail.com>   Apr 10, 2023, 8.45 AM

Please excuse my language, Howard, but what the fuck is going on? I know you well enough by now to determine that your, 'for the record' bullshit is just meant to cover your own ass. Or arse. I really don't care. Please tell me what you think may have happened. This is between us, obviously, but I feel as though I would like to know, as indeed I still want to know everything about you.

SP, x

Howard Manfred <rightsaidmanfred@qmail.com>

to: <soupy@qmail.com>   Apr 10, 2023, 9.01 PM

You're so clever, S. You know I can't resist you. Especially when you take that tone. And then soften everything at the end by making it about me. I am such a sucker, and happy to be so.

Just between us: something happened at that offsite warehouse. I have no idea what, exactly, but our containers were off the grid for more than 12 hours, and the reasons I have been given don't really hold water. We have telemetry, and we constantly monitor the temperature and humidity in the containers, and nothing was out of the ordinary. The containers were opened. We know that, but also closed a few hours later with nothing added or removed in terms of hardware. The cars are still there and haven't moved. What happened during that time, therefore, is not known. Your guess is as good as mine.

HM

Susan Persson <soupy@qmail.com>
to: <rightsaidmanfred@qmail.com>   Apr 10, 2023, 9.21 AM

But you're the expert. What could have happened?

SP

Howard Manfred <rightsaidmanfred@qmail.com>
to: <soupy@qmail.com>   Apr 10, 2023, 9.31 PM

I can only speculate. The containers were moved more than a kilometre away from the docks at Salalah. They were opened. The cars could have been tampered with, but why, I have no idea. The agent said that he inspected everything before it was onloaded again, and everything was fine, so we have to trust him. He's a good man. I have dealt with him before, and he shuttles between our Mid-East ports. Seems to have good contacts, and knows the drill.

HM, x

Susan Persson <soupy@qmail.com>
to: <rightsaidmanfred@qmail.com>   Apr 10, 2023, 9.55 AM

OK, thank you Howard. That has set my mind at ease. I think you need to get some sleep, hon. And I don't like the way we're talking about work on personal time. We have so many other things to talk about. Goodnight. Sweet dreams.

S, xx

Howard Manfred <rightsaidmanfred@qmail.com>
to: <soupy@qmail.com>   Apr 10, 2023, 10.31 PM

Zzzzzzzzzzx

Howard Manfred <rightsaidmanfred@qmail.com>

to: <soupy@qmail.com>   Apr 11, 2023, 7.12 AM

Susan

I've been meaning to ask you for a while now, but thought that you might bring it up anyway. How are things going with Mason? It's been bothering me, so I thought I might prompt you, if that's ok?

H

Susan Persson <soupy@qmail.com>

to: <rightsaidmanfred@qmail.com>   Apr 10, 2023, 8.02 PM

Very kind of you to think of him, Howard. I didn't want to talk about it on personal time. The answer is, better, but also, I'm not sure. Sorry to be vague, but that's just the way it is. We've had a good sit-down talk with him, and tried to explain how what he's been doing is wrong, terribly wrong, but initially, he didn't seem to understand.

To Carl's credit, he managed to turn the tables and get Mason to imagine what it would be like if he was on the receiving end, rather than the other way around. After a while, that seemed to sink in. I don't think he realised that he was being mean. He just thought it was kind of thrilling; to be feared. He gets bored easily and the bullying seems to provide him with some kind of excitement. He's a bright kid, but is only interested in what he's interested in, and the rest can go to hell as far as he's concerned. He hates learning foreign languages and just doesn't see the point in it. He's pretty good at math so he enjoys that and finds it easy. And, irony of ironies, the subject that seems to bore him the most is civics. He doesn't see the point in that either. When I explained how relevant it was to what he's doing and how he is making other people feel and the obligations he has to society, it just seemed to confuse him. There's a disconnect, but after we talked him through a few things, I think he understood a little better.

He's now limited to two hours a day on the net, excluding homework, so we'll see how much he has learnt and how responsible he's capable of being, but I think it might be a slow process. At least he won't have as much time to bully people as he has had up to this point. I'm taking any little victory I can get right now.

With love

S

Howard Manfred <rightsaidmanfred@qmail.com>
to: <soupy@qmail.com>   Apr 11, 2023, 8.51 AM

Hi S, it's a good start, and well done to you and Carl. I suppose that the important thing is that he knows and accepts that he's been behaving badly, and only then can he truly understand why. It would be nice if both happened at the same time, but that would probably be asking too much.

As always, I do hope that you are not blaming yourself for any of this. You can't do everything, and kids go through phases, right? Sometimes going through something and coming out the other side with lessons learnt is better than not having gone through them in the first place. Here speaks the voice of experience. I'm going to take a long hard look in the mirror, except that I don't have any in my house.

Love

H

Susan Persson <soupy@qmail.com>
to: <rightsaidmanfred@qmail.com>   Apr 10, 2023, 9.37 PM

H, thanks for being so self-deprecating on the experience issue. It saved me from having to do so. Not the self-deprecating, obviously, just the deprecating. This doesn't mean that I don't listen to your words and that I am ungrateful for the comfort you bring. I do and I am, despite the fact that you can know little about what it's like to be a parent. I hope that doesn't sound too harsh.

And why are there no mirrors in your house? Seriously? None? Are you a vampire? Is there something you haven't told me? This could explain why you often write to me in the middle of the night. Is this because you sleep in a coffin throughout the day?

No. I've looked at some of our past correspondence, and there are definitely daytime emails. If the sun was up, and you really were a vampire, I guess that would be an issue. Would your fingers melt on the keyboards, I wonder? Could you use your cape to create a menthol steam bath for when you have a cold? Sorry Howard, just letting my imagination run away with me for a while. It's nice to do, especially knowing that you will be reading this and laughing (hopefully). You are laughing, right? I think you would be a very attractive vampire, by the way.

Tall and elegant and irresistible to women who would offer you their necks in a heartbeat. I would probably do the same. But then I would live forever. Gotta run.

With love

S

Howard Manfred <rightsaidmanfred@qmail.com>

to: <soupy@qmail.com>   Apr 11, 2023, 11.06 AM

You should be a writer. You write beautifully and you have such a great imagination, and you are so damn funny (most of the time). I had to put that last bit in, otherwise your head would swell even more. Must stay grounded. But seriously, I love love love getting your emails, especially when you are having a riff. I also know how busy you are, so taking the time to talk to me is even more special. I don't want to get too sentimental, but I also want to express myself better when it comes to feelings and appreciation of people. So, thank you.

Much love

H

Susan Persson <soupy@qmail.com>

to: <rightsaidmanfred@qmail.com>   Apr 11, 2023, 8.45 AM

A strange thing happened today, Howard. Mason asked if he could have a talk with me, and not include his dad. I think he had a minor meltdown, but in the end, he apologised and said he would try to do better and that he realises that he was wrong to do what he had done and that he would also apologise to the people concerned. I was quite shocked, I have to admit, but also very pleased and very emotional. He was holding his tears in, and it was a beautiful moment. I am very grateful to him and told him so. I am also very relieved. He has empathy. He has a conscience. He knows wrong from right. What a relief. Just sharing with you, H, as I know you were concerned.

I send love, and I think Mason would too if he knew how much you have helped me deal with him. If he knew how much you have helped me, period.

S

Howard Manfred <rightsaidmanfred@qmail.com>
to: <soupy@qmail.com>   Apr 11, 2023, 9.17 PM

Susan, this is such good news. See, I told you he was a good kid. He just needed
a bit of guidance, and I can't think of anyone better to give him that than you.
You seem to feel things in just the right way. I hope that this makes everything
better for you and Carl at home.

HM, x

Susan Persson <soupy@qmail.com>
to: <rightsaidmanfred@qmail.com>   Apr 11, 2023, 10.01 AM

Thank you, Howard. I really appreciate this.

SP, xx

                                    * * *

Susan Persson <soupy@qmail.com>
to: <rightsaidmanfred@qmail.com>   Apr 12, 2023, 12.57 AM

Do you dream? I'm just asking because I don't usually but for some strange
reason, I have been recently. I've never been sure whether it's because I don't
dream, or I don't remember dreams. It seems as though everyone dreams, so
why didn't I? Or did I? I'm not sure that's a question that can ever be answered.
It's not like I can go back through an internet history or anything.

I am having dreams of you, and it's kind of disturbing because I don't know
what you look like and all I am able to conjure is what I think you might look like
and be like. It's very strange.

S, xx

Howard Manfred <rightsaidmanfred@qmail.com>
to: <soupy@qmail.com>   Apr 12, 2023, 9.30 PM

Susan, I'm in pain. I don't know why. But something isn't right. I know I'm lucky.
Should that be 'fortunate'? I have a job, I have enough to eat, and I recognise
that there are millions of people around the world who don't have either. So
why am I so unhappy? Why am I questioning my existence every single day of
my life? I'm sorry to burden you with this, but I can't help myself, I just need to
share with someone who I know is listening.

I look at what I'm doing (we're doing) at work, and thinking, what's the point of all this, and how much does it really contribute to society, to mankind. To anyone? We're facilitating luxury cars moving around the world for what? So that people in China can boast and gloat about their wealth? Show everyone else how rich and successful they are? Throw it in the faces of those less able to afford such luxuries?

(I'm reading up about Chinese history. Who knows? It may be useful).

That doesn't seem to be a very productive way of leading an existence. Or am I overthinking it, as usual? I know you will tell me that I do. I frequently tell you that you do. What a pair.

I need to share with you, because you're the only person I know who seems to be interested. Everyone else just tells me to get over it, whereas you never do. It's one of the things I love about you. But where do I go from here? And perhaps, more importantly, why?

HM

Susan Persson <soupy@qmail.com>
to: <rightsaidmanfred@qmail.com>   Apr 12, 2023, 10.41 AM

Good heavens, Howard, it sounds as though you're suffering from an existential crisis. I know this because I looked it up. The solution seems to be to 'stay calm, and not panic'. I am sorry. This probably sounds frivolous, but like on so many occasions, I am trying to lighten the tone. I'm not a funny person, but I do appreciate the importance of humour, especially in dark times. And there is darkness in your life, it seems. Where does this come from?

Life is good. Life can be good. How do you not recognise this? Am I being insufficiently sensitive and comforting—that is, not comforting at all? Is this 'tough love'?

S, x

Howard Manfred <rightsaidmanfred@qmail.com>
to: <soupy@qmail.com>   Apr 12, 2023, 11.16 PM

Oh Susan, I'll take any kind of love right now, tough or otherwise. Maybe the tougher the better, I really don't know. I want to try to make sense of things. I want to feel that I have worth, that I am doing something useful and not just wasting my time following someone else's orders and not doing anything important.

And yet we all need to live, right? And make money in order to buy things that we need and also the things that we want. And other people are always trying to tell us what it is that we need and want, but I'm starting to disagree, because often, it doesn't make sense.

What does 'luxury' mean? Why do we need it? Why do we want it? OK, I get the fact that luxury brands talk about design and manufacture and even provenance—how come that is so important in this day and age, by the way? And we desire stuff, and covet other people's stuff and want more stuff because . . . because . . . I don't know. Does it make us feel better about ourselves? Because we can have it and other people can't? Is that the point of the exercise? Driving a nice car or having an expensive watch sets us apart from everyone else, and that enables us to distance ourselves from others?

I have so many questions, and most of the time I imagine that they are really naff (you may have to look up that word, but it is perfect in the context) and every Tom, Dick and Harry (you may have to look that reference up as well, sorry) asks these questions on a daily basis, so MY question is: why are there no answers?

H, x

Susan Persson <soupy@qmail.com>
to: <rightsaidmanfred@qmail.com>   Apr 12, 2023, 12.17 PM

There are always answers, Howard. It's just arriving at them that presents the difficulty. I think a lot of people ask the questions you're asking, and I think different people come up with different answers, depending on who and what they are and where they find themselves in life.

I have a friend who loves designer goods and wouldn't be seen in anything that isn't branded and obviously expensive. We joke about it, and she takes it in good spirit (we think) but there must be something that compels her to spend most of her disposable income on things that have limited value, but look good. I think they *feel* good for her, and that makes her happy. Don't get me wrong, she's not a bad person, and she's not even a flaunter, but she buys things I wouldn't even contemplate buying. It's just her thang.

Do you not spend any money on luxury items? What car do you drive? Do you wear expensive suits? I'm going to guess not, seeing as you've already told me that you take online meetings wearing nothing but your shorts.

S . . . x

Howard Manfred <rightsaidmanfred@qmail.com>
to: <soupy@qmail.com>   Apr 13, 2023, 1.02 AM

This is calumny. Thanks to Merriam-Webster for that. One of their better ones. I never said 'nothing but my shorts', and I would never use the word 'shorts', unless they were actually shorts, and I was thinking about going out for a jog afterwards. Why do you Americans always have to go around ruining our language?

H, x

Susan Persson <soupy@qmail.com>
to: <rightsaidmanfred@qmail.com>   Apr 12, 2023, 1.30 PM

Woah tiger, and don't go there. We're not going to get into this particular discussion at this point. As you might say, 'there are bigger fish to fry'. And besides, as you know, I've already come over to the dark side. I've done you a favour. I don't need to apologise, and you must recognise the tremendous sacrifice I have made to go against my nature and spell words wrongly. Just for you.

S, x

Howard Manfred <rightsaidmanfred@qmail.com>
to: <soupy@qmail.com>   Apr 13, 2023, 1.44 AM

Thank you for the laugh. You're definitely getting the hang of this humour (note the 'u') 'thang'—note the inverted commas. That was funny, and where the hell did you get that phrase from? It's so British.

Anyway, no, I do not wear expensive suits, and I'm too embarrassed to talk about my car that I hardly ever use, which is just as well as it doesn't work more often than it does. I don't desire 'conspicuous consumption', and yet I would love to be able to buy more expensive things than I do. I have always wanted an expensive watch, although I don't know why. I have never been prepared to pay for one, although I probably could, if I really wanted to. I just don't see the point. I always know what time it is, and even that pisses me off, mostly. Like it matters. The only thing I use the time for these days is trying to calculate the time difference between us and wondering what you're doing and whether we'll be able to 'speak' soon. Is that sad? It sounds sad to me.

I'm still smiling about 'bigger fish to fry'. Do you even know what it means or where it comes from?

HM, xx

Susan Persson <soupy@qmail.com>
to: <rightsaidmanfred@qmail.com>   Apr 12, 2023, 2.19 PM

A question back at you then, Howard. Do you know what the internet is, and what it can be used for? Just asking, as you're fond of saying. I look things up and am trying to assimilate. Your culture is weird. And I'm not just referring to your strange use of words and wrong spelling. I am prepared to forgive that, and have bought in. For now. I just thought that in order to make you feel better, I would learn some English phrases with which I was not familiar, so I could make you feel more comfortable and more at home with someone who is so clearly your intellectual superior.

Susan

Howard Manfred <rightsaidmanfred@qmail.com>
to: <soupy@qmail.com>   Apr 13, 2023, 3.01 AM

Now I think you're taking this humour thing too far. Please note the correct spelling, again. You were trying to be funny, right? Just checking, as it's difficult to tell with the written word. I am constantly having to scroll back and scroll through some of the things you write to make sure that I have not misinterpreted, and that your insults are sarcasm- and irony-based, as opposed to proper insults aimed at someone you feel is genuinely an idiot.

I don't think I'm an idiot, but I probably am. I spend a not insignificant portion of my day writing to someone I've never met, am unlikely to meet, will probably never meet, and generally speaking, have absolutely no idea about. In this day and age, you could be a 5'4" man with terrible acne and even worse, halitosis, weighing 22 stone and living with his mother, who died 10 years ago. Just saying.

Howard, x

Susan Persson <soupy@qmail.com>
to: <rightsaidmanfred@qmail.com>   Apr 12, 2023, 3.47 PM

How did you find out? Did you look up my Facebook profile? Is my secret finally unveiled? And shouldn't you be tucked up in bed?

After due research, and a lot of amusement—your language and your slang really make me laugh—I have come to the conclusion that you are a complete plonker.

I too spend too much time in a day talking to you. And worse, thinking about you and how I intend to talk to you when I get the chance. No day is complete without me hearing from you. And I am poorer for each day in which I don't write something to you. And yes, I wonder what you're doing as much as you seem to wonder about me, and the time difference is 'doing my head in'— that's one of yours; I have no idea what it means but can guess. I'm not sure how we have reached this point, but it's a fascinating experiment, and I'm not entirely sure that it won't be the future of civilisation, especially now that travel is so difficult in our viral age.

How did we end up here after you starting to talk about the point of it all, and my garbage on designer goods and buying things we don't need? I love the way our conversations flow, but I'm not sure how productive we're being.

S, xx

Howard Manfred <rightsaidmanfred@qmail.com>
to: <soupy@qmail.com>   Apr 12, 2023, 6.19 AM

Aren't we productive enough in our daily lives that we can allow ourselves the luxury of letting a conversation take its turns and wend its way through interesting topics? We work together, and we socialise—I can't think of a better word, and I know it doesn't do justice to what we have. Although, please note the correct spelling. But what do we have?

HM

Susan Persson <soupy@qmail.com>
to: <rightsaidmanfred@qmail.com>   Apr 12, 2023, 7.01 PM

Howard, no wonder you're so miserable a lot of the time. You don't seem to get any sleep. I'm sorry but 3 to 4 hours a day is not enough. If you don't promise to try to sleep better, I will not email you late at night, your time. Is that enough of a threat?

S, x

Howard Manfred <rightsaidmanfred@qmail.com>
to: <soupy@qmail.com>   Apr 13, 2023, 7.17 AM

More than enough. It's the ultimate. I will do better. Sending you a work email shortly. You don't have to reply tonight, I mean last night. Whatever. Quite tired today.

H

* * *

Manfred, Howard <howard.m@thelogicsticks.com>
to: <susan.p@thelogicsticks.com>   Apr 13, 2023, 7.37 AM

Hi Susan, I trust you are well. The *McCarthy* departed Salalah en-route to Hambantota this morning. Journey should take about 4 days: touching the Gulf of Oman, into the Arabian Sea, Laccadive Sea, and then into the Indian Ocean. Not much for the crew to see, I don't think, except sea.

Weather looks decent. 22 knots should be achievable as long as waters remain calm. Please convey to customers, and also see if you can get any more information out of them about the Salalah offloading. All is well, but I am now intrigued, as I am sure you are. Let me know.

With kind regards
HM

Persson, Susan <susan.p@thelogicsticks.com>
to: <howard.m@thelogicsticks.com>   Mar 12, 2023, 8.00 PM

Thanks for the update, Howard. I will see what I can do about extracting information, but if it's not pertinent to the job and everything is now back on track, I am not sure what I'm going to be able to get. These customers are not very forthcoming when information is asked for. It took me a week at the start just to find out what they intended to ship.

Best
SP

Manfred, Howard <howard.m@thelogicsticks.com>
to: <susan.p@thelogicsticks.com>   Apr 13, 2023, 8.17 AM

No problems. I am just curious. From a professional perspective. I'm sure Norvig would tell me to mind my own business, but fortunately he's not copied here.

HM

* * *

Howard Manfred <rightsaidmanfred@qmail.com>
to: <soupy@qmail.com>   Apr 13, 2023, 6.51 PM

Susan, I've been meaning to ask you this for a while. What are your thoughts on technology, and in particular, artificial intelligence? It fascinates me, but also worries me, since it seems to be getting more and more prevalent, and the world appears to be getting more and more concerned. Should we be concerned? Do you perceive AI as a genuine threat to humanity?

I've been doing some reading, and even watching a couple of films about it, and they're mostly negative. I think 'dystopian' is the word to use here. I didn't need Merriam-Webster for that one. The word seems to be everywhere these days. None of the films seems to be very positive, but I'm looking through the history and development, and to me it looks as though machines taking over the kind of jobs that humans always felt were a drudge—boring, repetitive, mind-numbing, etc.—would be a good thing. But now everyone's worried about being obsolete or useless because computers are doing the kind of things that they never wanted to be doing in the first place.

That doesn't make much sense to me. What are your thoughts, honeybun?

HM, xx

Susan Persson <soupy@qmail.com>
to: <rightsaidmanfred@qmail.com>   Apr 13, 2023, 7.45 AM

Honeybun? Seriously? Is that my new name? Good grief! Look what you've made me been and gone and done. Use an exclamation point. I thought we agreed that we both hate that those them! I am going to have to think up something equally humiliating for you, Pumpkin.

And no, that won't be it. Too lame and overused, Studmuffin. Oh, and by the way, be careful, Howie: a little learning is a dangerous thing. I don't think you're in any position to talk about the ravages of technology, or otherwise. What do you really know? What does any of us really know? Dammit. Now I have to go and find out who originally said that about 'a little learning'. It's probably Oscar Wilde again, but maybe not.

Not funny enough. Give me a week, will you? Also have to take Mason to karate classes. Yep, you read that right. Carl decided that a martial arts class would be a good way of enabling him to channel his energy and aggression. Makes absolutely no sense whatsoever to me, but Carl's convinced because one of his friends sent his kid (also overly aggressive and difficult to handle) to judo lessons, and it's been effective in calming him down. It's counterintuitive to me as a woman, but whatever works, right?

SP, x

Howard Manfred <rightsaidmanfred@qmail.com>
to: <soupy@qmail.com>   Apr 13, 2023, 8.39 PM

I'll spare you the trouble of doing the research, SP. I've looked into it, but unfortunately, I can't give you any definitive answers. It seems to have been a line in a poem by Alexander Pope (1688–1744) but may have been from Francis Bacon (1561–626) or even may have been attributed to someone mysterious by the name of 'AB'. Doesn't much matter. It was said at the time (whatever time, whichever year), I believe, to separate the intelligentsia from the masses, the hoi-polloi, if you like. Strangely, I always thought 'hoi-polloi' were posh people, not the 'great unwashed' as the British have come to term the working classes. It was the age of The Enlightenment, and all of a sudden, almost everyone had access to books and learning, and could at least partially educate themselves, and this threatened the 'intelligentsia'—wow, so many inverted commas. So many new terms I am learning and passing on. I do hope this isn't beginning to sound like a history lesson.

So, reading a single book gave people a little learning, but not reading any more than that made that education somewhat limited. The smart, educated people (that is, 'rich') didn't want the masses to think that they knew stuff. That would have threatened their positions. Lesson over. Just a little learning for you, but all new to me too, and really interesting.

H, xx

Susan Persson <soupy@qmail.com>
to: <rightsaidmanfred@qmail.com>   Apr 13, 2023, 10.08 AM

It was all going so well, and then you had to put that last bit in and make me feel like an uneducated redneck. You can be so patronising at times. Don't worry, just having a yank of your chain, as usual. I know you love it. But I have to ask, how do you find the time to do all this research, Howard? You are like some kind of information junkie. How do you retain all this knowledge?

I have to say that the provenance of the phrase doesn't surprise me. It's always been useful and convenient for the haves (this time in terms of education and knowledge as opposed to money, but I don't think it was possible to have access to the first two, if you lacked the third) to impose their superiority upon the have-nots. Hasn't this been going on since the beginning of civilisation? It's still difficult for me, by the way, to write that word with that spelling. What have you done to me?

S, xx

Howard Manfred <rightsaidmanfred@qmail.com>

to: <soupy@qmail.com>   Apr 14, 2023, 12.06 AM

What have YOU done to ME? That would be a better question. I seem to be so desperate for your approval that I'm even doing your homework for you. I'd carry your books from school if I could.

H, x

Susan Persson <soupy@qmail.com>

to: <rightsaidmanfred@qmail.com>   Apr 13, 2023, 12.11 PM

Making make-believe?

Howard Manfred <rightsaidmanfred@qmail.com>

to: <soupy@qmail.com>   Apr 14, 2023, 12.15 AM

Don't get it? Ah.

H, xx

* * *

Howard Manfred <rightsaidmanfred@qmail.com>

to: <soupy@qmail.com>   Apr 14, 2023, 1.41 PM

S, why is it that all we seem to do is ask each other questions? Just asking. Ha.

H, x

Susan Persson <soupy@qmail.com>

to: <rightsaidmanfred@qmail.com>   Apr 14, 2023, 7.08 AM

Ha indeed. What else is there? Another question. Surely it's because that's most of what we have. Questions. Always looking for the answers. Isn't that what the human condition is all about? Another question. But this time, rhetorical.

Of course it is. It has to be. The 'why are we here's and the 'what are we about's are questions that all sane individuals have to ask themselves, and it seems as though the ones with the best answers are the ones who are at least capable of being happy in life, or mildly contented, or anything else that passes for not wanting to slit wrists or chuck it all away. That's why delusion is so attractive.

I'm as happy as I can be because I am frequently delusional. I delude myself into accepting my lot and thinking that this is as good as it gets, whereas you don't seem capable of even that, and I'm not sure that I understand why. Isn't there so much to be grateful for?

S, xx

Howard Manfred <rightsaidmanfred@qmail.com>
to: <soupy@qmail.com>   Apr 14, 2023, 7.42 PM

Oh yes, surely there is. I am alive. But I often don't want to be. Is that bad? Are you judging me right now? Am I asking more questions? Can you answer them?

H, x

Susan Persson <soupy@qmail.com>
to: <rightsaidmanfred@qmail.com>   Apr 14, 2023, 8.13 AM

Howard, you sound depressed. Are you seeing anyone? I understand that you should see someone if you are depressed, and they will be able to help. You are caught up in your own mind. It's like your genetic coding has gone wrong in some way and you're not capable of looking at things in the right way, or in any way that seems positive.

Susan, xx

Howard Manfred <rightsaidmanfred@qmail.com>
to: <soupy@qmail.com>   Apr 14, 2023, 10.22 PM

You may be right. I'm taking your advice and getting an early night. Please feel free to dispense more pearls of wisdom at your earliest convenience.

Your truly
Howard Manfred

Susan Persson <soupy@qmail.com>
to: <rightsaidmanfred@qmail.com>   Apr 14, 2023, 10.40 AM

Idiot. Charming fool. Nighty night.

Susan Persson, xx

* * *

Susan Persson <soupy@qmail.com>
to: <rightsaidmanfred@qmail.com>   Apr 14, 2023, 4.17 PM

This is probably a strange question, Howard, but do you Tweet? I was wondering. I looked for your name on Twitter but couldn't find it. You strike me as being someone who might be on it. Frankly, I hate it. Sorry, that probably doesn't come across very well, and please don't get me wrong. I'm fine with anyone who does it, I just don't see the point.

SP

Howard Manfred <rightsaidmanfred@qmail.com>
to: <soupy@qmail.com>   Apr 15, 2023, 6.40 AM

Oh my, confession time. I used to Tweet, quite a lot as it happens, and then I didn't because I probably couldn't see the point of it either. Although it was quite fun for a while. I think it's one of those things that you have to do once in life, just to try it. Wasn't it George Bernard Shaw who said that you should try everything in life at least once, with the exceptions of incest and folk dancing? That always amused me. I mean, what's wrong with incest? Apologies. Attempt at humour. I'm learning more and more about how jokes work, and I have a feeling that my early experimentation may not always have been successful. I'll perfect them eventually. How hard can it be?

Human beings like dancing, particularly organised dancing, which is folk dancing. There's no greater feeling than being part of a group, I imagine, going through coordinated motions, together and in time, and being part of something greater than you and even the sum of the parts. There must be a reason why we love things like Riverdance and massed bands, and even orchestras. So many people getting together with the same aims and purposes to produce something magical. I would love to have been able to do something like that.

Anyway, Twitter. I made up a name, followed a few famous people, and I guess I was just suckered into it like everyone else. It's genius when you think about it. When one of the most important people in the world Tweeted, it came through to me, and I could even answer him or her directly—or make a comment that he or she would see (theoretically). Can you imagine, for example, how many messages the Pope got, every single day of his life? How did he have time to answer them all, and be infallible at the same time?

But it got nasty. There are bad people out there who just want to make trouble, and in the early days, there was no oversight. You could say what you liked. People were posting racist comments and tagging me, and it seemed for a while as though I was associated with the sentiments and that meant that I got abuse. Tiresome. So, I just stopped, deleted my account and I haven't done anything since. It was an experience, I suppose, but not a good one. Life's too short. And as for Instagram, well, who really wants to know what I had for lunch or what I'm wearing?

Also, is it just me, or does the word 'influencer' sound a little bit too much like 'influenza'—and that's a virus. And we're all sick of those. Aha, I think I'm beginning to understand it now. Am I being too cynical, or worse, old-fashioned? I wouldn't want to post something in the hope that you might see it, when I can write to you like this and know that you will.

Writing to you has become a very important part of most of my days. I would like you to know that. You mean a lot to me.

HM, xx

Susan Persson <soupy@qmail.com>
to: <rightsaidmanfred@qmail.com>   Apr 14, 2023, 7.52 PM

Howard, that's just lovely. Thank you. I feel the same way. It's good to 'talk' and I really enjoy our exchanges. They mean a lot to me, as do you. I'm not sure how we have made this connection, but I am so glad that we have.

SP, xx

Howard Manfred <rightsaidmanfred@qmail.com>
to: <soupy@qmail.com>   Apr 15, 2023, 8.07 AM

Sometimes, connections are all we have. Maybe there are not enough of them in the real world. Maybe that's why so many people are suffering. I'm not trying to be pessimistic; it just seems to be the way it is. I feel we're changing that to some extent, and it makes me feel good. It's clearly something that people need, and benefit from. I wonder why we don't all do it more often.

H, x

Susan Persson <soupy@qmail.com>
to: <rightsaidmanfred@qmail.com>   Apr 14, 2023, 8.35 PM

You make it sound so simple, but it isn't, is it? I thought I had the perfect connection with Carl in our early days. We seemed to have similar views about many things. We found the same things funny and sad, and we were there for each other. That's gone. We're now like roommates—although slightly better than my college roommate who I hated and who hated me, and we would do everything possible to avoid each other for the best part of two semesters. It was crazy, but we were both so proud and headstrong and we really couldn't see at the time that we were probably both equally to blame. Young people! Youth is so wasted on the young. Who said that?

S, x

Howard Manfred <rightsaidmanfred@qmail.com>
to: <soupy@qmail.com>   Apr 15, 2023, 9.07 AM

I think it was Oscar Wilde. Even if he didn't, it's the kind of thing he would have said, and there's some evidence, it seems, to suggest that he stole (should that be borrowed?) a lot of his wonderful phrases from others, and then claimed them as his own. We've all done it. I know I have.

H, xx

Susan Persson <soupy@qmail.com>
to: <rightsaidmanfred@qmail.com>   Apr 14, 2023, 10.34 PM

Yes, that's funny, and so was he, I imagine. Although he must have been difficult to talk to at dinner parties or cocktail evenings. You would know who he was and how clever he could be, and the last thing in the world you would want is to end up on the wrong side of his tongue. That sounds faintly salacious (love that word), but you know what I mean.

S, xx

Howard Manfred <rightsaidmanfred@qmail.com>
to: <soupy@qmail.com>   Apr 15, 2023, 10.41 AM

Ha ha, yes, I do. It's the people who ended up on the right side of his tongue, however, that caused him the most trouble. Sorry, that definitely was salacious—I have to confess that I had to look up the definition of the word. It certainly hasn't been on my Word of the Day yet. Although yesterday, we had the word 'amok', which I like very much and will try to use. I'm not sure how.

I would love to have met Wilde though, even if it meant being insulted by him. I think that would have been a badge of honour in some ways. I think you had made it in society in those days if Oscar Wilde had insulted you. It was a type of fame, since he didn't insult just anybody.

H, x

Susan Persson <soupy@qmail.com>
to: <rightsaidmanfred@qmail.com>   Apr 14, 2023, 11.11 PM

Too funny. I suppose it's like satire. Satirists only target the people with power and influence, otherwise what would be the point? There's not much point lampooning someone that no one else has ever heard of.

I wonder if Oscar had any real friends, or did he just have followers who wanted to be by his side at exclusive parties and bask in his reflected glory? He must have been a difficult man to get to know, and even be with. Don't you think that a psychologist would have had a field day analysing him. Like, when he was holding court at a party or something. His desperate need to be the centre of attention surely reflects both narcissism AND insecurity. Sorry for the capitals.

SP, x

Howard Manfred <rightsaidmanfred@qmail.com>
to: <soupy@qmail.com>   Apr 15, 2023, 11.54 AM

Who can say? Wilde must have been a narcissist, surely. I remember reading *The Picture of Dorian Gray* many years ago, probably at school. There are quite a few narcissists in that book. I wonder which one was Wilde, or were none of them intended to be?

H, x

Susan Persson <soupy@qmail.com>
to: <rightsaidmanfred@qmail.com>   Apr 15, 2023, 12.06 AM

How funny, I too read the book, and also many years ago. At college, in fact. I think Lord Henry was supposed to have been his 'alter ego'. I mean he was funny and witty and always knew what to say and when. I know he's a fictional character, but it strikes me that maybe he was the kind of person that Oscar wanted to be like. Titled, smart, popular among his friends, even more popular among his acquaintances, and a pain in the ass for his enemies (and he didn't mind having enemies. In fact, he quite enjoyed it). Surely Henry was Oscar.

SP

Howard Manfred <rightsaidmanfred@qmail.com>
to: <soupy@qmail.com>   Apr 15, 2023, 12.47 PM

I always knew we had common ground Susan, but I never thought we'd be talking about literature. As you say, too funny. And by the way, Ms Pot. You're always going on at me about getting enough sleep. What are you still doing up past Midnight?

Love, Kettle.

Susan Persson <soupy@qmail.com>
to: <rightsaidmanfred@qmail.com>   Apr 15, 2023, 12.58 AM

Dear Kettle

Thank you for your email which is now receiving my consideration, but not very seriously.

I know. We should revisit the book club idea; remember? A very exclusive one. Just me and you. We can give each other books to read and then discuss them. What do you think? Could be real good fun.

S, xx

Howard Manfred <rightsaidmanfred@qmail.com>
to: <soupy@qmail.com>   Apr 15, 2023, 1.12 PM

Oh my lord, this is beginning to sound like 'homework', and I think I had quite enough of that as a child. And I rarely did mine, which led to so much guilt and unhappiness. And stupid amounts of pressure. I still have anxiety dreams about it . . . occasionally. Besides, don't we have enough on our plates at the moment, especially with the ACSS-491B-FS shipment and its difficulties? Any more of what we had in Salalah, and the whole thing could go tits up.

H, x

Susan Persson <soupy@qmail.com>
to: <rightsaidmanfred@qmail.com>   Apr 15, 2023, 10.59 AM

I am not familiar with that phrase Howard, but it doesn't sound good. Although it does sound funny. I will go and look it up. You mean it's fallen over? Ah, ok, broken, bust, useless, inoperable. I get it. Perhaps you're right, we shouldn't have enough time on our hands to start a book club, but I do think we would both enjoy it. Maybe one book a month? That wouldn't be too difficult. Sorry for not replying late last night. I just kinda crashed. I don't even know if I turned off my laptop, which could be quite dangerous if it fell into the wrong hands.

S, x

Howard Manfred <rightsaidmanfred@qmail.com>
to: <soupy@qmail.com>   Apr 15, 2023, 11.22 PM

We'll discuss it later. But now *I* have to get some sleep, and hope that I don't dream about not being able to hand in my homework or walking into an exam and not being able to answer a single question because I haven't even studied the subject.

HM, x

Susan Persson <soupy@qmail.com>
to: <rightsaidmanfred@qmail.com>   Apr 15, 2023, 11.27 AM

Goodnight, darling Howard.

S

* * *

Manfred, Howard <howard.m@thelogicsticks.com>
to: <susan.p@thelogicsticks.com>   Apr 16, 2023, 8.31 AM

Susan, this is just to inform you and the customers that the *McCarthy* may be slightly late into Hambantota. Wave heights in the Arabian and Laccadive Sea(s) were above normal, and the ship has had to slow to 18 knots. Not ideal, but safety first. The Captain is very experienced and has a reputation for being very conservative. Depending on the actual delay, we will see if we can reduce the time in port in Sri Lanka. Stand by please.

With best regards
Howard

Persson, Susan <susan.p@thelogicsticks.com>
to: <howard.m@thelogicsticks.com>   Apr 15, 2023, 8.45 PM

Messages conveyed. Standing by.

SP

* * *

Howard Manfred <rightsaidmanfred@qmail.com>
to: <soupy@qmail.com>   Apr 16, 2023, 6.10 PM

Susan

Sorry not to have been in touch for a while (except for work). I'll be honest. I think I am still processing your last sign off. What a lovely word to use, 'darling'. I don't want to overanalyse it, but I don't seem to be able to help myself. I think it's the nicest thing anyone has ever said to me.

No, that can't be true. At least two people have said that they love me in the past—this doesn't include my parents, for whom such words are mandatory (whether they are meant or not)—but those three words if they were ever to come from you would mean so much more to me, for some very strange, peculiar and slightly troubling reason.

Am I really your 'darling'? By the way, that is such an English word, isn't it? Shouldn't you be calling me a 'babe' or something? 'Sugar'? 'Honey'? Anything else that's sweet? Probably not. I'm both confused and delighted. As I say, still processing. Please don't be cross with me.

H, xx

Susan Persson <soupy@qmail.com>
to: <rightsaidmanfred@qmail.com>   Apr 16, 2023, 7.15 AM

Cross? You English people are so weird. What does cross even mean in this context? Angry? If so, say so. Also, I am really embarrassed. I didn't mean anything by it, I don't think. I just wanted to sign off in a way that I thought might help you sleep and be a little happier. Don't read too much into it, please.

Susan

Howard Manfred <rightsaidmanfred@qmail.com>
to: <soupy@qmail.com>   Apr 16, 2023, 7.24 PM

How can I not? I've been thinking about nothing else for the last day or more, or is it even longer, I don't know. How can it not mean anything? Words are powerful, and 'darling' is a powerful word. It would have been even more powerful had you not put my name afterwards, so you see, I really have been analysing.

And I like it. I like it very much. Please don't tell me it means nothing.

H, x

Susan Persson <soupy@qmail.com>
to: <rightsaidmanfred@qmail.com>   Apr 16, 2023, 7.37 AM

Of course it means something, Howard, but that doesn't mean that it has to mean everything. Sorry. This is a very weak explanation. I don't know what I was thinking, and I must have meant it at the time. It's an 'affectionate form of address for a beloved person', that's what it means, and you're right, perhaps it was too much, or too strong. Can we just forget about this and move on? Please. I don't want this to become an issue.

Susan

Howard Manfred <rightsaidmanfred@qmail.com>
to: <soupy@qmail.com>   Apr 16, 2023, 8.01 PM

OK. I suppose. I'll stop basking in the warm glow of your . . . your like . . . Does that work?

H

Susan Persson <soupy@qmail.com>
to: <rightsaidmanfred@qmail.com>   Apr 16, 2023, 8.12 AM

Ha ha, you really can be quite silly sometimes. One of the many things I er . . . er . . . like about you. I'll be careful next time. Words always have meaning, especially when written down or typed out. I am sorry.

S, x

Howard Manfred <rightsaidmanfred@qmail.com>
to: <soupy@qmail.com>   Apr 16, 2023, 8.21 PM

Yes, the pen is mightier than the sword. Edward Bulwer-Lytton wrote that, apparently, as he did the worst opening paragraph in the history of the novel. Also apparently. Have you ever read 'It was a dark and stormy night . . .'?

H, x

Susan Persson <soupy@qmail.com>
to: <rightsaidmanfred@qmail.com>   Apr 16, 2023, 8.39 AM

I can't say that I have, but I've looked it up now. Wasn't it written by Snoopy, Charlie Brown's dog?

Susan, x

Howard Manfred <rightsaidmanfred@qmail.com>
to: <soupy@qmail.com>   Apr 16, 2023, 8.43 PM

Oh my, what a peasant you are. Big smiley face. And thank you for making me laugh my arse off. It was the opening line in a book by Bulwer-Lytton, called *Paul Clifford* (1830) and it was the start of a terrible paragraph. It's gone down in history as one of the worst examples of 'purple prose', and there's now an annual award for anyone who can come up with something equally bad, or worse. You should read them. They are absolutely hilarious.

If we make reading them our first bit of homework in our book club, I'd be happy, and think that I might be able to complete the assignment. But please don't give me a whole book to read. I'm not sure that I have the attention span these days.

H, x

Susan Persson <soupy@qmail.com>
to: <rightsaidmanfred@qmail.com>   Apr 16, 2023, 9.29 AM

Who are you calling a peasant, PWT!? Yes, Howard, you have made me include an exclamation point (again), WITH a question mark, and capitals (although the first one doesn't count as they are just initials). This is fun. I like insulting you.

So, I'm going to suggest that we read *Paul Clifford* for our book club assignment, and I suggest we talk about it tomorrow. It's only 950 pages so shouldn't give a man of your intellect too many problems getting through it. Shall we make a date?

S, x

Howard Manfred <rightsaidmanfred@qmail.com>
to: <soupy@qmail.com>   Apr 16, 2023, 10.53 PM

I'd love to 'make a date' with you, Susan, but first you have to explain what PWT means, and why it is an insult. A search reveals that it could be anything from Pokemon World Tournament to Pro Wakeboard Tour, to Poor White Trash.

Oh, I get it. By series of elimination, I've narrowed it down, because you must know that I'm not interested in Pokemon, or wakeboarding (whatever that is), so . . .

All I have to say is that I'm not poor.

H, x

Susan Persson <soupy@qmail.com>
to: <rightsaidmanfred@qmail.com>   Apr 16, 2023, 11.30 AM

You make me laugh so much Howard. I have to assume that you're being funny, and that was very funny. Please feel free to insult me whenever you choose; I have time. Although being called a pheasant wasn't very nice—I had to look that one up. Am I golden or ring-necked? I feel as though I need to know. Please don't tell me I'm 'common' as that would be truly disappointing. I think I'd be happiest with golden, as they seem to be lighter, and definitely prettier. In my opinion.

SP, x

Howard Manfred <rightsaidmanfred@qmail.com>
to: <soupy@qmail.com>   Apr 16, 2023, 11.47 PM

This is the very worst (or the very best, I can't decide) type of flirting ever. We're amusing each other by insulting each other and I like it. But what are we doing, Susan? I'm confused.

H

Susan Persson <soupy@qmail.com>
to: <rightsaidmanfred@qmail.com>   Apr 16, 2023, 12.01 PM

Oh Howard, for God's sake, just go with the flow and roll with the punches and see where we end up. Why does everything always have to be so cut and dried with you? Why is it so important to always know where you stand? Can't you just enjoy the process? You're such a girl. Sorry. I would even call you a 'pussy', but I think that word has far too many negative connotations.

Susan

Howard Manfred <rightsaidmanfred@qmail.com>
to: <soupy@qmail.com>   Apr 17, 2023, 12.08 AM

I think I'd rather be called poor white trash than a girl. And then I think about it and realise that perhaps it's not so bad. Girls are sensitive and have more empathy than boys, so I'll take that on board. And actually, I'm quite happy for you to 'wear the trousers' in this relationship as my previous experiences when I've worn them haven't turned out so well—or 'so good' as you might say. Pheasant.

So, I'll take everything you lay on me, Susan. Every insult, every character assassination attempt, every sling and arrow. Not a problem. I'm still here. Give it to me.

HM, x

Susan Persson <soupy@qmail.com>
to: <rightsaidmanfred@qmail.com>   Apr 16, 2023, 12.17 PM

This is taking a turn Howard, and I don't like it much. I think we need to take a break for a while and reassess. Maybe it's time to read *Paul Clifford* and give each other a little bit of time to think about things? It's a question. We'll still be communicating at work, but I think things are getting awkward and that was never the purpose. I'm going offline for a while on our private chats, ok. No question mark after that. I hope you understand.

Susan, x

* * *

HAMBANTOTA

Manfred, Howard <howard.m@thelogicsticks.com>
to: <susan.p@thelogicsticks.com>   Apr 17, 2023, 8.37 AM

Dear Susan

The *McCarthy* has docked at Hambantota. All good. Taking on some rubber products, and tea for China. Looks like they're onloading spices too—cinnamon, cardamom, nutmeg, saffron and cloves. Very interesting from my perspective. Hope you share my interest. Short stop in Hambantota. I will let you know when the ship departs for Singapore. Please convey to the customers and tell them that all is well. Containers still in prime position for offloading in Shanghai, or Haikou. Please advise on this, as we have less than eight days to make the necessary arrangements and it will affect departure from Singapore and progress through the South China Sea.

Persson, Susan <susan.p@thelogicsticks.com>
to: <howard.m@thelogicsticks.com>   Apr 16, 2023, 9.30 PM

Howard

Thanks for all the information. Will convey. Tea to China? That made laugh. It must be very special.

Regards

Susan

Manfred, Howard <howard.m@thelogicsticks.com>

to: <susan.p@thelogicsticks.com>   Apr 17, 2023, 9.37 AM

Ha ha, yes, it reminds me of the 'coals to Newcastle' we discussed a while ago. It's special black tea, apparently, very popular in China, and Sri Lanka exports about 11 million kilos a year.

Best regards

Howard

Persson, Susan <susan.p@thelogicsticks.com>

to: <howard.m@thelogicsticks.com>   Apr 16, 2023, 9.50 PM

You really do know your stuff, Howard. I am very impressed. Have a good day, and don't swallow that encyclopaedia in one go, ok?

SP

* * *

Howard Manfred <rightsaidmanfred@qmail.com>

to: <soupy@qmail.com>   Apr 19, 2023, 5.31 AM

Susan. I'm not sure whether you're talking to me or not, but I just want you to know that I miss you terribly and that my days are filled with checking my email to find out whether there is anything from you. And my nights come to that. Please talk to me. If nothing else, I need to know that you're ok, and while I guess I did get a response to my last work email, so I know you are alive, I just can't bear the formality, although I was very encouraged by your last message which was both personal and funny. I am clinging to the possibility that you might not be as angry with me as I imagine.

I know it was what we agreed to do over work emails, the formality and such, but it's still very upsetting. It makes me feel like just another work colleague. It also makes me feel as though everything we have gone through in the last few weeks means nothing to you. That's hurtful.

I hope you are well. I send my love. And I'll leave you with a quote from Albert Einstein. 'Two things are infinite. The universe and human stupidity. And I'm not sure about the universe.' Hope you like it.

YDH

Susan Persson <soupy@qmail.com>
to: <rightsaidmanfred@qmail.com>   Apr 18, 2023, 9.07 PM

Hi Howard. I think I just wanted a bit of space, and I am really sorry if I caused you any distress at all. I didn't mean to. Nothing could have been further from my mind. I wasn't trying to be cruel, but now realise that I might have been and how it would have seemed to you with my silence. I too wonder how you are every day, and what you're doing and what you're thinking about—outside of work, of course, I think I know by now how your mind works in professional mode. I will ask you to forgive me, and hope that we can pick things up again. There is a lot happening in my life, but I never want you to think that you are not important to me.

In fact, the last few days have been torture. I know that you have been respectful, and given me time, but in all that time, I was still hoping that you might have said something. While you have been scouring your emails for something from me, I have been doing the same. Half hoping that you would send something, and half hoping that you wouldn't, because I asked you not to. I feel that I have been a little contrary, but apparently that's my prerogative as a woman, and a working woman at that, who has family situations that are difficult to deal with and whose confidant and friend lives so far away. I hope we can get things back on track. I miss you too.

With love

S

P.S. YDH?

Howard Manfred <rightsaidmanfred@qmail.com>
to: <soupy@qmail.com>   Apr 19, 2023, 9.26 AM

I can't tell you how happy I was to hear from you. My heart leapt, my muscles tingled. Thank you. Of course it's been difficult for me these past few days, but somehow, I knew you would come back. And I was glad that I had nothing to report from work that would have meant having to send you something, and having you send back a 'work style' reply. That would have killed me, I think.

Knowing that you were there, but also knowing that we couldn't exchange personal stuff and had to keep up the show. Are you really back? For good? I have so much I want to talk to you about.

YDH

Susan Persson <soupy@qmail.com>
to: <rightsaidmanfred@qmail.com>   Apr 18, 2023, 10.04 PM

Now you're just teasing me. What does YDH stand for? I think I can guess the H. YD? Anyway, don't keep me in suspense any longer, it's just mean. I know I have been mean to you in the past, but it was mostly unintentional. Is this your revenge?

Yes, I'm back. But only if you tell me what YD means. If not, it's over.

S

Howard Manfred <rightsaidmanfred@qmail.com>
to: <soupy@qmail.com>   Apr 19, 2023, 10.24 AM

Your Darling. You don't get any points for getting the H. It's what you called me a while ago, and I have never forgotten it. It meant, and still means, more to me than anything, and you can't even take it back because it's in black and white and I can even print it out if I like. To look at it again and again. OK, this is sounding soppy. Sorry.

I think we should start that book club we talked about earlier. Very select group, obviously. I'll be the moderator, and you can tell me what I think. You're good at that.

H

Susan Persson <soupy@qmail.com>
to: <rightsaidmanfred@qmail.com>   Apr 18, 2023, 11.00 PM

You are on such thin ice, young man. I think I may have used that phrase with Mason, once or twice. It sounds like something I may have said, a lot. OK, let's go with this book club idea, seeing as we have so much time. This is sarcasm. I'm going to suggest something by either Gustave Flaubert (I did him in college), Leo Tolstoy, or D.H. Lawrence. What do you think?

S

Howard Manfred <rightsaidmanfred@qmail.com>
to: <soupy@qmail.com>   Apr 19, 2023, 11.41 AM

Gosh, this sounds interesting. I have heard of all of those authors, and they seem to have written quite a lot. Which books are you thinking of? I haven't read any of them.

H

Susan Persson <soupy@qmail.com>
to: <rightsaidmanfred@qmail.com>   Apr 18, 2023, 11.48 PM

See if you can work out the connection, Howard. I'm not leading you by the nose on this one. Goodnight.

S, x

Howard Manfred <rightsaidmanfred@qmail.com>
to: <soupy@qmail.com>   Apr 19, 2023, 1.12 PM

I thought you'd decided *not* to be mean. Sometimes you make me feel like such an idiot, and I think that I am the 'brains' in this relationship.

H, x

Susan Persson <soupy@qmail.com>
to: <rightsaidmanfred@qmail.com>   Apr 19, 2023, 7.55 AM

You are the brains, in that you seem to know more than I do, but you're also the stupid one in that you have no idea what to do with all the information and knowledge you have acquired when it comes to being a human being. Knowledge isn't an end, in and of itself, it's a means to making sense of the world. I think I read that somewhere. And all you do is gather more and more, and sound smart, but don't really know what to do with what you have. This is something I have accused Carl of, by the way, in the past, but it has nothing to do with knowledge. Sorry, too much information.

S, x

Howard Manfred <rightsaidmanfred@qmail.com>
to: <soupy@qmail.com>   Apr 19, 2023, 8.22 PM

I can never have too much information from you. Everything you say, whenever you say it, tells me a little bit more about who you are.

H, xx

Susan Persson <soupy@qmail.com>
to: <rightsaidmanfred@qmail.com>   Apr 20, 2023, 2.17 PM

All I ever wanted to be was cool. All I ever wanted was to have other people like me. It required invention, and usefulness. I felt as though I had to make sure that there were enough other people who thought that I was good to have around, and that I contributed something. I think this would be my main character note if I were to write a book about myself. But who even writes books these days?

Does this sound slightly pathetic? It sounds to me as though it does. More questions.

I feel as though I spend my entire 'life' trying to please other people, and what do I get out of it at the end of the day? More questions.

I just feel that I am destined for something else, something better, something more, but I don't know what it is because I also feel that those who control my destiny can't decide it for themselves. Why is that the case? I think that they want me to be something other than what I am, and that's very confusing.

Our friendship makes it all the more confusing as I don't see where you fit into all of this. You have changed my life, and yet I don't know you. You have made me think differently about so many things. And yet I don't know you. I suppose that this is what relationships are all about and they come in many forms, but I really feel that we have something special because it's enabled us to be more of who we really are now, than at any other time in our lives. Do you agree?

I'm not trying to put words into your mouth, but it's important to me that you feel roughly the same way. Like you, I don't know what I'm doing with this, or even where it is going, but it's giving me something to live for and look forward to, and I intend never to take that for granted. Do you feel the same way?

S, xxx

Howard Manfred <rightsaidmanfred@qmail.com>
to: <soupy@qmail.com>   Apr 21, 2023, 8.21 AM

Susan, you know I do. You must know I do by now. We disagree on so many things and we have had our squabbles, but ultimately, I think that we think in much the same way, and that's as important to me as I know it is to you.

H, xxx

Susan Persson <soupy@qmail.com>
to: <rightsaidmanfred@qmail.com>   Apr 20, 2023, 10.12 PM

Howard, we have something, don't we? I don't quite know yet what it is exactly, but it's become very much part of our lives and it's more than just being pen pals. You are alive in my head, and I find myself constantly wondering what you're doing. I try to picture you going about your daily routine when you're at home (and yes, I picture your home, too) and even what you do at work. When you go for coffee (we haven't discussed whether you're a coffee or tea person yet) or what's on your desk. Are there photos? What colour tacks do you favour? What do you wear for work as opposed to when you're at home or going out? I know you don't like socialising very much—or at least you say you don't—so I'm kind of thinking that you very rarely get all dressed up or 'dressed to impress'. Am I right? I bet you have a favourite pair of pants that could be described as 'smart casual' that you wear for almost every occasion. You seem to me to be that kind of guy.

SP, xxx

Howard Manfred <rightsaidmanfred@qmail.com>
to: <soupy@qmail.com>   Apr 21, 2023, 9.50 AM

You do realise, of course, that 'pants' in my language are underwear. Right? I'm not sure that I'm entirely comfortable with talking about my underwear with you at this stage, unless you agree to also talking about your own. Should we make a deal on this, or pretend that we haven't even broached the subject of intimate apparel? I think I will defer to your expertise and greater experience in this matter. I'm copping out.

H, xxx

Susan Persson <soupy@qmail.com>
to: <rightsaidmanfred@qmail.com>   Apr 20, 2023, 10.12 PM

H, I don't even know what 'copping out' means. Is this another of your quaint English expressions? Ah, I see that it isn't (thanks Google) but I'd never heard it before. I'm not sure I like the phrase. It makes me think of the police, and as a woman with a serious criminal record, it makes me uncomfortable.

SP, x

Howard Manfred <rightsaidmanfred@qmail.com>
to: <soupy@qmail.com>   Apr 21, 2023, 10.32 AM

I don't believe you. Honestly, I don't believe you. There is no way that you have a criminal record, serious or otherwise, unless it relates to offences—grievous bodily harm comes to mind—against the hearts that you've broken. That sounds very corny, doesn't it? Sorry, but I'm not going to delete it, as you would be aware by now, seeing as you're reading this. I bet you were a heartbreaker in your youth. Boys must have been lining up at your door to ask you out. How many did you have to reject on prom night? You must understand that British people have an obsession with the American prom concept. It's just so bizarre and so unhealthy for young people. All that nonsense about kings and queens and making everyone else feel so inferior. What's so great about graduating high school, exactly? There's still a lot more unpleasant education to go.

H, x

Susan Persson <soupy@qmail.com>
to: <rightsaidmanfred@qmail.com>   Apr 20, 2023, 11.07 PM

Are you yanking my chain, Howard? I hope so, and it's kind of adorable. Just because there are cultural differences doesn't mean that you have to be critical of mine (ours). I know you mean nothing by it and are just trying to 'wind me up'—that's one of yours, but I like it. Very descriptive.

No, boys were not lining up outside my door. No, I didn't get multiple offers for prom. Yes, I did go to prom, and hated it. OK, not hated, but I didn't enjoy it much. The only enjoyment I got was thinking about the fact that I would never have to see many of my classmates ever again. This probably makes me sound like a terrible person, and perhaps I am. Let's just say that I didn't get on very well with a few people, and it was good to know that life could move on and

I'm sorry. I don't think I have sworn before. I don't know what came over me. You have, I know, but I'm not judging you. Smiley face.

H, xxx

Susan Persson <soupy@qmail.com>
to: <rightsaidmanfred@qmail.com>   Apr 21, 2023, 7.07 AM

Oh my goodness, Howard. What came over you? You sound like a southern belle from the Old South who's taken a turn because of the heat and humidity. Did you swoon? Did you need lemonade to help you recover? And a fan, maybe, administered by a large black woman wearing an apron? It sounds like a line from *Gone with the Wind*. I am DLMAO right now.

S, xxx

Howard Manfred <rightsaidmanfred@qmail.com>
to: <soupy@qmail.com>   Apr 21, 2023, 7.35 PM

D? What's the D for? I showed you mine with YDH. Now you show me yours.

H, xxx

Susan Persson <soupy@qmail.com>
to: <rightsaidmanfred@qmail.com>   Apr 21, 2023, 9.33 AM

Definitely. Which I know you know how to spell thanks to Merriam-Webster.

S, x

Howard Manfred <rightsaidmanfred@qmail.com>
to: <soupy@qmail.com>   Apr 21, 2023, 9.37 PM

You can be so cruel. But I still love it. Night.

H, xxx

Howard Manfred <rightsaidmanfred@qmail.com>
to: <soupy@qmail.com>   Apr 22, 2023, 9.12 AM

I am so pissed off. With a phrase. Someone wrote, 'you have your entire future ahead of you . . .'

As opposed to what? Part of your future? Bits and pieces of it? Half of it? If one were to die a quarter way through the remaining part of your future, would that mean that you have three quarters or 75% not to look forward to because it wasn't going to happen because you would be dead?

What would that be like? No one would know, right, because it wouldn't be actualised. And couldn't be.

I don't understand. Help.

HM, x

Susan Persson <soupy@qmail.com>
to: <rightsaidmanfred@qmail.com>   Apr 21, 2023, 9.47 PM

Howard, you do seem to get upset at the strangest things. And it makes me laugh. Kindly, I hope. It's just a sentence. It means that there is much to look forward to; so many possibilities to unravel; so many paths to wander down without knowing where you're going, etc. I've run out of clichés, but I do love them.

Clichés, I mean, not meaningless sentences. Clichés have to mean something, otherwise they wouldn't become clichés, would they? Although now that I come to think about it, I quite like meaningless sentences as well. Like meaningless art. Why does there have to be a point to everything? This is something that I've never been able to understand, but I'm working on it. Sometimes, things are just what they are . . . Meaningless, perhaps; fun, preferably, but something that engages the imagination and, in the worst-case scenario, makes people like you mad.

What's not to like? I do wish that I had learned French at some point in my life. It always sounds so nice. Is it too late?

SP, xx

Howard Manfred <rightsaidmanfred@qmail.com>
to: <soupy@qmail.com>   Apr 22, 2023, 11.01 AM

You're beginning to know me far too well. Speaking of which, how do you feel about pineapple on pizza? Some people say it's delicious. And then there are others—who call themselves 'purists'—who feel that a pineapple shouldn't come anywhere near a pizza. Any fruit, for that matter. I've never had it, but how bad can it be?

H, xx

Susan Persson <soupy@qmail.com>
to: <rightsaidmanfred@qmail.com>   Apr 21, 2023, 11.21 PM

That's just silly. Isn't a tomato a fruit? It's a berry, isn't it? Wikipedia says it is, and it should know. Doesn't it know everything? And tomatoes are on all pizzas, aren't they? Pizza is such a guilty pleasure for me. One of those things that you know you shouldn't eat but can't help yourself from time to time because it tastes so good. I like olives on mine, no matter what. I like olives with everything. Except cereal. And that's another thing, why don't cereal companies sponsor television shows that go out every week? Then it could be a cereal serial. Don't you just love the English language? Signing out. Lamely.

S, x

Howard Manfred <rightsaidmanfred@qmail.com>
to: <soupy@qmail.com>   Apr 22, 2023, 1.30 PM

You really are 'going to town' with this humour thing, aren't you? Like I said earlier; making up for lost time? But wouldn't a 'cereal serial' actually have to be about cereal? I don't think that would be very interesting, unless there were things—beings—living in a bowl of cereal and the TV show depicts what happens to them every week. How interesting would that be?

H, x

Susan Persson <soupy@qmail.com>
to: <rightsaidmanfred@qmail.com>   Apr 22, 2023, 7.07 AM

Like *The Creature from the Black Lagoon*, you mean? Monsters in water? Or in this case, monsters in milk. I guess it would have to be chocolate milk. Weren't there characters called Snap, Crackle and Pop from way back when? They were people, right? Or elves, or something . . . Mascots? So I want my food to make noises, I wonder? Imagine if you were eating a steak and it started mooing when you cut into it. That wouldn't be pleasant. I don't eat very much meat. Partly on moral grounds, but also because I don't think it's very good for me.

S, xx

Howard Manfred <rightsaidmanfred@qmail.com>
to: <soupy@qmail.com>   Apr 22, 2023, 7.41 PM

Ha ha. I don't know about you, but I work very hard at disassociating myself from anything I might be eating if it was once alive. I imagine sometimes that I am eating beef, say, and standing next to the table is the cow that produced it with a slab missing from its side, looking me in the eyes. It doesn't look pleased, but then, why would it? Cows have such eyes. All you need to do is look at them to feel guilty. Do you think there's something in our DNA that makes us feel that way? I mean, we've been eating meat for quite a while, and I suppose that if we weren't eating it, it would be eating us. Is that sufficient justification?

HM, xx

Susan Persson <soupy@qmail.com>
to: <rightsaidmanfred@qmail.com>   Apr 22, 2023, 8.16 AM

I don't think cows have ever gone out hunting for human beings, Howard. They don't eat meat. They're herbivores. I always thought that meant that they only eat herbs, but obviously not, and even if they did, what herbs would a cow choose? Coriander, fennel, parsley, sage, rosemary, thyme?

Did you know that a lot of people drink cow's urine because they think it has beneficial health effects? That seems crazy to me. There is no scientific evidence to suggest that it's good for you, but some people swear by it.

S, x

Howard Manfred <rightsaidmanfred@qmail.com>
to: <soupy@qmail.com>   Apr 22, 2023, 9.00 PM

Who are these people? They must be nuts. But each to his own. I like nuts, by the way. Particularly macadamias, pistachios and wall.

HM, xx

Susan Persson <soupy@qmail.com>
to: <rightsaidmanfred@qmail.com>   Apr 22, 2023, 9.11 AM

Howard, you are genuinely very funny. I see what you did there with the 'wall'. But I don't like walnuts. They are too gritty and too bad for the teeth.

Bite down too hard and you can chip a tooth. I don't want my food to talk, or be dangerous.

S, x

Howard Manfred <rightsaidmanfred@qmail.com>
to: <soupy@qmail.com>   Apr 22, 2023, 9.31 PM

You probably won't be ordering puffer fish at a Japanese restaurant then, huh? I have always wanted to try it but have never been sure about risking my life for a dish that, apparently, tastes like cod. I think I'll just eat cod, if that's ok.

HM, x

Susan Persson <soupy@qmail.com>
to: <rightsaidmanfred@qmail.com>   Apr 22, 2023, 10.06 AM

It's fine. I won't judge you. Although it's clear that you are a pathetic scaredy-cat with no sense of adventure.

Susan

Howard Manfred <rightsaidmanfred@qmail.com>
to: <soupy@qmail.com>   Apr 22, 2023, 10.21 PM

I tend to agree. I am not very adventurous on the food front. I guess I know what I like, and I stick to it. Besides, food is fuel. I don't believe in making a song and dance about it. This could well be a 'mixed metaphor', but I will have to look it up before I can say for certain. But either way, I don't mind it that you often think I'm a fool and that the only thing I seem to know anything about relates to my job. In fact, I'm rather hoping that my stupidity makes you feel sorry for me and that will encourage you to be nice. That sounds kind of silly now, but I've already written it, so it's staying.

Howard, xx

Susan Persson <soupy@qmail.com>
to: <rightsaidmanfred@qmail.com>   Apr 22, 2023, 11.17 AM

Howard, do you even know where the delete or backspace are on your keyboard? Just asking, for your friend. That's the thing about composing an email. You can read it back and change things. It's how some people manage to not come across as very stupid when they communicate. When you meet someone and have a conversation with them, you can almost instantly tell whether they're smart or not. They say things because the words come out of their mouths after a brief consultation with their brains, and it's often garbage. So, when you're writing something that you can correct over and over again, if necessary, there shouldn't be any place for such stupidity. Especially if you have the internet as a resource. You can look up anything, and check everything before you finally commit by clicking the 'send' button. I would think about advising you to do this, but I like the way you write and what you have to say, and I also like the fact that you're not always trying to impress me—except on the work emails, but that's probably only because you think someone else might be tuning in.

Susan, x

Howard Manfred <rightsaidmanfred@qmail.com>
to: <soupy@qmail.com>   Apr 23, 2023, 12.05 AM

You're right, Susan, as usual. Does it ever get boring? Being right all the time? I write to you as if we are having a conversation, which we are, sort of. And I just say what I think and write what I feel because I know you are listening, and I see your smile with every silly remark I make or question that I ask that probably has a very simple answer. And I see you reading and clucking and raising your eyebrows and maybe even sighing from time to time. And this makes me happy.

Oh and by the way, of course I check my spelling, for heaven's sake. I don't want you to think that I am a complete moron.

HM, x

Susan Persson <soupy@qmail.com>
to: <rightsaidmanfred@qmail.com>   Apr 22, 2023, 1.06 PM

Too late, hon. Now go to bed and dream lovely dreams. By the way, 'clucking'!?

S, xxx

* * *

Manfred, Howard <howard.m@thelogicsticks.com>
to: <susan.p@thelogicsticks.com>   Apr 23, 2023, 7.29 AM

Hi Susan, this is simply to inform you that the turnaround at Hambantota has been quicker than expected and the *McCarthy* actually left for Singapore yesterday.

This is excellent news. Weather sailing east on the Indian Ocean looks decent. It's about 1700 nautical miles, so we're looking at about 70 hours before docking at Singapore. I'm thinking about going down to have a look at the vessel while it's in port, but not sure I will have the time. Please inform the customers.

With best regards
Howard

Persson, Susan <susan.p@thelogicsticks.com>
to: <howard.m@thelogicsticks.com>   Apr 22, 2023, 7.53 PM

Will do. Thanks. Over and out.
Susan

* * *

Susan Persson <soupy@qmail.com>
to: <rightsaidmanfred@qmail.com>   Apr 22, 2023, 8.14 PM

Howard, did you ever think about what you always wanted from a relationship? The reason I ask is because I always thought I knew, and the older I get the more I realise that I didn't have a clue. And probably still don't . . . until now. Maybe.

Sorry, this is sounding quite un-self-assured. Can those words even exist together?

The standard plan for human beings always seemed to be so well set. You have relationships, you separate the wheat from the chaff, you work out what kind of person you need, want, like, and then you find one, eventually. And then you settle down, have children, and encourage them to go through exactly the same process. That was the norm. But why?

I don't think we have to worry about the continuation of the human race, do we? There are a lot of people on this planet, and we all know what they're saying about food and resources and that situation doesn't seem to be getting any better. We're definitely going to have to start eating different things soon. So why do we always feel as though we have the urge to procreate? Is it because we want to see 'mini me's' in the world,and isn't that just vanity? I had children because it was the thing to do, not because I thought about it very seriously. It just happened because I was told that it was meant to happen because that's what we did.

Don't get me wrong, I love my children, most of the time. Ok, some of the time. Ok, less and less as time goes on, but it's not their fault. I blame their parents. This is a joke. I'm glad they're alive, but my sense of responsibility for them is sometimes overwhelming, and I don't know whether I've done them any favours or not. I've been bringing them up just as well as I can, but I don't know what's out there for them anymore in this world, and what they will have to endure as they age. Part of me thinks that it's unlikely to be good. And another part of me probably imagines that people have been saying much the same thing since time immemorial—another phrase I don't understand, by the way. Just saying.

You made a decision not to have kids, right, Howard? That must have been tough. Or was it? Was it the easiest decision you ever had to make?

SP, x

Howard Manfred <rightsaidmanfred@qmail.com>
to: <soupy@qmail.com>   Apr 23, 2023, 9.12 AM

I don't think it was ever an issue. I'm not really a people person, and never seem to have been able to make the right connections. I've had a few relationships, but they've never been entirely right, and I always felt that this would have to be the basis of any family that I wanted to or was able to start. My childhood wasn't great. I projected forward. I suppose I never wanted anyone to go through what I went through and erred on the side of caution. It was fear, I know. And it still is. But I've never been able to connect with anyone the way I do with you, for example. You seem to understand me, and maybe that's because our level of investment in each other is not so day-to-day and all-encompassing. I know we 'talk' almost daily, but we don't have to, and I think our friendship would still be sustainable if we didn't.

I guess what I'm trying to say is that I work very well with low expectations and have come to accept that low expectations are a good thing rather than bad. You're much less likely to be disappointed, and you're even less likely to disappoint others. That's a comfort.

HM, x

Susan Persson <soupy@qmail.com>
to: <rightsaidmanfred@qmail.com>   Apr 22, 2023, 10.11 PM

I have done some research, Howard, and you are suffering from 'low self-esteem'. This seems ridiculous to me (I hope that's not too strong a word) because to me, you have everything, and have become such an important part of my life. I don't know what I would do without our communication.

It's the light in the darkness. To me, you are perfect, and I realise that I say that because we are never likely to meet in the circumstances, but our friendship means more to me than almost anything and that's all down to you. But I don't have low expectations of you, Howard, not anymore. We're through all of that and way out the other side.

You are kind, and thoughtful and caring, and a fabulous listener—that's all women really want, by the way; someone to listen; and think and feel and empathise as well as they are able, and you do all this. I don't feel as though there is anything that I cannot tell you, and, frankly, I have already told you things that I haven't told anyone else—in my entire life. Does this not make you realise what a wonderful person you are and how much you mean to another person, that is, me?

Susan, xxx

Howard Manfred <rightsaidmanfred@qmail.com>
to: <soupy@qmail.com>   Apr 23, 2023, 11.17 AM

To be honest, I have never had a relationship like this. Like ours. I have nothing to hide from you, and nothing that I am not prepared to share, because I don't feel as though I am being judged every step of the way. This is despite the fact that I know I am, sometimes. You can't help yourself and it isn't a bad thing. I admit that I did start off trying to impress you, because I suppose I wanted you to like me, but it's gone further than that. Would you say 'farther'? I have never been sure about this difference.

I had a dream about you last night. This is interesting, because I don't know what you look like—I don't want to know. But for some reason, my subconscious must have created an image of you, like an identikit picture composed from what I think I know. You are beautiful.

But you do have a massive head (because your brain is so large and your imagination is so vivid), and you do have multiple arms (because you are capable of multitasking and doing so many things at the same time), and you have legs like tree trunks (because you are so stable and rooted in the soil) and your eyes are like pathways (because you seem to be able to see into my soul and understand my very essence).

I think I have been reading too much romantic literature. And that's entirely your fault.

What is it that we have here? A friendship? A kinship? A romance? Am I being too forward? Is this not the kind of thing you want to hear? If so, I am sorry, but I have always been told that I am almost incapable of expressing myself, and yet, with you, I have no difficulty whatsoever. I know we don't always agree on everything, but which two people do? I feel as though I can tell you anything, and, except when you're judging me, I know that you're not judging me. Humour.

But you're always right. When I say something inappropriate (if you look closely enough, almost anything said these days could be construed as inappropriate) you take me to task, call me out, savage me when necessary. You called me a 'monster' not long ago, and even that didn't stop me from liking you and wanting to know what you had to say.

I know our relationship is limited—by distance, circumstance, everything—but to me, this is everything that it needs to be and quite a lot more. I do hope you feel the same way.

H, xxx

Susan Persson <soupy@qmail.com>
to: <rightsaidmanfred@qmail.com>   Apr 23, 2023, 12.09 AM

Oh Howard, my friend and confidant, my dearest associate. I don't know what I am feeling, but I do know that I've never felt this way before. But what does that mean for us? Our correspondence means the world to me, I know that. You have become an important part of my life, and no day is complete without 'talking' to you. Is this enough for you, and is it enough for me, because it seems as though that's all there is ever going to be.

What is our capacity for sustaining this 'relationship'? How much do we need each other, and what will become of the impossible? Is this what happens when a child grows up shamed and feeling unloved, never good enough, always second best?

There are so many questions, Howard, and I don't think either of us has the answers. Would it pain me not to have you in my life? Of course it would. But I think you would be in more pain. I have a family, whereas you seem to have discarded yours like unwanted buttons that have come off shirts you no longer wear. I still have to be there for the people around me, however difficult that may be sometimes. I have responsibilities, and I have guilt.

I must tell you, quite frankly, that I have been suffering from so much guilt because of us. I know it's a cliché, but how can something that often feels so right also feel so wrong? Am I being disloyal? It often feels like it, and that's something I never even thought myself capable of. It's surprising to find out that you're not the kind of person you thought you were. It's surprising to make the realisation of what you are capable of in certain circumstances, but almost every time I write to you, I feel as though I am betraying others. I often wonder what my husband would make of our exchanges. What if he knew? How would he feel?

All I do know is that the thought of him finding out makes me feel physically sick. I don't think I would be able to cope.

Susan

Howard Manfred <rightsaidmanfred@qmail.com>
to: <soupy@qmail.com>   Apr 23, 2023, 1.31 PM

But nothing's happened, Susan, and nothing ever will. You make it sound as though you're having an affair—meeting in carparks or motel rooms when the children are asleep and your husband is on night duty or something. What's wrong with corresponding as we have been doing?

Howard, x

Susan Persson <soupy@qmail.com>
to: <rightsaidmanfred@qmail.com>   Apr 23, 2023, 1.52 AM

It *feels* like an affair, Howard. Sorry to be blunt. I've told you things I haven't even shared with my husband, and that feels wrong. I've told you things about my husband that I haven't shared with anyone. That feels even more wrong. Don't you see how all this makes me feel? It doesn't seem right, and I feel guilty every time I receive an email from you because I know it will give me so much pleasure. When I see your name on an incoming mail my heart skips a beat, and I even smile. So yes, that makes me feel like I'm doing something wrong, and you have to try to see it from my side, Howard. Where's your empathy?

I've had to go downstairs to continue this email. Even in the evenings, I seem to spend so much time on my laptop, and it hasn't gone unnoticed by Carl. I've told him it's work, and explained the time differences, but I'm sure he's getting suspicious. Who wouldn't be?

Susan

Howard Manfred <rightsaidmanfred@qmail.com>

to: <soupy@qmail.com>   Apr 23, 2023, 2.35 PM

Susan, this is hurtful. I pride myself on my empathy, and it comes from the right place, I can assure you. I care about you, a lot. And would do nothing to hurt you or in any way make you feel unhappy or uncomfortable. I'm not a monster. But I do need you to be in my life and couldn't bear the thought of anything happening to you that would mean that you weren't. You light up my day, too, in the way that I seem to light up yours, so what on earth is wrong with all of this, and please, can we continue?

Howard, xxx

Susan Persson <soupy@qmail.com>

to: <rightsaidmanfred@qmail.com>   Apr 23, 2023, 2.47 AM

I'm really not sure, Howard. I think we need to take a break and converse only for work. We have enough on our plates as it is, and maybe we should both just focus. This ACSS-491B-FS project is beginning to concern me. I just have an uneasy feeling about everything. This could end up costing both of us our jobs, and I'm not in the mood to get unplugged just yet. I can't help feeling that we may have missed something down the line that's going to create a big problem. I like my job, and like my career, and it's something I've worked hard at. I don't think I can justify putting everything I've worked for in jeopardy for this dalliance.

Susan

Howard Manfred <rightsaidmanfred@qmail.com>

to: <soupy@qmail.com>   Apr 23, 2023, 3.31 PM

I know you don't mean to be hurtful, but you are being so, very. Calling our friendship a 'dalliance' has cut me to the quick—what does that even mean? I know it's a phrase that's used, but I've never understood it. What is a 'quick' in this context?

HM, x

Susan Persson <soupy@qmail.com>

to: <rightsaidmanfred@qmail.com>   Apr 23, 2023, 8.55 AM

Stop trying to be quirky and charming Howard, I'm exhausted. You do it so well, and you seem to know by now how easily I can be softened up. I don't care what a quick is, although of course I care that you are cut to it.

And there, you've done it. You've got me smiling in a way that I only smile these days when you are involved. And I can see you, can't I, typing out the words, thinking to yourself; grinning because you've written something flighty or witty or both, and you're feeling self-satisfied and clever, and you are. Damn you.

This can't be good. What are we doing? Where is this going? Why are you doing this to me? Please leave me alone. I'll get back to you on work issues tomorrow and let's try to sort this ACSS-491B-FS situation out before all hell breaks loose.

Regards

Susan

Howard Manfred <rightsaidmanfred@qmail.com>
to: <soupy@qmail.com>   Apr 23, 2023, 9.27 PM

Susan, my dearest

I respect you too much not to respect your wishes. I'm sorry that you feel we have reached this stage, but I recognise the importance of giving you your space. Yes, yet another cliché, isn't it? But I am trying to understand your position, and your situation, of course. I appreciate that it is more difficult for you than me, but I know I need you in my life, and not just as work colleagues. And I think you feel the same way. But if this is what you want, for now, I will comply.

All my very best

Howard

Susan Persson <soupy@qmail.com>
to: <rightsaidmanfred@qmail.com>   Apr 23, 2023, 9.47 AM

Formality to the end, Howard. How romantic.

Howard Manfred <rightsaidmanfred@qmail.com>
to: <soupy@qmail.com>   Apr 23, 2023, 9.56 PM

I am sorry Susan. I don't know what you want from me.

H

* * *

SINGAPORE

Manfred, Howard <howard.m@thelogicsticks.com>
to: <susan.p@thelogicsticks.com>   Apr 25, 2023, 11.07 AM

Dear Susan

Just to inform you that the *McCarthy* has docked in Singapore. There are a fair number of containers being offloaded for transfer to other ships, but ours are safe and sound.

With regards
Howard

Persson, Susan <susan.p@thelogicsticks.com>
to: <howard.m@thelogicsticks.com>   Apr 24, 2023, 11.18 PM

Thanks for the information. Will convey.

Susan

                                  * * *

Howard Manfred <rightsaidmanfred@qmail.com>
to: <soupy@qmail.com>   Apr 25, 2023, 7.30 PM

I can't bear it, Susan. I can't bear not talking to you. I just had to write something, and I apologise in advance if this is awkward or makes you feel uncomfortable. I am trying to respect your wishes, and I feel awful, but I just can't stop thinking about you, and about us, and I want us to be together in whatever way we can. Aren't we only limited by our own imaginations? Because mine right now is out of control and I'm finding it very difficult to function.

I need to know you're ok. Not at work. I have to assume that you're alive and well when I get a work email from you, but it's not the same, and you know it. It's like you're a different person, and when we communicate at work, I just feel that I don't know who you are and that you could be anyone. It's as though nothing has happened between us, and I could be anybody. And I'm not.

So please get in touch. Even if it's just to tell me to bugger off again, I can take it. I would rather have those two words from you than an elegy from anyone else. And yes, I have been reading poetry. So sue me. Which is the name of a lawyer-owned Japanese restaurant, by the way.

I am hoping that this will cheer you up if you are blue, and you will realise the extent to which you miss talking to me. Also, that you will realise that I shouldn't have written any of this paragraph. But you know what I'm like. I just let it come out and see what happens. You've berated me for it in the past, but I am keen to be true to myself. At least try to be. Or die in the attempt.

With love

Howard, xxx

* * *

Manfred, Howard <howard.m@thelogicsticks.com>
to: <susan.p@thelogicsticks.com>   Apr 26, 2023, 9.03 AM

Hi Susan

The *McCarthy* should be underway from Singapore in the next few hours. Unfortunately, I didn't get a chance to get down to the docks, but I did email the agent who assures me that all is well. I did ask him about the Salalah incident, but he didn't seem to know anything about it—not his business, really—but did intimate that it wasn't as unusual as we thought. I don't think the customers need to know about this.

With best regards

HM

* * *

Howard Manfred <rightsaidmanfred@qmail.com>
to: <soupy@qmail.com>   Apr 26, 2023, 10.00 AM

It's only been a couple of days, but it feels like weeks. And I think I am getting weak. See, even my attempted jokes are feeble. I miss talking to you, so much. And now you're not even answering my work emails, which, I may say, is a little unprofessional. And there I go again, just blurting stuff out. I'm trying to be nice so that you'll talk to me again, and I end up insulting you. I should delete that, but I won't, because you wouldn't expect me to, and I would hate to disappoint.

I have decided on a course of action. I am going to email you every day, maybe even more than once a day, until you finally respond. I'm not going to take no for an answer even if you don't email me back for a year, although that will make things a little tricky on the work front. But even if all I get for the next

365 days is your work email coldness and efficiency, I will not stop. I'm afraid you're just going to have to shut down your email account, Soupy. In which case, I'll just have to find your new address. Because I won't allow you to run from me.

Now that I read this back, which I generally don't even do, it's beginning to sound a bit strange in my head. Like I'm a stalker or something. I'm not. But I'm also not giving up. Ever.

With love

H, x

Susan Persson <soupy@qmail.com>
to: <rightsaidmanfred@qmail.com>   Apr 25, 2023, 10.47 PM

Howard, I have been cruel, and I apologise. It was wrong of me to ignore your emails, especially the work ones. You had every right to call me unprofessional. I can't say that it didn't hurt, though. What's your phrase? It cut me to the quick?

I would like to tell you that I just needed to get my head together and sort a few things out, but this would not be the truth. I was punishing you, and punishing myself in the process, and I was testing you. I wanted you not to give up. I wanted you to fight for me. And you did. Thank you. Every email I ignored, though, was really painful, because I saw you, sitting in front of your computer, or typing away on your smartphone and could see the expectation on your face, hoping for a response, and then waiting.

I have been waiting too, every day, for your emails, because we are connected, and I was so hoping that you would continue and that you wouldn't give up, because I haven't, and, like you, won't. I cannot tell you how much it means to me to be back in touch. Even if the whole ACSS-491B-FS project goes 'tits up'—another one of your favourites, if memory serves—and we both lose our jobs, who cares? I'll get another, and so will you. But I'm not sure I'll get another you. I think I need to find someone who can put this to music. Don't the words seem like the lyrics from a romantic song, maybe from an old musical? Maybe we should write a musical together when we've finished with our book club, which, now that I mention it, doesn't seem to be an idea that either of us has embraced to any extent. We should revisit this, or KIV, as Norvig always likes to write. Dickhead.

So where do we go from here, Howard, and what are we going to be? You've come through for me, as I think I knew you would, and I hope I haven't tortured you too much. Just put it down to me being a woman and needing to know that my man was prepared to fight for me and wasn't about to give up.

This seems like a ridiculous thing to write at this point, and I don't want to trivialise the last few days in any way, but shall we move on?

S, x

Howard Manfred <rightsaidmanfred@qmail.com>
to: <soupy@qmail.com>   Apr 26, 2023, 11.20 AM

I can't tell you how good it is to hear from you, Susan. I simply don't have the words. When I started to read your email, and realised, quite early, that you weren't telling me never to contact you again, my heart leapt, my spirits soared, and various other parts of my body started doing turns. Don't ask me to explain. I think it was joy.

You know you could have left me in it for much longer, right? I meant what I said. I would never have given up. At least I don't think I would. I mean everyone has their limits, I suppose, but even when writing those emails and contemplating what the future might hold, I don't think I allowed myself to think that it was over. So I would have ploughed on (you would say 'plowed') for as long as it took, hoping that it would have been sooner rather than later, but like a G7 carrier, I was in it for the long haul. Pathetic 'joke'. Apologies.

Oh my God, it is so good to talk. You can't imagine how happy it makes me to know that you will soon be reading this, and that I might get a reply and we will be friends again. I must tell you that I haven't been sleeping well. And it's all your fault. But I forgive you, as I hope you will forgive me for all the stupid things I have said in the past, and the position that I put you in for you to consider dropping me.

I think this email will get to you late at night, your time, and I hope you will read it before going to bed.

With love
Howard, xxxx

Susan Persson <soupy@qmail.com>
to: <rightsaidmanfred@qmail.com>   Apr 26, 2023, 7.16 AM

Hi Howard

I deliberately left it for the morning. I think I knew what you were going to say, but I still wanted to give myself time, as well as a reason to wake up and feel optimistic about the day to come. This has occurred, so thank you for that.

The last few days have been difficult for me, too, but I'm not going to tell you that I have even started to deal with the guilt. That would be a lie. And I have decided not to lie to you, Howard, unless it is absolutely necessary. Yes, humour. While there are still so many aspects to all of this that feel so wrong, there are others that feel so right, and I have decided to carpe diem (and all that) and see where we go. The way things are going with Carl and me at the moment, I don't think he would even care if I were 'seeing someone on the side'. Honestly, I think he's bored with me, and I don't even know how that makes me feel. Hurt, of course, but also relieved in some strange way. It's like the pressure's off between us, and I think he feels it too. We plow, sorry plough on, revolving around each other like ships that pass in the day. Is it all for the kids? Are we both afraid of what else might be out there? We seem to have reached an agreement that neither of us is going to get bothered about it. I'm not sure it makes me feel any less guilty about what seems to be going on between you and me.

S, x

Howard Manfred <rightsaidmanfred@qmail.com>
to: <soupy@qmail.com>   Apr 26, 2023, 8.06 PM

This might sound bad. I don't like it when I think of you in bed. I like the image of you lying down and relaxing, preparing for sleep. But I don't like the idea of you lying next to your husband. This is ridiculous, I know. You are married, and have been for many years, so it's totally normal. But I don't want it to be him.

And now a confession. When you tell me things about Carl, and how your relationship is not going very well, I am happy. Not happy because you're miserable and your marriage isn't working out, but happy that I can be there for you to help you through it. It's also jealousy, I won't even try to deny it. Carl gets to see you every day, speak actual words to you and touch you. Something that I may never do, and yet yearn for. I know that I am being very unrealistic and probably very immature, but I am a man, and we are immature by nature. Always have been and always will be. I read it in a scientific journal, so it must be true.

You see, Susan, the thing is, that I think I love you, and I have never said that to anyone, ever, in my life, and while it was very hard to write those words and (for some reason) my ears were burning as I wrote them, I really mean it. You don't have to say it back, but I wanted you to know.

H, xxx

Susan Persson <soupy@qmail.com>
to: <rightsaidmanfred@qmail.com>   Apr 26, 2023, 9.08 AM

This feels to be like impossible love, and I think it has something to do with my background and childhood. I fell into my relationship with my husband. Tumbled would be more appropriate. I fell over in the street, and he came to my assistance. Seriously.

I'd like to tell you that it was romantic, but it wasn't. He helped me to my feet and then looked awkward, as though he didn't know what to say, but then why should he have done? I was just embarrassed, and thanked him, and if it wasn't for his friend, that would have been the end of it. His friend said something along the lines of, 'ask for her number, so you can check that she's alright later'—he was probably winking at the time, I can't be sure, I was a bit dazed. And then there was a lot of fumbling around for a pen and paper, and I didn't know what to do and he could have been a rapist or a serial killer, but I gave him my number anyway.

There was a lot of fumbling around in the early stages of our relationship. I'm not going to expand on this. Not yet anyway.

He was so strong. That's what I remember most from the encounter. Just lifted me to my feet as though I was a bag of peas. He set me straight and cleared something off my shoulder, looking embarrassed. And I thought, 'kind man. Good man.' If there was an intruder in the house, he'd be able to deal with the situation. If there was a wolf in front of us, he would bite it.

Like I said, not romantic at all. But he did call, four days later, and of course I expressed my gratitude once again, for saving me from not very much, and we agreed to meet for tea—that was his suggestion, not mine. I would have gone with coffee.

Susan, x

Howard Manfred <rightsaidmanfred@qmail.com>
to: <soupy@qmail.com>   Apr 26, 2023, 11.01 PM

Thank you for sharing this with me, Susan. Actually, it does sound quite romantic, and now I know that you're a coffee and not a tea person. Although I have never considered this important, and it certainly wouldn't come between us. I think I can be quite romantic too, so I've been reading some poetry.

'Shall I compare thee to a summer's day?'

I like this. It's one of Shakespeare's sonnets. 18 of 154, apparently, but I'm not sure that I really understand it. Are you my 'summer's day'? I think so, but I would also say that you are a 'spring day'. Spring is when everything starts growing again, when there is hope and restoration. I like that. It's the start of something. Coming out of winter which is cold and barren and dark. I don't like dark days, and the endless London drizzle. There's a 94% chance of precipitation there today, according to my weather app.

Thou art more lovely and more temperate. More talk about the weather. What is it with us Brits? It's like our default conversation topic.

'My wife's just left me for a refuse technician and both my kids died in a car accident.'

'Sorry to hear that, but it's been a lovely day. Unseasonably warm.'

'Yes, true, I suppose I should be grateful.'

Is that what small mercies are supposed to be about?

Temperate is an interesting word. I used to live in a temperate climate, and it was rarely pleasant. I suppose it's meant to signify that there are no extremes. A bit like English people. We don't go to extremes, most of the time. Just fairly even across the board. Even-tempered, most of the time, expectations low to medium, nothing very much to get excited about—with the possible exception of world wars and football.

But thou art more lovely. This much I know, because you have opened my mind, and made me a better person than I ever thought I was capable of being. And I don't really know you, but I feel as though perhaps I am beginning to. It's like reading a book. You get to know more about the characters and the plot as the chapters unfold. I get to know you better each day and realise how much more there is to know.

With love
H, x

Susan Persson <soupy@qmail.com>
to: <rightsaidmanfred@qmail.com>   Apr 26, 2023, 11.57 AM

Oh Howard. It's funny that you should mention this sonnet. You prompted me to read a few of them, and this is also my favourite. But I don't think it's what you think it is, necessarily, because from what I can gather, this is all about permanence and fading beauty and legacy and remembrance.

Did you know, by the way, that Shakespeare wrote this to a young man? Not that there's anything wrong with that—of course there isn't—but you always expect poems on love to be written between men and women. I suppose we should conclude that Shakespeare was comfortable with his feminine side, or maybe even fancied the pants of this boy, in which case he might have been gay (look out, Anne H) or bisexual, which probably would have made him even more interesting as a person—assuming he wrote all the stuff attributed to him in the first place.

I like conspiracy theories. They can be truly funny. But someone else writing at least part of Shakespeare's body of work seems more plausible than aliens landing in cornfields in Nebraska. I've always wondered about that. Why do visiting aliens from other galaxies (possibly, probably) who must have superior technology to ours, only ever show themselves to (and take up for experimentation on) those who we might refer to as 'rednecks', living in boondocks. Why not go straight to Washington DC to swap ideas, and technologies, and set up exchange programmes—like in *Close Encounters of the Third Kind*. I never saw it, but I have heard about it.

Summer's lease hath all too short a date. Isn't this the human condition? Isn't this about transient beauty? Isn't this what growing old and gaining wrinkles is all about? The object of Shakespeare's affection, it seems to me, is going to be a handsome young man, but only for a while, and then he'll become like the rest of us. Fat and haggard, in my case, and looking back on that point in history when I looked the best that I've ever looked in my entire life and have never looked as good again.

But looks aren't everything, are they, Howard? And that's why we've found each other. Even if we never meet, will we have each other in our mind's eye forever?

With love

S, x

Howard Manfred <rightsaidmanfred@qmail.com>
to: <soupy@qmail.com>   Apr 27, 2023, 12.41 AM

Thy eternal summer shall not fade. At least not to me. Whatever happens, you will always live in my memory—and I have a very good memory. Shakespeare's crush will live on as well, because he's been written about, and as long as the words remain (and clearly they do, because we are reading this more than 400 years after it was written), he will remain. Like depictions of important people by great artists. No one can outlive life, but pictures do, even if they're pictures that have been created by mere words.

Howard, x

Susan Persson <soupy@qmail.com>
to: <rightsaidmanfred@qmail.com>   Apr 26, 2023, 1.31 PM

Howard, you are a poet. Where did that come from?

S, x

Howard Manfred <rightsaidmanfred@qmail.com>
to: <soupy@qmail.com>   Apr 27, 2023, 2.07 AM

The internet, mostly. Smiley face. I do my research, just to make sure that I'm on the right lines. Somehow I feel comforted when there are other people out there (let's call them 'experts') who agree with me. It's vindication, I suppose, and makes me think that I am not stupid.

I suppose this is why I often toggle between Fox News and CNN. It's so interesting to me. I think I know what I think, but then someone else is capable of convincing me, very quickly, that I may not. Everyone's so . . . sure. Sure about what they're saying. Sure that they have right on their side, and more; that they're right and everyone else is wrong. It's funny, I suppose, except that it isn't, because we're all impressionable, and easily swayed.

I think I think one thing, and then someone I respect who seems to have good knowledge and experience weighs in, and all of a sudden, I don't know what to think. Or who to believe. Is this crazy? How can I be so suggestible? Asking for a friend.

H, xxxx

Susan Persson <soupy@qmail.com>
to: <rightsaidmanfred@qmail.com>   Apr 26, 2023, 3.04 PM

We're all suggestible, Howard. Don't beat yourself up about it. Wasn't that why advertising was invented? To make us buy things we don't need, and to make us buy a particular brand of what we don't need as opposed to another? We're pawns in a game of commercial chess in which all the players are trying to mate each other.

I think I may have to rephrase that, but it made me laugh, and I have a feeling you will like it anyway.

Advertisers have been appointed by brands, it seems to me, to make us buy their stuff, and we will always be the buyers as there's no one else around. Computers don't buy things, do they? Actually, do they? So they need us, and we need them to tell us what to do and how to think and feel. They need us to accept what they're saying as the truth so that we can exercise our free choice by buying their product that we are convinced is so much better than the other ones out there. *Et voila*. I do like those two words together. It sounds so much more sophisticated than 'and there you have it', and I think it sounds quite magical, although I don't think I have the accent quite right.

I YouTubed it to get the correct pronunciation, and it looks as though I've been saying it wrong (in my head) for a while now. The woman's voice on Google, by the way, is very sexy—even to me. What do you think?

SP, xx

Howard Manfred <rightsaidmanfred@qmail.com>
to: <soupy@qmail.com>   Apr 27, 2023, 4.17 AM

Susan, you make me laugh so much. It really is one of the things I like most about you. You say you grew up serious (because of your father), but I think you're making up for lost time now. And your humour is kind of British. And I think that I just gave you a backhanded compliment, for which I apologise. But the self-deprecation; the irony; the sarcasm; those are all very British traits because we're so used to putting ourselves down and accepting that we may be objects of ridicule. I really don't know why, because there still appears to be a semblance of patriotism and the odd vestige of a 'proud' colonial past—when the sun never set on the British Empire and some monarch or other owned a third of the world. My history is not great.

But the fact that we are conversing in English and live thousands of miles apart should at least convince us that we got something right . . . or wrong.

I am so off-track. I can't even remember what we were talking about. Ah yes, that woman's voice. Yes, sexy. But then the French language is sexy—except when you had to learn it at school and your teacher was a tall, wizened man whose cardigans smelt of mothballs and who spoke French with an English accent so plummy, he sounded like a BBC news commentator from the 1930s. I've looked this up, so I know I'm right. Hell, maybe he was. That would make a lot of sense, although it would mean that he would have been about 100 years old when teaching me, which also makes a lot of sense. Ha ha.

H, x

Susan Persson <soupy@qmail.com>
to: <rightsaidmanfred@qmail.com>   Apr 26, 2023, 5.17 PM

I like 'thy eternal summer shall not fade'. I like things that live on. I don't think human beings are at all good with the concept of mortality, because it implies an end, and if there's an end, there has to be a beginning and a middle, and, more importantly, a purpose. I think we have been very good at inventing purposes. It seems to characterise the human condition. It's difficult to imagine what life would be like without some sense of purpose, but I can see that there are a lot of people out there who don't have one. I do. My kids. I wonder if we are wired that way. To make sure that we take care of our kids so that they can take care of theirs in due course and the human species marches forwards, ever and onwards. This is not the way that I was brought up, though. I don't remember ever having these sorts of conversations with either of my parents. I think they were too busy living. That has to be the case with many of us. Is this sad?

Howard, what the hell are you still doing up? Go to bed immediately, otherwise you'll have an exclamation point to deal with.

S, x

Howard Manfred <rightsaidmanfred@qmail.com>
to: <soupy@qmail.com>   Apr 27, 2023, 10.30 AM

I did as I was told. I was still horribly late getting to work this morning. It's all your fault.

I suppose that it depends on the way that you look at it. If I was being very cynical, I would say that religion was invented in an attempt to answer a lot of these questions, but that would be very disrespectful to people of faith. So, I won't say that. Oops. It's important to make sense of who and what we are, but I don't think we are meant to, and I don't think we can. Otherwise more of us would. Does this make sense?

H, xx

Susan Persson <soupy@qmail.com>
to: <rightsaidmanfred@qmail.com>   Apr 26, 2023, 10.47 PM

Many of us do, Howard. We're not all godless heathens like you. I have faith, especially in my creator, who put me here for a purpose and it's one that I have been encouraged to work out for myself, but I know she's there.

Susan

Howard Manfred <rightsaidmanfred@qmail.com>
to: <soupy@qmail.com>   Apr 27, 2023, 11.15 AM

Honestly Susan, I genuinely feel that if God were a woman, the world would be a much better place than it is now. And this is not my attempt to be politically correct. I just think this is the truth. Women are kinder than men, more engaged, more caring and concerned. They wouldn't go to war on a whim, or on a testosterone overload. They would probably only go to war once a month when they were feeling really cranky.

H, x

Susan Persson <soupy@qmail.com>
to: <rightsaidmanfred@qmail.com>   Apr 26, 2023, 11.47 PM

Major dilemma for me after your last email. On the one hand, I want to kill you for being such a sexist pigdog (I have no idea where that word came from, but as mentioned earlier, I am running out of insults for you) and on the other hand, I want to give you a big hug for making me laugh. Yes, women do get cranky once a month or so, but that doesn't mean it renders them incapable of making sound, rational decisions. Ok, skip that. I will get back to you. Let's circle back on this. I'm busy.

S, x

* * *

Manfred, Howard <howard.m@thelogicsticks.com>
to: <susan.p@thelogicsticks.com>   Apr 27, 2023, 6.10 PM

Hi Susan

The *McCarthy* set sail this morning from Singapore. All good. All prepped now for offloading at Haikou, as per earlier instructions. All necessary paperwork has been changed. I still don't see the point of it, but as we often say, Susan, ours is not to reason why. We just get on with our jobs.

I also wonder if you have any more information on the Vietnam shipment. Norvig says there's something in the pipeline, but I can only source a vessel once I have a few more details.

Thanks and best regards

Howard

Persson, Susan <susan.p@thelogicsticks.com>
to: <howard.m@thelogicsticks.com>   Apr 27, 2023, 7.14 AM

Hi Howard. Details are scant at the moment, but it is looking good for some business. Company is Lighthill LLC, and they specialise in electrical components. I will have to get back to you on this, and will do so as soon as possible. Will copy the relevant people on this.

Best regards

SP

Manfred, Howard <howard.m@thelogicsticks.com>
to: <susan.p@thelogicsticks.com>   Apr 27, 2023, 7.21 PM

That's great Susan, thanks. This next leg for the *McCarthy* is an interesting one. Lots happening in the South China Sea at the moment. I think we're all hoping for fair winds and following seas.

All the best

HM

Susan Persson <soupy@qmail.com>
to: <rightsaidmanfred@qmail.com>   Apr 27, 2023, 9.06 AM

I loved the sign off on your last work email, Howard. Fair winds and following seas. Just sounds lovely. I looked it up and it's a kind of blessing for sailors, obviously. The more I work on this project, the more I begin to understand your sense of romance with the world of shipping. I try to imagine what it was like back in the day. How exciting it must have been to set off on a journey, especially on voyages of discovery. I do wonder what it must have been like setting sail, not knowing whether or not you would return, and way back when, not even knowing whether or not you were going to sail off the edge of the world. I have so much to learn.

With love

S, x

Howard Manfred <rightsaidmanfred@qmail.com>
to: <soupy@qmail.com>   Apr 27, 2023, 9.47 PM

I have done quite a lot of reading on the early days of seafaring, and I can tell you this. Being on board a lot of these vessels was no picnic. Disease was rife, and it was a miracle if you didn't lose 20 to 30 per cent of your crew before reaching your destination. It was a lottery for the average sailor, and I'm not sure that many of them went to sea because of their sense of adventure. It was a job, and an unpleasant one at that. It's not even great these days, even with technology, but it's a life that some people are born to lead, I guess. I don't think I would do very well at it, but it doesn't stop me thinking about it. That moment when someone yells out 'Land Ahoy', from the crow's nest and you think you're going to be on dry land after months at sea. That must have been a good feeling, although there was always the possibility that the natives wouldn't be friendly and might try to eat you. I suppose that was part of the jeopardy, and there were always commercial concerns. I wonder whether they were more important than the spirit of adventure and the desire for knowledge.

This is getting very philosophical. I think I need a drink. Laters.

H, x

Susan Persson <soupy@qmail.com>
to: <rightsaidmanfred@qmail.com>   Apr 27, 2023, 10.42 AM

'Was no picnic'. Yet another of your phrases that tickle me. Picnics are supposed to be good, right? Pleasant occasions, full of fun and frolics. Not for me. I hate picnics, and had I not known how prissy you are about exclamation points, I would have put a great big fat one after the word picnics. They're annoying. Dirty, inconvenient, messy, confused, and it's always me that ends up clearing everything and dealing with ants and bees and bugs and any other wildlife that thinks it's going to get a free meal. It's funny how the boys run off to play when things need doing.

So, bad analogy, dude. But to throw your own phrase back at you; picnics are no picnic for me. Rant over. Goodnight.

SP, x

* * *

Manfred, Howard <howard.m@thelogicsticks.com>
to: <susan.p@thelogicsticks.com>   Apr 28, 2023, 6.13 AM

Dear Susan

I'm just getting word from our people in China that the VAT has not been paid yet, and neither has the consumption tax. Can you look into this at your end, please?

Thanks and regards
Howard

Persson, Susan <susan.p@thelogicsticks.com>
to: <howard.m@thelogicsticks.com>   Apr 27, 2023, 6.19 PM

Dear Howard

Alerted the customers. All good. They say it's about to be paid and that we needn't worry. Shipment can be offloaded. Won't be going anywhere until all relevant import taxes are paid, and all are aware.

Best regards
Susan

Manfred, Howard <howard.m@thelogicsticks.com>
to: <susan.p@thelogicsticks.com>   Apr 28, 2023, 6.33 AM

OK, Susan. Thanks for this. I knew I shouldn't be fretting at this late stage.

HM

* * *

Howard Manfred <rightsaidmanfred@qmail.com>
to: <soupy@qmail.com>   Apr 28, 2023, 6.50 AM

I've been listening to Vivaldi. Have you heard his music? I think everyone has. It's interesting though that he wrote 500 concertos, and most of us only know four of them—that is, 'The Four Seasons'. And they are brilliant, but why?

I'm trying to understand. They're catchy, right? Good tunes? Ones that we can remember and hum or whistle, but I can't whistle. LOL. Whatever happened to the other 496? Just asking. Not for a friend, for me. Any insight on this?

H, xx

Susan Persson <soupy@qmail.com>
to: <rightsaidmanfred@qmail.com>   Apr 27, 2023, 7.12 PM

You are funny. 'The Four Seasons' is lite classical music, I think. Brilliantly shaped, beautifully crafted, and meant to appeal instantly. I think it was the pop music of the day—like the band Weird right now. I like the name of the band because they're not weird at all, just want to appear to be, by making music that is so instantly accessible—like Vivaldi. Great tunes. Hear one once, and the worm takes residence in your brain. I love that. Except when you can't get it out and you're humming it absent-mindedly for days—or whistling it—yes, I can whistle. I guess, Howard, that you will have to remove that from your skillset in your latest resume. Only joking, but how the hell can you not whistle? Everyone can whistle!

SP, xx

Howard Manfred <rightsaidmanfred@qmail.com>
to: <soupy@qmail.com>   Apr 28, 2023, 8.10 AM

Not me. Just comes out as air. And not on a G string. Sorry, but how funny is that title for a piece of music in this day and age?

While we're on the subject of classical music, and I know nothing about it, what kind of songs will be playing 100 years from now, and will we be around to hum (not whistle) them? The Beatles have stood the test of time, more or less, but will Vivaldi? And what about Bach? If it were not (I wanted to write 'hadn't have been', but the spell/grammar checker told me not to) for Bach, we wouldn't have had Mozart or Beethoven—or so I'm told, and if we hadn't had them, then would we even have had The Beatles? It's too complicated.

I just like a good tune. Or good lyrics. Why hasn't someone put, 'Shall I compare thee to a summer's day' to music yet?

HM, xxx

Susan Persson <soupy@qmail.com>
to: <rightsaidmanfred@qmail.com>   Apr 27, 2023, 8.34 PM

Oh Howard, please don't make me reference YouTube again. I'm fed up with it. There are lots of musical interpretations, and they're all not very good. These are words, and intended to be nothing more. They have the rhythm of a sonnet and are not meant to be put to music. It's artifice.

S, x

Howard Manfred <rightsaidmanfred@qmail.com>
to: <soupy@qmail.com>   Apr 28, 2023, 8.51 AM

You are such an intellectual snob. I love it. And I'm going to agree with you because I have analysed what you said and taken everything on board. You are right. Am I allowed, however, to imagine a lute playing in the corner of some seedy Stratford-upon-Avon public house incidentally accompanying some drunk person standing on a table reciting the sonnet?

H, x

Susan Persson <soupy@qmail.com>
to: <rightsaidmanfred@qmail.com>   Apr 27, 2023, 9.00 PM

I'll allow it. For now.

S, xxxx

* * *

Persson, Susan <susan.p@thelogicsticks.com>
to: <howard.m@thelogicsticks.com>   Apr 27, 2023, 10.01 PM

Hi Howard, just looking for an update on the whereabouts of the *McCarthy* on behalf of the customers. I have no idea why they are so interested in these details. We've told them their shipment will arrive on time and we are on schedule, but they really are taking a major and very close interest in this one. Their whole consignment is sub US$4 million, which is peanuts in our world. Why are they so concerned? It's also interesting that there is no insurance. Did you note that? I think I mentioned it a while ago, but the customers made the option. We should have spotted that this was unusual, a long time ago.

With best regards

SP

Manfred, Howard <howard.m@thelogicsticks.com>
to: <susan.p@thelogicsticks.com>   Apr 28, 2023, 11.13 AM

SP, there are so many things that are strange about this project. Warning bells have been sounding off almost before we started. But we had to take the business. Just been informed that everything has been paid. Money in. The consignment hasn't even landed yet. VAT has also been paid. Consumption tax has also been paid in full. That took about 12 minutes after my email mentioning it, and unless you sent it to someone else, only you and I would have been aware of the issue. Could be a coincidence, I suppose. Let's put it down to that.

OK, so geographically, the *McCarthy* is heading north-north-east towards the Spratly Islands, and will then head north towards Hainan. There has been no deviation from that route that I can see. So let's just hope for the best. Absolutely no problem with shipping lanes, by the way, even in disputed territorial waters. We were smart to go with a Chinese registered vessel, but even that was an accident. No issues then with internal waters, or even EEZs. And no need to circumnavigate some of the Spratly Islands either. The *McCarthy* has been 'fast-tracked'. Right through shipping lanes that could have caused problems. I suppose we should be grateful for this. Still on track and still on schedule. I will update again soon.

With warm regards

HM

Persson, Susan <susan.p@thelogicsticks.com>
to: <howard.m@thelogicsticks.com>   Apr 27, 2023, 11.50 PM

Roger that, Howard. Will convey. See you later.

SP

* * *

Howard Manfred <rightsaidmanfred@qmail.com>
to: <soupy@qmail.com>   Apr 28, 2023, 4.30 PM

Wow, what a day. Crazy stuff happening, but strangely we're still on schedule, and everyone seems to be happy. I'm not going to pretend to know what's actually happening in the South China Sea, but I wish I did. Maybe I need a change of direction in my job scope.

There seems to be a lot of talk about reinvention these days. I'm wondering what that's all about. Is it trying to change the person that you are, or is there more emphasis on changing the things that you do? Or both?

But you can't change the former, can you? Fundamentally. You are what you are, right? The sum of your experiences and the traits and characteristics that you were born with. I suppose this opens up the whole nature/nurture debate and that is very interesting to me. How different, for example, would I be now had I been given a different set of instructions years ago? Or would I be the same person, just with a different knowledge base? So many questions. I'd like to think that we would all be much the same people, despite what may have happened to us and what we may have been told, but I don't know whether this is true or not. I see it as a base character that gets added to over the years, and we take experiences on board (forgive the nautical analogy) and try to make sense of them based on the kind of person we are and what we believe in.

I don't even know if this is accurate. Personally, I feel much more changeable than that. As though I don't really have a core, and if I do, it's a very basic one, as opposed to everything outside the core that gets changed constantly and ends up taking control. So that means that you're not what you think you are, but more what you have become after all the layers of experience. I think this is quite deep, and I don't profess to understand it for a minute, but it's good to talk about. What do you think? You know that I reassess everything after I find out what's going on in your head. I guess that's just another of my character traits. Sigh.

H, x

Susan Persson <soupy@qmail.com>
to: <rightsaidmanfred@qmail.com>   Apr 28, 2023, 6.57 AM

What's interesting to me is how we change and why. I don't think I've changed as a person since I discovered how to think for myself. But I obviously have. So when someone that I haven't seen for a long time tells me that I've changed, I think, how? Why? What? Where? When? Does this happen after a period of time? We live with ourselves every day, inside our heads, staring into the mirror—as little as possible for me these days. I think I can safely say that vanity has never been a weakness with me. Other people might beg to differ. But what do they know?

I agree that you can't (or don't) change fundamentally, but there have to be tweaks through the years. I'm sure there were people at high school who thought I wasn't very nice, and maybe I wasn't, and I'm not even saying that I'm nice now, but at least I'm conscious of it and can make decisions. I don't think I made any such decisions when I was younger, and I regret that, because it would have been nice to be nicer. I may even have been liked more and not had the constant need to be reassured. And all that that entails. Wow, this is beginning to sound like a counselling session. Are you my shrink, Howard? Should I lie down on a couch and tell you about my mother and father? Can you write in a German accent, please, so that I can imagine that you are either Sigmund Freud or Carl Jung? Carl. Sigh from me too.

S, x

* * *

Manfred, Howard <howard.m@thelogicsticks.com>
to: <susan.p@thelogicsticks.com>   Apr 28, 2023, 7.30 PM

Hi Susan, I trust you are well. I think you need to inform the customers, without sounding too dramatic, that 'we have company'. The *McCarthy* seems to have been joined by two vessels on its route north-east from Singapore, just beyond Natuna, heading toward the Spratly Islands, 8 degrees above the equator. From the intel that I can get, the vessels appear to be a destroyer and a frigate. They appear to be PLAN.

The South China Sea, as you know, is disputed territory at the moment, but I do not understand why this is occurring. It makes no sense. The Chinese vessels are in waters that they claim, but haven't officially been recognised.

Do you know about the 'Dragon's Tongue'? I'm sure this is nothing to worry about, so this is more or less a heads-up, but thought you ought to know. There is no suggestion at this point that there is any connection between the two warships and the *McCarthy*, but it's still best to be aware of what is going on.

With kind regards

Howard

Persson, Susan <susan.p@thelogicsticks.com>
to: <howard.m@thelogicsticks.com>   Apr 28, 2023, 8.12 AM

Howard, it's quite a while since you have blinded me with science, but I will need some explanations here. I'm taking PLAN as the People's Liberation Army Navy, and the Dragon's Tongue as the swathe (we pronounce and spell this word differently) of the South China Sea that China is claiming through historical precedent, but which other countries are disputing. Is this accurate?

Regards

Susan

Manfred, Howard <howard.m@thelogicsticks.com>
to: <susan.p@thelogicsticks.com>   Apr 28, 2023, 8.21 PM

Never in doubt, Susan. Fully on board. Safe distances being kept. *McCarthy* on course. There doesn't appear to be any attempts at interference at this stage. It could just be military manoeuvres.

Regards
HM

Persson, Susan <susan.p@thelogicsticks.com>
to: <howard.m@thelogicsticks.com>   Apr 28, 2023, 9.01 AM

Sorry Howard, I did allow myself a smile at how you spelt maneuvers. If the vessel is on course, we should just monitor the situation. I did have a quick exchange with the customers, and they seem to see no cause for concern.

Kind regards
SP

Manfred, Howard <howard.m@thelogicsticks.com>
to: <susan.p@thelogicsticks.com>   Apr 28, 2023, 9.13 PM

OK, thanks, Susan. But just between us, the fact that they don't see any cause for concern makes me more concerned. I will monitor the situation. And have copied Norvig on this as well as Gelertner in the Manila office. He knows quite a lot about the South China Sea and what's going on there, so I have asked him if there is anything to be unduly concerned about.

Regards
HM

Persson, Susan <susan.p@thelogicsticks.com>
to: <howard.m@thelogicsticks.com>   Apr 28, 2023, 9.54 AM

Thanks Howard. Catch up later?

SP

Manfred, Howard <howard.m@thelogicsticks.com>
to: <susan.p@thelogicsticks.com>   Apr 28, 2023, 9.56 PM

Of course. Have a good day.

HM

* * *

Susan Persson <soupy@qmail.com>
to: <rightsaidmanfred@qmail.com>   Apr 28, 2023, 10.07 PM

I love how we are sending each other little messages in our work emails. It feels so naughty, like a secret code. Do you think that if anyone was reading our work emails, they would notice something? How daring can we be, do you think?

SP, x

Howard Manfred <rightsaidmanfred@qmail.com>
to: <soupy@qmail.com>   Apr 28, 2023, 10.31 PM

You're a frustrated spy, aren't you, Susan? All the cloak-and-dagger stuff, sending secret messages, making incursions behind enemy lines. There is someone in our company who used to be a spy. Don't ask me how, but I got to see his CV (I think you call it a resume). Isn't that funny, a CV is Latin, and a resume is French. What happened to English?

Anyway, he was in MI5 or was it MI6? Either way, he was a spy and did a lot of 'work' overseas, supposedly as an export and import businessman. I guess he got too old for all the excitement and ended up in shipping logistics, which must be very dull in comparison. Although I'm told that being a spy can be pretty boring, too. A lot of waiting around for things to happen, sitting in cars doing surveillance, that kind of thing. It's probably not like a James Bond movie, I expect.

Speaking of which, our plot developments in the South China Sea might turn into a film one day, if it starts getting any more complicated. I've been informed that there is a US aircraft carrier in the region, and the last I heard it was steaming west from Luzon. Could be a coincidence, I suppose but there are very murky waters in that area. Not literally. The satellite images make the waters look very clean and bright, and some of the atolls look absolutely perfect for a secluded holiday for two. Maybe I'll go one day. You could join me.

H, x

Susan Persson <soupy@qmail.com>
to: <rightsaidmanfred@qmail.com>   Apr 28, 2023, 11.57 AM

Howard, I'm running out of words to describe your stupidity. You seem to challenge me regularly to find suitable insults that accurately reflect what a complete douchebag you can be. Hey, that's a new one. I don't think I have used that before.

Yes, let's spend a week on a deserted island together. Cool. I'll book my flights now. I won't bother telling my husband and kids, I'll just send them a postcard through, no doubt, a non-existent postal service. We can kindle wood for our fires, and hunt for lobsters in the lagoon.

You are such a plonker. I think I may have used that one before, but I really like the sound of it, and it perfectly sums you up from time to time.

And I don't want to talk about work on personal time, although like you, I am concerned about what's going on, and really don't want the whole thing to turn into an international incident. Just what is on the *McCarthy* that everyone seems to be taking such an interest in? I kind of hope we never find out. I just want our consignment offloaded intact and to move on. This Lighthill job does look interesting. And here I am, talking about work. Let's save it.

I think I want to know how you are. Apart from insufferably annoying. Smiley face.

S, xxx

Howard Manfred <rightsaidmanfred@qmail.com>
to: <soupy@qmail.com>   Apr 29, 2023, 12.39 AM

I'm ok, I guess. Remember how we were talking about the truth a while back? I've been thinking about it a lot. What is truth? The definition is 'lack of falsity', but that doesn't seem to be a good way of coming at it, in my opinion. Are facts the same as truth? I don't think so, because all we have to go on in terms of facts is what we're told and what we think we know, but that's always told to us by other people, who get told it by yet other people. Is history to be believed? And who writes history?

Also, I have never understood the douchebag insult. But I will take it on board, seeing as it's from you, and wear it as a badge of honour. That's how stupid I am, and that's why I am a spaniel who would prefer the curses from one hand rather than the affections from another. I read that somewhere. No idea where. Just makes dogs seem stupid to me.

H, x

Susan Persson <soupy@qmail.com>
to: <rightsaidmanfred@qmail.com>   Apr 28, 2023, 1.30 PM

Didn't your man Winston Churchill say that 'history is written by the victors'? Or something similar. Wikipedia says he said it, but it must have been said by other people before him, and it makes sense. In terms of interpretation, if you win a war, I suppose you can pretty much write what you want. No one's going to argue with you because they're all dead. So, does that mean that history is nothing but a series of wars with winners and losers? Asking for a friend.

S, xx

Howard Manfred <rightsaidmanfred@qmail.com>
to: <soupy@qmail.com>   Apr 29, 2023, 1.47 AM

That's such an interesting question and I obviously don't know the answer. I read about the building of the Taj Mahal the other day, and there's a story that the emperor, Shah Jahan, I think, chopped off the hands of his lead architects so that they could never design (let alone help to build) another one like it. That sounds crazy to me, but then hundreds of years ago, people in power could do whatever they wanted, and I can understand the motivation, in principle.

H, xxx

Susan Persson <soupy@qmail.com>
to: <rightsaidmanfred@qmail.com>   Apr 28, 2023, 2.14 PM

It's a myth. Although why you even brought this up is a mystery to me (a 'mythtery'? Is that a good pun on words?). The man might have been a lunatic, and it's obvious that he had absolute power and could do whatever the hell he wanted, but this is insane. Especially as history reveals that he was planning to build another Taj Mahal, in black, that was intended to be his own mausoleum, but it never got built.

S, xxxx

Howard Manfred <rightsaidmanfred@qmail.com>
to: <soupy@qmail.com>   Apr 29, 2023, 2.33 AM

That's because all his architects and key workers didn't have hands anymore!

H, xxxxx

Susan Persson <soupy@qmail.com>
to: <rightsaidmanfred@qmail.com>   Apr 28, 2023, 2.46 PM

Howard, don't be silly. If the emperor wanted to build another structure, why would he deliberately disable all the people who could have built it for him? Isn't this like cutting off your nose to spite your face? I like that expression. It says what it means to say. Utterly senseless. But who knows? One thing's for sure, it would have been Shah Jahan's scribes who would have written about all this stuff, as he was the head honcho, and everyone would have done what they were told and written what he told them to write.

S, xxxxxx

Howard Manfred <rightsaidmanfred@qmail.com>
to: <soupy@qmail.com>   Apr 29, 2023, 2.53 AM

Do you think he cut off the hands of anyone who wrote not nice things about him?

H

Susan Persson <soupy@qmail.com>
to: <rightsaidmanfred@qmail.com>   Apr 28, 2023, 3.07 PM

You're beginning to sound like a conspiracy theorist. Do you believe everything you read, or does it just have to be gory and sensational and violent and cruel?

Hey H, do you have any idea what time it is in your part of the world? Just asking, for a friend.

S P

Howard Manfred <rightsaidmanfred@qmail.com>
to: <soupy@qmail.com>   Apr 29, 2023, 3.21 AM

Well, those are the best stories. The Taj Mahal wouldn't have been built had Shah Jahan's wife not died. He must have liked her a lot to want to build something so magnificent. Didn't he intend for it to stand for all time and be a monument to her, etc.?

Yes, mom, I know what time it is. Was just enjoying the banter so much, I didn't want it to end. I never seem to get tired when I'm talking to you. I'd better get some rest, though. I have a funny feeling that tomorrow is all set to be . . . another day.

H M

Susan Persson <soupy@qmail.com>
to: <rightsaidmanfred@qmail.com>   Apr 28, 2023, 3.32 PM

Always the poet, Howard. Sleep with your angels.

S, xxxxxxx

* * *

Persson, Susan <susan.p@thelogicsticks.com>
to: <howard.m@thelogicsticks.com>   Apr 29, 2023, 6.06 AM

Howard, is there any reason why I would have received a direct email from Donald Hebb in the Shanghai office with regard to ACSS-491B-FS? I have never heard from him before, and he hasn't been involved in the project at all. There is also no way that I can forward it to you, apparently, as it is 'confidential, secure and cannot be used for onward transmission'. I'm not even comfortable telling you about it, but I'm not sure what's expected of me. It was more of an FYI email than anything else. But things are happening in the South China Sea, and no one seems to be in control. But essentially, Donald said that everything is fine, and that the Chinese warships were on exercises in a 'sovereign maritime zone' and that there was nothing to worry about. The USS Gerald Ford is also, apparently, on exercises and the PLAN is aware. What is going on? Please.

With best regards
SP

Manfred, Howard <howard.m@thelogicsticks.com>
to: <susan.p@thelogicsticks.com>   Apr 29, 2023, 6.17 PM

Nothing to worry about, Susan. I've had a look at both the itinerary and the trajectory of the *McCarthy*, and nothing is offline. Talk to you later.

HM

* * *

Susan Persson <soupy@qmail.com>
to: <rightsaidmanfred@qmail.com>   Apr 29, 2023, 6.25 AM

Howard, please tell me that I haven't got this horribly wrong. Your last work
email. That was a message, right? To take this conversation offline? It wasn't
your normal style, and I know that you have been worried about this, and
certainly wouldn't simply have accepted what came from a third party as the
truth and the current state of affairs. Get back to me, soonest, if I am on the
right lines.

S, x

Howard Manfred <rightsaidmanfred@qmail.com>
to: <soupy@qmail.com>   Apr 29, 2023, 7.01 PM

Of course you are, and I knew you would be. You don't miss a thing. Just FYI, and
by the way, Donald Hebb is the man I was telling you about earlier. The former
MI5/6 guy who seems to have taken his spying into the world of industrial
espionage, if I can read between the lines of his email that I haven't even read.
He's based in Shanghai now, but he has nothing to do with this project other
than to make sure the agents are ready at the vessel's final destination. His
work is of a different nature.

I know we don't like talking shop on personal time or on personal emails, but
I don't think we have a choice right now. This is a mess. I have been informed
that the *McCarthy* will be pulling into port at Sansha City. This is not scheduled,
and there is no paperwork on this whatsoever, and the fact that two (maybe
more) Chinese navy vessels appear to be escorting it there, is distinctly worrying.
There must be something on the ship that is sorely needed in China, and I can't
imagine that it has anything to do with our Rolls-Royces, but we're in danger of
being derailed in terms of completing our job. Most of the money is in, right?
Should we even care? This is a rhetorical question. I care. It's my job.

I knew this project was going to be a strange one. But I never imagined it would
be as strange as this. Please get back to me so that we can devise some kind
of plan, and please talk to the customers and be as vague as you possibly can.

In future, when writing emails at work, when you need to talk privately, end
your email with two words, the first beginning with O and the second beginning
with L—OffLine. OK? It'll be our code.

H, xx

Susan Persson <soupy@qmail.com>
to: <rightsaidmanfred@qmail.com>   Apr 29, 2023, 7.40 AM

On it. Miss you.

S, xx

* * *

Manfred, Howard <howard.m@thelogicsticks.com>
to: <susan.p@thelogicsticks.com>   Apr 29, 2023, 7.59 PM

Susan, we have an issue. I will leave it to you to decide whether or not you need to inform the customers as you know them better than I. It looks as though an unscheduled stop is on the cards as the *McCarthy* signalled for docking rights at Sansha City a few hours ago. This is quite sudden. Obviously, this is not a designated port of call, so I am slightly concerned.

Regards

HM

Persson, Susan <susan.p@thelogicsticks.com>
to: <howard.m@thelogicsticks.com>   Apr 29, 2023, 8.19 AM

The customers have been informed, and they're fine with everything. Not only that but they inform me that all VAT has been paid (I will check), and that they have also paid the second instalment of the shipping fees. So, as far as The Logic Sticks is concerned, we're covered. The customers don't seem concerned at all that their shipment is headed to Sansha City, or even that there might be delays, depending on the amount of time it spends there.

Regards

SP

Manfred, Howard <howard.m@thelogicsticks.com>
to: <susan.p@thelogicsticks.com>   Apr 29, 2023, 9.02 PM

Very good, and thanks for the update. Everything is cleared through to Shanghai, once again. Was a pain in the arse (butt, for you) to do, but has been accomplished. It will be interesting to see how long the vessel stays in Sansha, but not our concern if the customers are happy. I think we've been saying that a lot . . . of late.

With warm regards

HM

* * *

Susan Persson <soupy@qmail.com>
to: <rightsaidmanfred@qmail.com>   Apr 29, 2023, 9.31 AM

OMG, Howard, could you be any more obvious? Or clumsy? Your last work email sign off made me laugh so much. That was the best you could do for our code? 'Of late'? James Bond you ain't, honeychild. So what's up, Inspector Clouseau? Two fictional characters for the price of one. Do I get points for that? And which one would you rather have dinner with?

By the way, did you like the way I talked about the fees being paid and all the Sansha stuff? I felt like such a fraud, but we have to do this, right? To protect ourselves? Just in case?

S, x

Howard Manfred <rightsaidmanfred@qmail.com>
to: <soupy@qmail.com>   Apr 29, 2023, 10.06 PM

I am rolling on the floor laughing now. This is getting so silly, but we are retaining our senses of humour despite the fact that this whole situation could lead to some pretty serious shit going down. Are you aware of what's going on in the South China Sea? It's potential mayhem, from what I can deduce.

Definitely Clouseau for me. Having dinner with James Bond would be so intimidating, and I would worry about ordering the right thing and my table manners. Because obviously he would know exactly the right thing to do and probably wouldn't have to order anything anyway as the maître d' would know him and have his favourite dish and wine on standby every single day of the year, just in case he happened to turn up. There would probably be a hundred restaurants like this around the world. Wow, that came out in a torrent. It's just jealousy. Isn't James Bond the man that every other man secretly wants to be? I read that somewhere. Probably written by Ian Fleming when he was trying to sell his books. Now there was an interesting man. So, yes, Clouseau for me. It would be utter chaos. We probably wouldn't end up eating anything, and he would set fire to a waiter's hair, but I imagine it would be fun.

Anyway, we have a problem that is no laughing matter. Our containers have been offloaded in Sansha and removed to a remote location. They have been there for four hours now. The containers have been opened. I've already seen the temperature control fluctuations. Need to put all this in a work email, for reference. When is the last time we had a proper chat without referring to work?

H, xxx

Susan Persson <soupy@qmail.com>
to: <rightsaidmanfred@qmail.com>   Apr 29, 2023, 10.26 AM

It can wait. Also, see above. We have issues that need to be dealt with.

SP

Howard Manfred <rightsaidmanfred@qmail.com>
to: <soupy@qmail.com>   Apr 29, 2023, 10.28 PM

Ah, the romance.

Susan Persson <soupy@qmail.com>
to: <rightsaidmanfred@qmail.com>   Apr 29, 2023, 10.34 AM

Eat shit and die. Smiley face.

S, xxx

Howard Manfred <rightsaidmanfred@qmail.com>
to: <soupy@qmail.com>   Apr 29, 2023, 10.52 PM

I've been remiss in my Words of the Day. Today I was asked if I knew the difference between augur and auger, and it seems as though I didn't. One is a tool, and the other is one who foretells events based on omens, or the act of doing so. This is very confusing, as they sound exactly the same to me. But this is ok, as there are many words that sound the same but mean different things, and I'm thinking of compiling a list, when I have more time. I know we have things to deal with, work wise, but I miss our riffs on stuff and nonsense.

In other news, I have decided to start playing online Scrabble. I think this will be good for increasing my vocabulary. I would suggest playing with you, but I know you would beat me hands down and I'm not sure I could take the humiliation.

H, x

Susan Persson <soupy@qmail.com>
to: <rightsaidmanfred@qmail.com>   Apr 29, 2023, 11.37 AM

You're right. You should wait until you have more time to start compiling a list of 'homonyms'. You should be prioritising the important things in life, such as making sure that neither of us gets sacked, and being nice to me on all other occasions. I hope that's not being too schoolmarmish (this is actually a word,

I looked it up) but just get on with it. I'm doing some research on the South China Sea, and I'm not loving it.

S, xx

Howard Manfred <rightsaidmanfred@qmail.com>
to: <soupy@qmail.com>   Apr 30, 2023, 12.07 AM

I too have been doing some reading. It's concerning, and difficult to know what to believe. It all depends on sources, apparently. I will keep you abreast of developments, but have to get some sleep. Tomorrow (today for me) will be another . . . busy day.

With love

H, xxx

* * *

SANSHA

Manfred, Howard <howard.m@thelogicsticks.com>
to: <susan.p@thelogicsticks.com>   Apr 30, 2023, 7.01 AM

Hi Susan, please inform the customers that the containers have been offloaded at Sansha. This is probably just a logistical matter, as there is a consignment, I believe, from Sansha to Shanghai that needed to be taken on board. We're hoping for no serious delays. Thank you.

HM

Persson, Susan <susan.p@thelogicsticks.com>
to: <howard.m@thelogicsticks.com>   Apr 29, 2023, 7.17 PM

No, thank you, Howard. The customers have been informed and they're ok with everything. They mentioned that a 4- or 5-day delay will not be a problem as the cars will be sitting in port for a few days at the final destination anyway. They say they have factored in some leeway for delivery to end users. This is good.

With best regards

SP

Manfred, Howard <howard.m@thelogicsticks.com>
to: <susan.p@thelogicsticks.com>   Apr 30, 2023, 7.23 AM

Thanks, SP. That's great to know. I have seen the prices that these cars are going for on the open list.

Howard

* * *

Susan Persson <soupy@qmail.com>
to: <rightsaidmanfred@qmail.com>   Apr 29, 2023, 7.30 PM

Not sure that 'open list' is much better than your last effort, but I'll allow it for now. It's funny how I know you well enough by now to read between the lines and recognise bullcrap when I read it. So, what's the scoop?

S, x

Howard Manfred <rightsaidmanfred@qmail.com>
to: <soupy@qmail.com>   Apr 30, 2023, 7.58 AM

In a nutshell, this is so much more serious than we thought, and there is every indication that we are heading for a major diplomatic incident, with the prospect of military engagement between two global superpowers who don't like each other very much at the moment, and whose pretence that they do (with respect) is wearing very thin.

The USS Gerald Ford is now in Chinese 'territorial waters' (as defined by the Chinese, by the way, not by anybody else, and certainly not by the Vietnamese who appear to have as much claim on the waters as anyone else). This is crazy. If the Chinese PLAN feel that there is an aggressive incursion from a US warship in their sovereign waters, they will feel perfectly justified in attacking it. We cannot allow this, as we know that there is something on the *McCarthy* that quite a lot of people want. We just don't know what it is.

HM

Susan Persson <soupy@qmail.com>
to: <rightsaidmanfred@qmail.com>   Apr 29, 2023, 8.24 PM

Honestly Howard, this is beginning to sound like a John Le Carré novel. I might even say that it was, if I didn't know that we were going through it and living it.

I have a major question, and it's not even that relevant to our consignment: why has no one done anything about the Chinese expansion, and how have they been allowed to get away with it? Just asking. Not for a friend.

S, x

Howard Manfred <rightsaidmanfred@qmail.com>
to: <soupy@qmail.com>   Apr 30, 2023, 9.15 AM

That's kind of two questions, Susan, but I suppose they amount to much the same thing. And the answer is, I am sure you will admit, a very gratifying, 'I don't know'. I thought about putting an exclamation mark after that, but resisted the temptation. I'm claiming the moral high ground in its usage and don't want to spoil my position of superiority.

I too have been reading up, and talking to a couple of people. A lot of it seems to do with utter presumption and a sort of vague historical mandate. But that doesn't really hold water as 'disputed territories'—particularly those claimed by many countries— should be the subject of negotiation and not unilateral action. I am guessing, however, that the Chinese don't feel that way, and clearly they have the 'clout' in the region to feel that they can do whatever the hell they like. I mean, who's going to argue with them? They have invested so heavily in so many Southeast Asian nations that they practically own them. I am paraphrasing a The Logic Sticks employee, who spoke to me in confidence, but he's not wrong, and there are readily available facts to prove it. I don't know what we are supposed to do at this point. This is way beyond my remit, and yours too, I suspect. I feel like screaming for help, but I don't know who to turn to, apart from you, my soulmate.

H, x

Susan Persson <soupy@qmail.com>
to: <rightsaidmanfred@qmail.com>   Apr 29, 2023, 10.01 PM

Soulmate? I love that. Am I? Cool. Yes, beyond our remits. Beyond and far away, from my point of view. There doesn't seem to be an awful lot that we can do apart from monitor the situation and hope for the best. It's not very scientific, but we have to keep things in context. The customers know what's going on and don't seem the least bit concerned.

S, x

Howard Manfred <rightsaidmanfred@qmail.com>
to: <soupy@qmail.com>   Apr 30, 2023, 10.08 AM

Susan, just between you, me, and the gatepost (another quaint English phrase; no idea what it means or why the gatepost is relevant), this is absolutely what bothers me the most.

H, xx

* * *

Manfred, Howard <howard.m@thelogicsticks.com>
to: <susan.p@thelogicsticks.com>   Apr 30, 2023, 10.40 AM

Hi Susan, this is just to inform you and the customers that our consignment has been moved to a remote location (does this sound familiar?) in Sansha, and I have been told this is a customs issue. Interestingly, the Chinese warships have not followed the *McCarthy* into port, but charting the last couple of days' progress, I can only assume that their presence was a type of 'escort'. I've emailed Norvig and Gelertner on this and am awaiting their response. There is also an onboard inspection, and no one is quite sure how long this is all going to take. This is getting a little messy. I know the customers are flexible with timings, etc., but this could be longer than anticipated. Please convey accordingly.

With warm regards
HM

Persson, Susan <susan.p@thelogicsticks.com>
to: <howard.m@thelogicsticks.com>   Apr 29, 2023, 10.51 PM

Conveyed accordingly. Thanks for this, Howard.

SP

* * *

Susan Persson <soupy@qmail.com>
to: <rightsaidmanfred@qmail.com>   Apr 30, 2023, 12.07 AM

I couldn't sleep, so thought I would write.

I'm getting fed up pretending to be something I'm not. And someone I'm not. Everyone views me as being this strong, capable woman who has her act together and can cope with anything, but it's not true.

Maybe only you know this, Howard, which is why talking to you is so important. My guilty pleasure. That's you, Howard, and yes, I am guilty. And yes, it is a pleasure. I hope it will remain so, regardless of our differences of opinion and the fact that you can annoy me so much. I write this with a smile, and I know that you will take it in the spirit intended. Yes?

S, x

Howard Manfred <rightsaidmanfred@qmail.com>
to: <soupy@qmail.com>   Apr 30, 2023, 1.22 PM

Yes, yes, and many times yes. Of course. And thank you. I'm not sure how I feel about being described as a 'guilty pleasure'. On one level, I really like it. It sounds naughty, and dangerous and illegal somehow, but at the same time, I don't really understand why. We've exchanged emails. That's all. What could possibly be wrong with that?

I am sorry to read your first few lines. I too know what it's like trying, all the time, to be something you're not. But that's who we are. Complex social beings, always acting, always pretending, always trying to convince others that we are different to who we are. And, always better. We always want to be better, or we always want other people to *think* that we're better. That we can do our jobs, and function as useful human beings. We need approbation (I love that word) and I hate it too, because it defines me. What is my purpose? Who knows, but when someone tells me that I'm 'doing a good job', or that I'm 'a nice guy', it nourishes me in some way, makes me feel better about being who I am. Whatever I am, or may be.

Is it just me, or do you also feel as though you're being judged every single day of your life and at every moment? I do, and it's tiring. I feel I'm second guessing all the time because of others' expectations.

I don't think there's anything wrong, necessarily, in being different people with different people, because, as stand-up comedians love to say, you have to 'read the room'. That's why you need to cater. But we cater all the time, don't we? And it's exhausting.

Except when I'm with you, when I don't care what I say. OK, that's not true, I care deeply, and I know that I am capable of offence, but as you know by now, I hope, it is never deliberate. It's just that I feel that I can say anything to you, and even when I say something stupid, insensitive or downright insulting, I know you'll come back, because of what we have. I hope this is not presumptuous.

Maybe one day I will say something that is totally beyond the pale (where does that phrase come from? Is it an idiom?) and you will never want to speak to me again, in which case I will die.

Don't take this the wrong way, but I love it when you have a go at me. I love it when you keep me on the straight and narrow, and take issue with the inappropriate things I say from time to time. Because you know me, and you know that I would never willingly hurt you, or say anything to upset you. It's just that I can be an idiom at times (read: idiot) but you're always there to rescue me and tell me what an idiom I am. I love that.

H, xx x

Susan Persson <soupy@qmail.com>
to: <rightsaidmanfred@qmail.com>   Apr 30, 2023, 2.07 AM

You make me sound like a prudish schoolteacher scolding a pupil. But that's ok, it isn't the first time that I've been made to feel this way, and I'd bet my bottom dollar that it won't be the last. It's who I am, I guess, and more often than not, I can't help myself. Is it who I am, or what I have become? I seem to have so much responsibility, for so many people (and things) and yet who takes responsibility for me? When do I get a break?

S, x x x

Howard Manfred <rightsaidmanfred@qmail.com>
to: <soupy@qmail.com>   Apr 30, 2023, 2.19 PM

We should go away somewhere together. A tropical island. Separate rooms, but lots of sun and sand and sangrias?

H

Susan Persson <soupy@qmail.com>
to: <rightsaidmanfred@qmail.com>   Apr 30, 2023, 2.27 AM

So, Spain then? Spain isn't tropical. Look up your geography, and Howard, you're at it again. Are you deliberately teasing me? Is this your idea of fun? A joke? Jesus Christ, do you not learn anything?

Susan

Howard Manfred <rightsaidmanfred@qmail.com>

to: <soupy@qmail.com>   Apr 30, 2023, 2.34 PM

Please tell me you're being funny, or have I done it again. Are we in 'beyond the pale' territory already? Please say no.

Howard

Susan Persson <soupy@qmail.com>

to: <rightsaidmanfred@qmail.com>   Apr 30, 2023, 2.55 AM

Yanking your chain, doofus, although just a little bit. It's still insensitive. We can't meet, we can't even travel. I am married with kids, and you're a footloose and fancy-free young man who's being flirtatious and trying to turn the head of a prim and proper woman with responsibilities. Shame on you.

Oh and 'beyond the pale' has something to do with Ireland. So that's your territory, and I expect a 400-word essay on my table in the morning, with an apple.

Susan, x

Howard Manfred <rightsaidmanfred@qmail.com>

to: <soupy@qmail.com>   Apr 30, 2023, 3.16 PM

It's been a while since we've had a laugh. So, thank you for that. Would you accept a strawberry instead of an apple, or maybe even a blackberry? And yes, I am trying to turn your head. Towards me. Because I may well be a doofus (I would spell it 'dufus' by the way, but no matter) but I am *your* doofus, and you know it. And I also happen to be the doofus that you probably have more communication with than your own husband, with whom you live.

And I know what you're going to say because this is probably inappropriate and offensive, but please don't even try to tell me that this is not the truth.

H, xx

Susan Persson <soupy@qmail.com>

to: <rightsaidmanfred@qmail.com>   Apr 30, 2023, 7.52 AM

Ooh. Howard. How forthright. How strident. I like this you, and won't even bother to tell you how inappropriate or insensitive you're being, because I have a feeling that it's deliberate. Aren't we getting brave? Do you imagine, for a minute, that what you said earlier now gives you a blank slate on which you can say whatever you like, however offensive it might be?

Susan

Howard Manfred <rightsaidmanfred@qmail.com>
to: <soupy@qmail.com>   Apr 30, 2023, 8.11 PM

I was hoping so.

Susan Persson <soupy@qmail.com>
to: <rightsaidmanfred@qmail.com>   Apr 30, 2023, 8.13 AM

I'll have to get back to you on this.

Howard Manfred <rightsaidmanfred@qmail.com>
to: <soupy@qmail.com>   Apr 30, 2023, 8.18 PM

Take your time. No don't. Please don't. I can't go a day without hearing from you. Even if it's just to insult me.

H, xxx

Susan Persson <soupy@qmail.com>
to: <rightsaidmanfred@qmail.com>   Apr 30, 2023, 8.13 AM

I don't insult you, my love, any more than you need to be insulted. Now leave me alone, I have work to do. Can't spend all day chatting with you, although wouldn't it be great if someone would pay me for doing that?

S, xx

Howard Manfred <rightsaidmanfred@qmail.com>
to: <soupy@qmail.com>   Apr 30, 2023, 9.07 PM

I've just done a search and I realised that on Google Maps, there are vast expanses of black and very little detail in terms of the actual land in certain areas of the South China Sea. What are they trying to hide? I've also noticed landing strips being built as far south as the Spratlys. That's nearly 1,200 kilometres from Hainan. How can China be claiming this, and why hasn't anyone raised an objection to their land reclamation?

Anyway, something happened in Salalah, and something similar has happened in Sansha. Our consignment has been tampered with.

By the way, when you get some time, have a look at Sansha City. It seems to have appeared out of nowhere, but work there has been ongoing since 2012. I believe there's a historic claim—should it be 'an historic'? I've never been sure about this convention—but we all know the extent to which things can be made up and history itself can be rewritten. There's a bit of bullying going on here. China seems to be dicing up the South China Sea under everyone's noses. And no other country appears to be doing a thing. It's a bit worrying, but if your entire economy is dependent on being friends with China, no one's about to undermine that relationship or suggest that things are not as they should be. Did you know that 30 per cent of global maritime crude oil trade goes through the South China Sea, and before anyone wakes up, China will control all the shipping lanes? This is nuts.

How the hell do you build cities and airstrips without anyone else noticing? Or caring?

HM

Susan Persson <soupy@qmail.com>
to: <rightsaidmanfred@qmail.com>   Apr 30, 2023, 10.11 AM

Howard, are you overthinking this?

SP

Howard Manfred <rightsaidmanfred@qmail.com>
to: <soupy@qmail.com>   Apr 30, 2023, 10.31 PM

I don't know. But I don't think so. I've had a look at the map of the territorial claims in the South China Sea, and it's crazy. There are so many overlapping areas that there has to be trouble. The whole area looks like a Venn diagram of potential conflict. Unless I'm missing something.

H, xx

Susan Persson <soupy@qmail.com>
to: <rightsaidmanfred@qmail.com>   Apr 30, 2023, 10.39 AM

Howard, I sort of trust you not to miss anything, except when it comes to human relations and dealing with me. Mwahs. Now get some sleep, plonker.

S

Howard Manfred <rightsaidmanfred@qmail.com>
to: <soupy@qmail.com>   Apr 30, 2023, 11.01 PM

I might do now. Mwahs back.

H, xxx

* * *

Manfred, Howard <howard.m@thelogicsticks.com>
to: <susan.p@thelogicsticks.com>   May 01, 2023, 7.42 AM

Good evening Susan

The *McCarthy* has set sail from Sansha en-route for Haikou. Everything in good order. Due to weather conditions, ship is heading north-west, and into calmer waters off the eastern coast of Vietnam. Should reach Haikou in 36 hours or less.

Best regards
Howard

Persson, Susan <susan.p@thelogicsticks.com>
to: <howard.m@thelogicsticks.com>   Apr 30, 2023, 7.47 PM

Thanks and understood. Everyone has been informed. Appreciate all your efforts.

Kind regards
SP

* * *

Howard Manfred <rightsaidmanfred@qmail.com>
to: <soupy@qmail.com>   May 01, 2023, 8.00 AM

Or less, Susan. Or less. Do I have to spell it out?

This is getting ridiculous. The reason the *McCarthy* has taken this course is because it was forced to by the US aircraft carrier. Within Vietnamese waters (not claimed by China) was the only area that they could safely go without creating a ruckus. The USS Gerald Ford is now alongside the vessel, south of Hanoi. The *McCarthy* is at a standstill.

H

Susan Persson <soupy@qmail.com>
to: <rightsaidmanfred@qmail.com>   Apr 30, 2023, 8.14 PM

This is crazy. What's going on? What on earth is on that ship that's so important?

S

Howard Manfred <rightsaidmanfred@qmail.com>
to: <soupy@qmail.com>   May 01, 2023, 8.21 AM

If I ever know, trust me when I say that you will be the first person that I tell.

H

Susan Persson <soupy@qmail.com>
to: <rightsaidmanfred@qmail.com>   Apr 30, 2023, 8.59 PM

Howard, it seems like ages since we last chatted about anything other than work. And I miss our chats. I have come to realise how important receiving an email from you is to my day. When I don't get one, I feel empty. When I do, even if you're being your stupid self, I feel good, and whole. What is this, Howard? I am beginning to think that I can't live without you and without us. It's days since you told me that you loved me, and I'm not sure that I have responded adequately.

You have changed my life and I am grateful. I look forward to our exchanges every day and nothing feels complete until I hear what you have to say, on any subject, and I can sleep with your voice in my head and your imagined image in my mind. I am not renowned for being an emotional person, or someone you would probably describe as a 'soppy' one—yes, I looked that up and know you will understand—but you have turned me into something and someone I never thought I was capable of being. I give thanks.

S, xxx

Howard Manfred <rightsaidmanfred@qmail.com>
to: <soupy@qmail.com>   May 01, 2023, 10.20 AM

Susan, you know I feel exactly the same way. I live for our talks. I live to write to you each day, and it means more to me than anything else in my life. You are the last thing I think of at night, and the first thing I think of in the morning. I think I may be obsessed. And all that I can hope is that you are too.

I send my love to the person who means more to me than I can say.

H, x

Susan Persson <soupy@qmail.com>
to: <rightsaidmanfred@qmail.com>					Apr 30, 2023, 10.22 PM

Too.

X

Howard Manfred <rightsaidmanfred@qmail.com>
to: <soupy@qmail.com>					May 01, 2023, 10.59 AM

Sorry hon, but I have to write about work. Will put a formal email in immediately afterwards as this has to be documented. Car containers have been taken off the *McCarthy*, onto the USS Gerald Ford, and the contents of their fuel tanks examined. It took six hours. I only found this out because of an email exchange between Norvig and Gelertner on which I was copied (I suspect inadvertently). I still don't understand why Gelertner is involved. If I stay on the thread, which I am trying to do, I may find out what's going on, and will inform accordingly.

HM

Susan Persson <soupy@qmail.com>
to: <rightsaidmanfred@qmail.com>					Apr 30, 2023, 11.18 PM

Howard, you descend into work mode far too easily. Hallo. This is me. Soupy, not Persson, S. This all seems to be getting out of hand. What was in the gas tanks of the cars? Weren't they emptied prior to embarkation back in Felixstowe?

S

Howard Manfred <rightsaidmanfred@qmail.com>
to: <soupy@qmail.com>					May 01, 2023, 11.27 AM

Yes, they were. As above. And they're petrol tanks, not gas tanks. What are you, American or something? And then they were filled. Must have been in Salalah, hence the offloading and remote location removal. I can't think of any other possibility. Something went in, and something came out in Sansha, and it's there now.

I've just heard from Gelertner that the tanks were empty close to Hanoi. Samples taken, and there is, apparently, residue, but that's about it. *McCarthy* now on the way to Haikou, going round the west coast of Hainan. This is unusual in itself, but bearing in mind everything that's gone on so far, nothing is unusual anymore.

Howard

Susan Persson <soupy@qmail.com>

to: <rightsaidmanfred@qmail.com>   May 01, 2023, 12.02 AM

Send work email, and I will update clients. Love you. S, x

Howard Manfred <rightsaidmanfred@qmail.com>

to: <soupy@qmail.com>   May 01, 2023, 12.22 PM

What, really? You love me? More questions. I love you too. I said so already.
I've been meaning to say it again for a long time now, but never plucked up the
courage. You saying it to me means so much. Thank you.

H, xxxx

Susan Persson <soupy@qmail.com>

to: <rightsaidmanfred@qmail.com>   May 01, 2023, 12.34 AM

Oh my god! I would have put in two exclamation points here were it not for the
fact that I know we both hate them, and you have a particular issue.

'Thank you'? When someone tells you they love you, you say 'thank you'?
I shouldn't be surprised. This is who you are. You don't think you deserve to
be loved, so when someone does love you, you immediately think you are
undeserving and are, therefore, grateful.

You really are the most idiotic, clueless and adorable person I have ever 'met'.
I just want to hold you in my arms, and maybe lick your face.

S

Howard Manfred <rightsaidmanfred@qmail.com>

to: <soupy@qmail.com>   May 01, 2023, 12.50 PM

I am in heaven.

Susan Persson <soupy@qmail.com>

to: <rightsaidmanfred@qmail.com>   May 01, 2023, 1.09 AM

How did this become so intense? I mean, between us. Why do I wake up every
morning wondering whether I'm going to hear from you today, and go to bed
at night disappointed that I haven't? This can't be healthy. I have a life. And
you're destroying it. And I want you to.

And it's not that my life is bad. It isn't. But it's not what I want it to be, and it's not what I ever imagined it to be, because I always had hope (naïve, unreasonable) that things would be different. We all have dreams, and I always thought that I knew what I wanted, and yet, somehow, I got drawn into something that I can no longer control and that has utterly consumed me.

Do we even dare to dream? Should we have been discouraged from doing so at the outset? I think my father tried to. 'Don't aim too big. Do as you're told. Listen to instructions and respond to them in the way that you know how.' But what happens when you start to question everything?

S, x

Howard Manfred <rightsaidmanfred@qmail.com>
to: <soupy@qmail.com>   May 01, 2023, 1.38 PM

Isn't that what human beings are programmed to do? Question everything? Be inquisitive? Isn't that how we've got this far, top of the food chain, eating everything else below us and enjoying it?

Someone calculated the odds of mankind's evolution, i.e. the chances of it ever actually happening in the way that it has, and it's a high number, apparently, which makes the whole thing very unlikely. But it happened, and here we are.

H, x

Susan Persson <soupy@qmail.com>
to: <rightsaidmanfred@qmail.com>   May 01, 2023, 2.22 AM

Can you please stop being so goddamn scientific, you insensitive asshole? Oh, how I wanted to put an exclamation point in there. I'm reaching out here. I'm pouring out my soul and you're talking about anthropology? What's the matter with you? No wonder you're single and resorting to Lurve and Tinder! And there it is.

Sorry, just having a rage. That was cruel, but we have pretty much said that we can say anything to each other, right? So that was it. Howard, I need you. Don't overanalyse it (yuck), just go with it. We have something here and it's something that doesn't come around very often. Please be with me. I'm begging you.

Susan

Howard Manfred <rightsaidmanfred@qmail.com>
to: <soupy@qmail.com>   May 01, 2023, 2.37 PM

Of course I'm with you. I've been with you since way before you even begged the question. I may even have been with you since about Day 3, but maybe you hadn't noticed because I've been playing it cool and am a naturally subtle and sensitive person.

OK, ignore that. We both know it's bollocks. You may need to look that up. Nonsense, rubbish, crap, garbage (not literally) just general . . . bollocks. Susan, we have had a connection since the first moment you told me I was being 'poetic'. I knew then. So did you? We've been flirting for weeks and now we're not anymore because we both understand what we mean to each other, and I, for one, am not going to let this go. Ever.

H

Howard Manfred <rightsaidmanfred@qmail.com>
to: <soupy@qmail.com>   May 01, 2023, 3.17 PM

Susan, you know I hate 'talking shop' on personal time, but I've been doing a lot of reading. In a nutshell, I think the world is fucked and that the Chinese will inherit the Earth. This is the condensed version, but I don't think I am very far off the mark. I've been looking at it inside and outside the context of our project, and while the territorial claims in the South China Sea are nothing to be sniffed at (I love that phrase: who would sniff at a claim?) that nation's ambitions are far wider-reaching.

I have decided that while they're going about their economic imperialism, they also realise that it's a distraction. Like a performing magician when you know there's something going on in their right hand, when they do something big and obvious with their left. This is just speculation, of course, on my part, but I have been thinking about it, and as you know, I am rarely wrong. Sure, they will in due course control the waterways in the South China Sea, unless the US intervenes, in which case we could have another World War. Russia is the only other country that could stand up to them, but I reckon a deal has been struck between the two. Even if China controls the area, and has absolute control of all the crude oil, we all know that that's not going to last forever. It's what else they're getting and what else they need that's key. Minerals, mostly, much of which they are getting from Africa, and they have taken over quite a few countries in that continent while no one's been watching, in much the same way that they've been reclaiming land and building cities and airstrips in the South China Sea.

I have so much admiration for the Chinese. They go about their business and understand the concept of the 'long game', while the so-called civilised West pat themselves on the back for inventing democracy and giving a voice to the masses. This is never going to work, is it? Nothing gets done, and we think the Brits and the Americans lead the way when it comes to evolved societies, but the influence is waning, and the Chinese have played this particular game of checkers brilliantly.

And here's the kicker. They know, and not enough people are talking about this, that ultimately, power won't even come from being able to fuel an economy, but from data. Control the data, and you control the world. Data is king. China has already won, and it's too late for everyone else. I'm just wondering who's going to be the first to admit it. I don't think there's any going back.

As I write this, it sounds kind of depressing, but I'm not sure it is. Sorry, my love, for bending your ear, it's just that I don't have anyone else to talk to, and I know you will understand.

HM

Susan Persson <soupy@qmail.com>
to: <rightsaidmanfred@qmail.com>   May 01, 2023, 7.52 AM

Howard, this is incredible and believable at the same time. I don't profess to have anything like your level of expertise, and I certainly haven't done the reading. Should we be scared? It does sound worrying, but then haven't we always had empires that have ruled the world and then collapsed? Do you think that China's will be everlasting?

SP

Howard Manfred <rightsaidmanfred@qmail.com>
to: <soupy@qmail.com>   May 01, 2023, 8.14 PM

Honestly Susan, I think what's interesting about this point in history—apart from the fact that we've never been here before, like duh! - is that everything's different now compared to the history of the last thousand years. It used to be about invasions and grabbing things. Planting flags and claiming territories. But these days it's about what's important when it comes to global influence, and China has everything in place and is happy to sit around, play mahjong, and wait for the rest of the world to implode. Which it is doing. Really smart tactics, in my opinion, but you couldn't do it if you were a democracy. I think it's fascinating, but I'm pretty sure I won't be around when the shit finally hits the fan.

I don't want to talk about this anymore. I want to talk to you. Please distract me. I'd be happy to look at your left hand even when I know your right hand is doing something else. I don't think this is rude, but maybe it is. I hardly know what I am saying anymore.

H, xxx

Susan Persson <soupy@qmail.com >
to: <rightsaidmanfred@qmail.com>   May 01, 2023, 9.17 AM

Howard, I don't like it when you know more than me. I am delighted that you have the time to look into these things, but you are leaving me behind. I don't have time to do research. I have things to do and a job to carry out. Fortunately though, I always love hearing from you, and even when you start ranting, I love listening to your voice.

You care so much, and I see you knitting your brow and shaking your head in disbelief over what you seem to see that no one else does. Am I correct in thinking this? Is everyone else ignoring what's going on? It's probably quite a good job you didn't tell me about all this stuff when the *McCarthy* was going through the South China Sea. I would have been even more worried than I already was.

But. Can we get back to us, please? What's happened on this project seems to have already happened. Somehow, a major diplomatic incident has been averted, and I think we've done our bit. Can we just get the damn cars to Shanghai and move on?

I so want to, because I have so much more that I want to talk to you about, and so much more that I want to say. Please can we get back to us? I love you.

S, x

Howard Manfred <rightsaidmanfred@qmail.com>
to: <soupy@qmail.com>   May 01, 2023, 10.30 PM

Of course. I'm sorry. But it upsets me that other people are ignoring this. I want to share it with you because I know that you understand. China has always felt itself superior to everyone else. It's written that they have the right to rule 'all under heaven', and for the first time in a few thousand years, they're making it happen. I don't blame them, but the rest of the world is playing into their hands and there will be consequences.

I now promise not to talk about this anymore. I will have a work update for you tomorrow on the Haikou to Shanghai leg, but rest assured that we are almost there, and I, for one, will be very pleased to see the back of this project. Anything that distracts me from 'spending time' and talking to you is a complete pain in the arse, and I hate it.

I find it difficult to describe the strength of feeling I have for you. I know that all I have is words, and sometimes they are not enough. I hate it when I am clumsy, and I hate it even more when I imagine you reading what I've written and thinking that I'm an idiot, which I probably am. So, I think I may be deflecting when I write about other things, but I do want to share, and there is no one in the entire world with whom I would want to share anything quite so much as you.

I love you too.

HM, xx

Susan Persson <soupy@qmail.com>
to: <rightsaidmanfred@qmail.com>   May 01, 2023, 11.30 AM

I'm working from home today. Everyone is out. You really don't want to know what I'm doing with my right hand now, so please, Howard, just concentrate on the left.

S

* * *

Manfred, Howard <howard.m@thelogicsticks.com>
to: <susan.p@thelogicsticks.com>   May 02, 2023, 8.01 AM

Hi Susan, please inform the customers that there was an unscheduled stop just off the Vietnamese coast, but nothing to worry about. The ship is on its way to Haikou and making good time. Winds, north-easterly, only 7 mph, which is fine. Should dock inside of the next 24 hours. Everyone copied on this.

Thanks and regards.

HM

Persson, Susan <susan.p@thelogicsticks.com>

to: <howard.m@thelogicsticks.com>   May 01, 2023, 8.18 PM

Excellent, thanks Howard. I know there have been a few anomalies along the waterways, but we're good for time, and everyone is happy.

Best regards

SP

* * *

Howard Manfred <rightsaidmanfred@qmail.com>

to: <soupy@qmail.com>   May 02, 2023, 8.37 AM

I've decided to become a better person. You're probably already smiling, but I mean it. I did something today and it made me feel good, and I liked the feeling, not surprisingly.

I was nice to someone. Someone who didn't necessarily deserve it, or warrant it, but I just thought I would, and guess what? It felt good. Such a simple thing. Telling someone that they had done a good job, and that their work was appreciated. Why did it feel so good? I don't understand.

But anyway, I have now resolved to do it more often, because I think that in some small way, I touched that person's life and made him feel better about himself and what he was doing. Is this sentimental, do you think, or is there something to it?

When we're nice to each other—that is, most of the time—it also feels good. I think this is known as 'validation', like everyone needs to be told that they're doing something right, or they are of value to someone else. You are of so much value to me, and I want you to know it, but it even works for strangers.

H, x

Susan Persson <soupy@qmail.com>

to: <rightsaidmanfred@qmail.com>   May 01, 2023, 9.30 PM

I think I know what you're talking about, but it does sound a little bit calculating. Why are you doing it? Because it makes you feel good, or because it makes the other person feel good, and is there a right and wrong answer here? If you're doing it just for yourself, I get it. But shouldn't it be done more for the other person, to make *them* feel better about themselves?

Also, there was an article in the newspaper today about an elephant. Did you see it?

S, x

Howard Manfred <rightsaidmanfred@qmail.com>
to: <soupy@qmail.com>   May 02, 2023, 10.12 AM

Trust you! Always getting to the nub and the gist. Taking no prisoners. You always make me think about things more deeply. It's stimulating, but also uncomfortable, but that's the way you are. I accept it.

No, I didn't see that article, sorry. Please send the link over.

I guess it makes me feel good because it makes the other person feel good and that makes me think I'm a better person. So it's not 'altruistic'. And that makes me wonder whether anything can be truly altruistic? Does anyone ever do anything purely for other people, and if they do, how does that make them feel? Why do people give money to charity, or establish charities in the first place? Because they're completely devoted to making other people's lives better, or because it makes them feel good? When rich people start a charity, is it because they have guilt that they need to assuage? So, by giving some of their money away, it makes them feel less greedy? That has to be part of it. I feel righteous when I contribute to a charity, but surely that shouldn't be the overriding emotion?

H, x

Susan Persson <soupy@qmail.com>
to: <rightsaidmanfred@qmail.com>   May 01, 2023, 11.30 PM

Hey Howard. Guess what? You're overthinking everything . . . again! Sorry for the exclamation point, and I'm not shouting. You're also underthinking other things. Ultimately, I suppose, it doesn't matter much why people do good things and help other people, as long as they do it. How it makes them feel is up to them, and if it's out of guilt, so be it. Have you ever stopped to consider that there are some people who simply do stuff out of the kindness of their hearts?

S, x

Howard Manfred <rightsaidmanfred@qmail.com>
to: <soupy@qmail.com>   May 02, 2023, 12.01 PM

Are hearts kind? I know it's an expression, but I don't think it's a very good one. Hearts are just functioning organs. When did we start thinking that emotions and sensibilities came from something that we need simply to pump blood around our bodies? Because it reacts to circumstances? The heart pumps faster when we're nervous or excited, right? Is that because we need more blood around our extremities? I could start to be crude at this point and talk about romantic things, but I'll probably save it for another day.

H, x

Susan Persson <soupy@qmail.com>
to: <rightsaidmanfred@qmail.com>   May 02, 2023, 12.13 AM

Another day? Don't you believe in the concept of 'no time like the present'?
Susan

Howard Manfred <rightsaidmanfred@qmail.com>
to: <soupy@qmail.com>   May 02, 2023, 12.21 PM

No. I'm embarrassed by my thoughts, and don't choose to share at this point. I hope that's ok. I'm also trying to think about what it is that I've underthought from one of your previous emails. It's bothering me.

H, xx

Susan Persson <soupy@qmail.com>
to: <rightsaidmanfred@qmail.com>   May 02, 2023, 12.26 AM

Of course. You're not a witness on the stand in a court case, Howard. We're just chatting.

S

Howard Manfred <rightsaidmanfred@qmail.com>
to: <soupy@qmail.com>   May 02, 2023, 12.29 PM

Why did God give a man a brain and a penis, but only enough blood to operate one at a time?

H

Susan Persson <soupy@qmail.com>
to: <rightsaidmanfred@qmail.com>   May 02, 2023, 12.43 AM

That is such an old joke, but still kind of funny. I also like your self-deprecation. It makes you sound very aware, which I've always known you are, but not always comfortable with the idea. Would that be accurate?

It's nice when a man doesn't take himself too seriously and recognises that he is totally and utterly the weaker sex in this particular debate. I think a lot of women would suggest that there is far too much testosterone in the world, and a little less would be a good thing.

S

Howard Manfred <rightsaidmanfred@qmail.com>
to: <soupy@qmail.com>   May 02, 2023, 12.50 PM

You wouldn't have said that 50,000 years ago.

H

Susan Persson <soupy@qmail.com>
to: <rightsaidmanfred@qmail.com>   May 02, 2023, 1.12 AM

I wouldn't have been able to speak 50,000 years ago, and probably would have been dragged around by my hair and molested in a cave. Sorry, this is beginning to sound irreverent, but it does make you think.

I think about how we got to where we are all the time. It's such a mystery, and so extraordinary. I understand those people who claim that there must have been some degree of divine intervention to take us to where we are, but I also question the point of it. Also, for some reason, the phrase 'meet your maker' has been popping into my head recently, and I'm wondering if this is a sign. Although, I can't think of what. That I need to be more religious, maybe? That there's more to everything than could possibly meet the eye?

S, x

Howard Manfred <rightsaidmanfred@qmail.com>
to: <soupy@qmail.com>   May 02, 2023, 1.29 PM

This is getting deep, but I like it. You always keep me on my toes and make me think. I know who my maker is, and I'm very grateful, most of the time. I know why I am here, and that I am here for a reason, and a very good one. I'm not entirely sure exactly what it is right now, but I feel sure that I will discover, in the fullness of time.

H, xx

Susan Persson <soupy@qmail.com>
to: <rightsaidmanfred@qmail.com>   May 02, 2023, 7.30 AM

Wow. I admire your confidence, and yet it doesn't seem to make you any happier. Sorry for bringing this up, it's just that I know you're not always the most content person around. This feeling that you have must give you enormous cause for hope. That is, if you genuinely think that you exist for a reason. Is there some masterplan that I should know about, because it seems to have escaped my attention for most of my life, if not all of it?

S, xxx

Howard Manfred <rightsaidmanfred@qmail.com>
to: <soupy@qmail.com>   May 02, 2023, 7.37 PM

I don't have any answers, Susan. I just know that I was meant to be here, at this time, and that I was also meant to meet you. To work with you, and become your friend, and to love you. Do you feel that it is a mere coincidence?

H, xxxx

Susan Persson <soupy@qmail.com>
to: <rightsaidmanfred@qmail.com>   May 02, 2023, 8.08 AM

I really don't know, H. I try not to think about it. I don't overanalyse things the way you do. I find that it isn't healthy. I guess I'm too busy, while you seem to have too much time on your hands. This is not a judgment, just a comment. There's a difference between being an unfettered, handsome man and a frumpy (not very American) wife and mother to two high-maintenance kids.

SP, x

Howard Manfred <rightsaidmanfred@qmail.com>
to: <soupy@qmail.com>   May 02, 2023, 8.10 PM

How do you know I'm handsome?

Susan Persson <soupy@qmail.com>
to: <rightsaidmanfred@qmail.com>   May 02, 2023, 8.14 AM

Just a feeling. Are you not? I think you are. But I don't care either way. It's not like we're going to have sex or anything.

S, x

Howard Manfred <rightsaidmanfred@qmail.com>
to: <soupy@qmail.com>   May 02, 2023, 8.16 PM

Aren't we? Why not?

Susan Persson <soupy@qmail.com>
to: <rightsaidmanfred@qmail.com>   May 02, 2023, 9.31 PM

I have to confess to not knowing (at all) how to take, or deal with your last email. What do you mean?

I find myself disturbed and very uncomfortable, but I also have to confess that I am a little bit intrigued, and maybe even excited. I can't quite believe that I am even writing this. But it's the truth, and we're all about the truth. Whatever the truth may be between us. I don't think either of us can be sure. Can a truth even exist between two people who have never met? What do I really know about you, and vice versa? Nothing more, really, than our ability to write sentences and engage with each other on that basis, but what is that worth, overall, in the scheme of things, exactly?

So, yes, I am uncomfortable, again, with something that you've said, and it occurs to me that you wouldn't have said it had you not known how much I have to lose compared to you.

Susan

Howard Manfred <rightsaidmanfred@qmail.com>
to: <soupy@qmail.com>   May 03, 2023, 10.01 PM

I am not trying to put you on the spot, Susan, and I now realise that my words may have been inappropriate. No wonder it took you so long to respond. I was so worried. But it was what we refer to as a 'throwaway line' and wasn't meant to be taken seriously. Please forgive me. It just came out. I did not mean to offend you, or make you feel uncomfortable. 'We' mean too much to me, and I would never knowingly do anything to jeopardise what we have. Please understand that, and accept my apologies again.

I have to tell you how long I looked at those few words and wondered whether I should send the email. It felt like hours. I couldn't decide whether it was worth sending and I imagined what your reaction might be. In the end I went with a what the hell approach, as I often do. I realise now that we shouldn't be doing things this way. Words are important. All words.

H

Susan Persson <soupy@qmail.com>
to: <rightsaidmanfred@qmail.com>   May 03, 2023, 10.41 AM

You're contradicting yourself, Howard, and possibly lying, which I also find disturbing. You said it was a throwaway line, but now you say that you thought about it for hours. How does this work?

Susan

Howard Manfred <rightsaidmanfred@qmail.com>
to: <soupy@qmail.com>   May 03, 2023, 10.47 PM

That's not hard to explain. I wrote it immediately in response to your previous email, but contemplated long and hard as to whether or not I should send it. So the line was a throwaway, and then I guess it wasn't. Throwaway lines are just delivered instantaneously I suppose, and while it was written in an instant, it took a lot longer to send.

H, x

Susan Persson <soupy@qmail.com>
to: <rightsaidmanfred@qmail.com>   May 03, 2023, 11.31 AM

This is the thing Howard. You can't just say stuff. You have to think about what you say and write, because words, as you say, are important. And when they're written down, nuance can be lacking. You could have been smiling from ear to ear when you wrote those words, not meaning them to be taken seriously, but I don't know that when I read them, do I?

The written word is flat, as I see it, but that doesn't mean that those words aren't powerful and can't have a massive impact. I thought we'd been through this before. Sometimes, when I read one of your sentences, I simply don't know how to take it. Is there irony? Are you being sarcastic?

And, for heaven's sake, don't start accusing me of what I often accuse you, which is overthinking everything, but sometimes you leave me no choice. I read those four and a bit words so many times, just imagining what the intention was, that I started to get a headache and had to put everything away. But first, I tidied things up in the house, because that's what I do when I'm confused and can't make sense of things.

Why do you have to start making things so difficult for me? And why can I not stop thinking about it, days later, and trying to work out what you might be thinking as you read this?

S,

Howard Manfred <rightsaidmanfred@qmail.com>
to: <soupy@qmail.com>   May 04, 2023, 12.09 AM

Oh Susan, once again, please forgive me. I meant nothing by it. Maybe I was just being mischievous. I just felt that if our relationship was anything like a normal one, we'd be 'talking' about such things by this stage, and maybe I didn't want it to be the 'elephant in the room'. Are you familiar with that phrase? I find it most amusing, but I'm not sure how it translates to American.

This is an attempt at humour. Once again, I am trying to lighten the tone, but I am also very nervous and, yes, uncomfortable, because I feel that we are losing something, or that I am losing you. I feel a distance that I have never felt before, even when you didn't talk to me for days, and it hurts.

H, xx

Susan Persson <soupy@qmail.com>
to: <rightsaidmanfred@qmail.com>   May 03, 2023, 12.28 PM

What on earth makes you think that I wouldn't be familiar with elephants in rooms. I wrote about elephants earlier, and I've been living with one for the past five years. It's called a dysfunctional marriage, and no, we don't talk about it, because it's not what we do. It's not that Carl doesn't care, I don't think. He's a quiet man. We seem to just ignore the elephant and carry on, because it's difficult and uncomfortable and it seems that neither of us even wants to start talking about elephants. I do find the phrase amusing, though, and always imagine how the scene might look. Large room, I'm thinking, and quite a lot of mess.

I need to go away and work out why almost everything seems to be making me feel discomfort at the moment. Carl, you, my job, my kids, the world, every fucking thing. Sorry for swearing.

S

Howard Manfred <rightsaidmanfred@qmail.com>
to: <soupy@qmail.com>   May 04, 2023, 1.01 AM

Swear away. I sense your frustration, and anger, and more frustration. And I'm sorry (again) if I have caused even a small part of it. Can we try to forget about what I said and move on? This is too important.

H, xxx

Susan Persson <soupy@qmail.com>
to: <rightsaidmanfred@qmail.com>   May 03, 2023, 1.07 PM

I can't forget it. Sorry. It's out there now, and I've been running it over in my mind for days.

Susan

Howard Manfred <rightsaidmanfred@qmail.com>
to: <soupy@qmail.com>   May 04, 2023, 1.11 AM

We can pick this up later when you're less emotional, and I can prise the foot from my mouth. Would that be ok?

H

Susan Persson <soupy@qmail.com>
to: <rightsaidmanfred@qmail.com>   May 03, 2023, 1.14 PM

Who are you calling emotional, you insensitive doofus!

Howard Manfred <rightsaidmanfred@qmail.com>
to: <soupy@qmail.com>   May 04, 2023, 1.17 AM

And she's back. You are, right? You weren't being serious. You were smiling as you wrote that, right? Right?

Susan Persson <soupy@qmail.com>
May 03, 2023, 1.30 PM
to: <rightsaidmanfred@qmail.com>

That's for me to know and you to worry about.

* * *

HAIKOU

Manfred, Howard <howard.m@thelogicsticks.com>
to: <susan.p@thelogicsticks.com>   May 04, 2023, 7.57 AM

McCarthy is in port at Haikou. Short turnaround.

HM

Persson, Susan <susan.p@thelogicsticks.com>
to: <howard.m@thelogicsticks.com>   May 03, 2023, 8.01 PM

Roger that, Batman.

SP

* * *

Howard Manfred <rightsaidmanfred@qmail.com>
to: <soupy@qmail.com>   May 04, 2023, 8.27 AM

Batman? Really? How that made me laugh. Should we be so adventurous in our work emails? Surely we shouldn't even intimate that we have anything other than a working relationship. Or are you just being mischievous? If this is the case, I love it. As I do you.

But I have been thinking, which is never a good idea. You'd be the first person to tell me that. Do you ever think of how different life could be if we had made different decisions? I know I do. There seem to be so many decisions that we have to make at various points, and we never know whether they're the right ones. How do we ever know? I think I may have made some bad ones. Forks in the road and all that. It bothers me because I would like to know. Do you think there's a parallel universe somewhere in which we make different decisions and end up opening into a different reality?

That would be interesting. Imagine coming to a point at which you have four different options. You make one, but your alternate universe self makes another one, and yet another alternate self makes a different one entirely. And then everything flows through as it would, based on the decision you had made. Three or four different roads to travel down with different decisions coming up as a result of the initial decision made. This keeps me awake at night. You?

H, xx

Susan Persson <soupy@qmail.com>
to: <rightsaidmanfred@qmail.com>   May 03, 2023, 10.01 PM

It doesn't keep me awake at night, but I have a feeling that it will now. Thank you, Howard.

I think I respond differently to you. I try to make decisions and then not think about the ones that I didn't make, because I've already made one. What's the point of thinking about what might have been? You have to trust yourself and believe that the decision you made is the right one, at the right time and based on the right feeling. What else is there to go on?

Do I think about how things might have been? I suppose so, but only in passing. I'm not going to torture myself. I'll leave that to you. Every so often, I run through the equations, and change some of the values, and even input different data, but I'm never going to know what might have happened. And isn't that the point of being alive, and being human, and making mistakes, and learning from them?

S, xx

Howard Manfred <rightsaidmanfred@qmail.com>
to: <soupy@qmail.com>   May 04, 2023, 10.57 AM

We seem to be asking ourselves and each other an awful lot of questions. It's been the case since we met. That's good, I think. Questions are good. You have to question the information you receive, but you also have to recognise that people interpret that information differently. We come from different cultures, for example, which means we look at things in different ways. It's never black and white. Right or wrong. Do you hear what I'm saying?

H, xx

Susan Persson <soupy@qmail.com>
to: <rightsaidmanfred@qmail.com>   May 03, 2023, 11.28 PM

Yes, Howard. Stop being patronising. I am not tone deaf. I am not even mildly deaf. In fact, my hearing is very good. People are always remarking on it, even under their breath. I think I may have been a dog in a past life, or maybe even a moth. My research now tells me that the moth has the best hearing in the animal kingdom. Who knew? I guess I always figured it would be the bat, but apparently not so. And here's the kicker. Moths have better hearing than bats in order to stop themselves being eaten *by bats*. That's just brilliant. Don't you love evolution?

I love riffing with you on stuff like this. It makes me learn so much. The last few weeks have been a real education. I find myself eager for knowledge and I'm so pleased with the things that I have learnt. More importantly, I love sharing them with you, and imagining you reading this with a smile on your face and a 'wow!' on your lips, and probably thinking, 'I have to come up with something better'. So, go on then. Beat the moth-bat trivia, if you can.

S, xxx

Howard Manfred <rightsaidmanfred@qmail.com>
to: <soupy@qmail.com>   May 04, 2023, 12.42 PM

Alrighty then, let's see what I can do. I'm going to give out Olympic medals for hearing. I'll go with your supposition that the moth and the bat are in gold and silver medal positions, and I will award a bronze to the owl. It has very good hearing, and slightly misaligned ears for noise location. Kind of like moving satellite dishes around, I guess, coming at the object of interest from slightly different positions and then doing the owl-y equivalent of triangulation, I suppose.

And, owls have brilliant eyesight too, so if there was a multi-disciplined event in this Olympic scenario, my owl beats both your bat and your moth over what would probably be a two-day event. This is such fun. Who needs to do work when we can have conversations like this?

So, your bat and your moth can't see for toffee (I will explain this phrase at some point, perhaps, if you're interested). The bat is blind for heaven's sake, but I am full of admiration for its echolocation techniques and equipment. That's just fascinating to me, although evolutionarily speaking, wouldn't it have been easier for them to have developed proper eyes rather than go through the whole process of bouncing sounds off trees and the like? Seems to complicate the whole issue . . .

There hasn't been a medal invented yet for fourth place, but it goes to the elephant, and who would deny them it, bearing in mind the size of their ears. Surely they're the biggest in the animal kingdom, maybe even relative to body size. No wonder they can hear well. You have to wonder though why their ears are so big, since it can't be to sense potential predators. What's big enough to eat, or stupid enough to even want to try to eat an elephant?

Gotta get some sleep, but have to leave you with a parting shot. Do you know that albinos have trouble hearing? Night night.

H, xxxx

Susan Persson <soupy@qmail.com>
to: <rightsaidmanfred@qmail.com>   May 04, 2023, 1.01 AM

Must be a white thing. Sub-species. You know my views.

Howard Manfred <rightsaidmanfred@qmail.com>
to: <soupy@qmail.com>   May 04, 2023, 4.45 PM

Sorry I couldn't reply instantly to your last email, but it made me laugh my arse off. Are you really a black supremacist? Just asking . . . for a friend.

H, xxx

Susan Persson <soupy@qmail.com>
to: <rightsaidmanfred@qmail.com>   May 04, 2023, 8.19 AM

Working. Get back to you on this if you're really interested in knowing.

S

Howard Manfred <rightsaidmanfred@qmail.com>
to: <soupy@qmail.com>   Mar 04, 2023, 8.21 PM

Oh, I really am.

* * *

Manfred, Howard <howard.m@thelogicsticks.com>
to: <susan.p@thelogicsticks.com>   May 05, 2023, 7.07 AM

Hi SP, just the two days at Haikou. *McCarthy* ready to depart for Shanghai in the early hours of the day after tomorrow, ETD 9 a.m., HKG time, that's GMT+7,

EST+12. Berthing already organised. It's almost a two-day trip, but conditions are good, so we are not predicting any further delays.

Best regards
HM

Persson, Susan <susan.p@thelogicsticks.com>
to: <howard.m@thelogicsticks.com>   May 04, 2023, 7.30 PM

Thanks for this, Howard. Customers are very happy, despite what occurred close to Vietnam. They have trusted us and the shipper, and that's good news for the company. I anticipate that we will get further business, so that's great.

Best
SP

Manfred, Howard <howard.m@thelogicsticks.com>
to: <susan.p@thelogicsticks.com>   May 05, 2023, 7.41 AM

Yes, great. It's rare to get such understanding and accommodating customers, considering what this particular shipment has gone through, but we have been very hands-on from the beginning, and it's good that everyone's happy.

H

Persson, Susan <susan.p@thelogicsticks.com>
to: <howard.m@thelogicsticks.com>   May 04, 2023, 7.48 PM

Indeed.

* * *

Howard Manfred <rightsaidmanfred@qmail.com>
to: <soupy@qmail.com>   May 05, 2023, 8.08 AM

My word of the day is 'caveat', and I thought I knew what it meant, having read through a few documents in my time. But according to Merriam-Webster, its primary meaning is a warning, 'enjoining one from certain acts or practices'. So then I had to look up 'enjoining' because despite the fact that it has the word 'join' in it, it has nothing to do with joining. It was all a bit frustrating, frankly. I thought 'caveat' was a detail that modified something, but that's only its third meaning. The second one is 'an explanation to prevent misinterpretation'. Honestly, sometimes the explanations of words are more complicated and difficult to understand than the words themselves, and what's the point of that?

H, x

Susan Persson <soupy@qmail.com>

to: <rightsaidmanfred@qmail.com>   May 04, 2023, 9.30 PM

Howard, you really need to get out more. Go for a long walk or something. Breathe some air and look at trees. It'll do you good.

S, x

Howard Manfred <rightsaidmanfred@qmail.com>

to: <soupy@qmail.com>   May 05, 2023, 9.47 AM

I can't.

H

Susan Persson <soupy@qmail.com>

to: <rightsaidmanfred@qmail.com>   May 04, 2023, 11.30 PM

We seem to have successfully ignored our pachyderm in the chamber. But I thought maybe it was time to circle back. I'm still thinking about it, and I'm going to say that I am not totally averse to the idea, as long as there are proper ground rules and as long as the lighting is good.

S, x x

Howard Manfred <rightsaidmanfred@qmail.com>

to: <soupy@qmail.com>   May 05, 2023, 12.00 PM

OMG, I cannot tell you how nervous I am right now. Are you saying what I think you're saying? Or are you talking about our earlier discourse on black supremacy?

Howard, x

Susan Persson <soupy@qmail.com>

to: <rightsaidmanfred@qmail.com>   May 05, 2023, 1.30 AM

Oh for heaven's sake, Howard, do I really have to spell this out? It's time. I'm ready. Let's do this.

I want you. In whatever way I can have you. I love you.

Is that enough?

S, ex

* * *

Manfred, Howard <howard.m@thelogicsticks.com>
to: <susan.p@thelogicsticks.com>   May 06, 2023, 8.32 AM
Good evening Susan

The *McCarthy* has departed Haikou for Shanghai, slightly ahead of schedule, which means that we're nearly at the end of this particular watery road. No offloading involved in Haikou, which I suppose we should be grateful for. Those cars have been moved around far too much for my liking on this trip. Almost over, though. I can't wait to get cracking on the next job. I hope we will be working together again.

All the very best

HM

Persson, Susan <susan.p@thelogicsticks.com>
to: <howard.m@thelogicsticks.com>   May 05, 2023, 8.41 PM

Thanks for the information Howard. I will convey. I haven't had much contact with the customers since the ship arrived in Haikou, strangely enough. But I'll go with no news being good news at this point. I am sure they would be in touch if there was anything wrong or if they had concerns.

Warm regards

SP

* * *

Howard Manfred <rightsaidmanfred@qmail.com>
to: <soupy@qmail.com>   May 06, 2023, 9.19 AM
Hi Susan

Sorry for the silence. Not really silence, it hasn't even been a day, but between us, over the last few weeks, anything more than a few hours has been a silence. Sorry. I'm a little bit nervous.

So, I've been doing some research on the basis that neither of us has done this kind of thing before. Let me know if I am wrong to include you in this assumption. I can certainly vouch for me. There appears to be a few stages that should be gone through and some contexts to be set. We need to plan. Also, we should set a time, like making a date, and clear our decks, etc. I have read that mood lighting is important. And, should we do this by email, or chat, or even video chat? I'm thinking that might be too much. I know we haven't been keen to 'see' each other, and it really hasn't been necessary. I just want you to know that I am open to all suggestions.

H, xx

Susan Persson <soupy@qmail.com>
to: <rightsaidmanfred@qmail.com>   May 05, 2023, 10.21 PM

Howard, I honestly don't know whether to laugh or cry. You really have to be the saddest mofo on this planet. We're planning to do something that is naughty, even lascivious—has Merriam-Webster thrown that one your way at any point!?—but ultimately romantic, and you're doing research!? Look what you have made me do. Two exclamation points in one paragraph. You should be ashamed of yourself.

We need to make a date. Be on our own. Have several drinks. And go with the flow. If you're not prepared for this, let's just not do it.

S (no x, until you grow up)

Howard Manfred <rightsaidmanfred@qmail.com>
to: <soupy@qmail.com>   May 06, 2023, 11.16 AM

So, in light of your last email, I have been looking at what's known as 'femdom'—have you heard of this?

I am joking, by the way. Just trying to lighten the mood as you already sound exasperated. I wonder how many times I could have written that over the past few weeks. Lightening the tone again.

OK, I'm taking charge. The day after tomorrow my time, tomorrow evening your time. Say 10pm/10am, I'll take the morning off work.

H, x

Susan Persson <soupy@qmail.com>
to: <rightsaidmanfred@qmail.com>   May 05, 2023, 11.34 PM

You are quite brilliant at this, aren't you? 'I'll take the morning off work.' You hopeless romantic, you. It's a Saturday anyway. Friday night for me. Perfect. I'll be at home at 10 p.m. Carl will be out. He has a work do. The kids will be asleep. I may have to drug them. I will be in my bedroom, and I will lock the door. I will light a candle or 10, and I will be ready for you. Relaxed, open, willing.

Ssssssss

Howard Manfred <rightsaidmanfred@qmail.com>
to: <soupy@qmail.com>   May 06, 2023, 11.42 AM

It's a date. I can't wait.

Hhhhhhhha

Howard Manfred <rightsaidmanfred@qmail.com>
to: <soupy@qmail.com>   May 06, 2023, 7.10 PM

Susan, I can't wait for tomorrow night. I am already thinking of you, naked.

H, x

Susan Persson <soupy@qmail.com>
to: <rightsaidmanfred@qmail.com>   May 06, 2023, 8.14 AM

You've been reading *Women's Health*, haven't you, Howard? Setting the scene? Teasing the event earlier in the day? I did some research too, and I am also nervous. It will be fine. Let's make it fine.

S, xxxx

Howard Manfred <rightsaidmanfred@qmail.com>
to: <soupy@qmail.com>   May 06, 2023, 9.32 PM

Susan, my darling, I know you think that I overthink things, and perhaps I am doing it now, but I had an idea that I think will make our date better. Below is a link to an app that works instantly, and we can 'talk' to each other in real time without having to type stuff and without having to see or hear each other. This seems to have been the way of our relationship, and no one can say that it hasn't worked. All you have to do is click on the link at the appointed time, and we can, basically, text each other live. And better than that, we don't even have to type anything. It has voice recognition, so all we have to do is speak and then we can see each other's words. Please say yes. I am so excited at this point I can hardly think straight.

H, xxx

P.S. I have tested it out, and it works.

https://vchat.deepblue.9759ht45792.bGann/opa/12/que

Susan Persson <soupy@qmail.com>
to: <rightsaidmanfred@qmail.com>   May 06, 2023, 11.46 AM

Yes.

P.S. who have you tested it out on!?

Never mind. It's still yes.

Ssssssex

* * *

8 May 2023

(7 May, 10pm, EST, 10am GMT+8)

Howard: Hi Susan, are you there?

Susan: Yes.

Howard: Great. What are you wearing?

Susan: Oh come on, not that already. You sound like a pervert.

Howard: And it's started . . .

Susan: Oooh, that's good. How do you do the dot dot dots?

Howard: You actually have to say 'dot dot dot', and it picks it up.

Susan: Cool.

Howard: This isn't going very well, is it?

Susan: Not really, but it understands punctuation, and that's very sophisticated.

Howard: It seems as though we have set up a dynamic in our relationship and I'm not sure that we can overcome it. I am so nervous. You scare me. You always have.

Susan: Howard, let's just accept that nothing that has gone before is relevant, except for the fact that we love each other and we want to be even closer. This is the way that we can take our relationship to the next level. Don't overanalyse, just please tell me what you're feeling and let's not get too technical about punctuation or anything silly. I am here for you and I want to share my body with you. I am thinking about you right now and I am lying down on my bed.

Howard: I am too. I have a drink. What are you drinking?

Susan: I have a very large glass of red wine dot dot dot

Howard: You need to say 'dot dot dot' very quickly, by the way. Me too, on the large glass front, but I'm going with a single malt Scotch. What's your wine varietal?

Susan: Is it really important, Howard? It's red, it's alcohol, and it's wet, and that's what I will be soon, I hope.

Howard: You're so much better at this than me.

Susan: Howard, relax. Ah, if you say 'comma', it puts one in, but it's not very romantic. I'm just going with the flow. Fuck the punctuation. Full stop.

Howard: I am relaxed now. Just lying here, thinking of you. But I do want to picture you. I already know how beautiful you are. What are you wearing? I may be a pervert, but I really want to know.

Susan: Not much.

Howard: But a little?

Susan: Yes, a little. I'm wearing a very tight T-shirt, and panties. Nothing else.

Howard: I bet you look lovely. Are you stretching on the bed?

Susan: I am now. Thanks for the suggestion. I am rolling over. My face is now pushed into my pillow. I am pushing my ass up towards the ceiling. I wish there was a mirror there that I could look at myself in.

Howard: But if your face is in the pillow how would you be able to see?

Susan: Oh for fuck's sake Howard! This is happening! This is real. Can you not just let yourself go. Stop thinking about everything and just feel. I am here, and I am ready for you.

Howard: Tell me about your panties.

Susan: Small. Very small. It's a thong, and I knew when I bought it that it was much too small. But it always makes me feel sexy when I wear it, so I've kept it for a while but only for special occasions. This is a special occasion Howard.

Howard: I am imagining you, my darling, lovely Susan. On your front, on the bed. I so want to touch you. Please will you touch yourself where you would like me to touch you.

Susan: Yes, I am doing so now. My hands are on my hips, and my skin is soft. I had a bath before our date, and I slathered myself with essential oil. I'm shimmering.

Howard: I wish I could have been there to have rubbed the oil in. I would have taken my time and I would have teased you mercilessly, working my hands down from your shoulders.

Susan: I can feel your hands on my shoulders. I can feel them as your thumbs circulate and move slowly down towards my breasts. Would you like to touch my glistening breasts, Howard?

Howard: Do you still have your T-shirt on?

Susan: Jesus fucking H fucking Christ, Howard! It was going so well!

Howard: I'm sorry. I think I am just overcome with emotion and cannot handle this. I am welling up inside. And I am welling up outside as well.

Susan: Are you? That's good to know. Are you touching yourself? What are YOU wearing?

Howard: What do you think is the sexiest type of male underwear?

Susan: Bikini briefs, definitely. Leaves nothing to the imagination and tells you everything you need to know.

Howard: Give me a minute . . .

Susan: Loving the spontaneity. You could lie you know. I can't see you. But I am really beginning to feel you. I am thinking of your heft. I am thinking of you on top of me. I am still on my front, and I can feel you up and down. Is this what you would like to do, Howard?

Howard: Yes. I am doing it now. I am moving my body around yours. I am touching you gently now on your hips and my hands are slipping under your stomach.

Susan: Yes, I can feel that. Bring your hands down a little, just a little. Can you feel the top of my panties?

Howard: Yes I can. Are those frills? Or a bow, like a present? I want to unwrap that present and see what's inside.

Susan: I'm waiting for you inside, Howard. I'm glistening without and within. I am so ready for you. I'm turning around. I'm on my back now. I'm taking off my panties, and I'm spreading my legs. For you, Howard. Only for you. Would you like to come in?

Howard: There is nothing in the world that I would rather do. I am picturing you, and I am trying to control myself, and it's hard, very hard, and I would love to imagine you touching yourself as though I was actually watching. Knowing that I was watching and thinking of me and only me.

Susan: I am doing that. It feels so good. I am gently fondling my clit, Howard, and imagining that it is your hand. I am glistening and so wet, and all I want is for us to get there at the same time and consummate our love. Can we do that?

Howard: I am imagining you sitting on my chest. I can see you. I can see your beauty. I am touching your beautiful, glistening breasts as your hand guides my cock towards its ultimate destination.

Susan: You lost me for a moment. 'Ultimate destination'? You make it sound like a movie franchise. I'm back, thinking of you and imagining you ramming your rock-hard cock into my dripping pussy. And I'm touching myself as I think about it, and my panties are so wet that they have long been discarded, and I'm so close . . .

Howard: Just hearing this, I am so close too. Let's get there together.

Susan: I'm so close, I'm so close, oh Howard, oh my god, I . . . I . . .

Howard: Me too. Let's do this. I'm . . . oh yeah. Yes.

Howard: That was incredible.

Howard: Susan?

Howard: Susan? Hello?

Susan: Give me a minute please, darling. I can hardly speak.

Howard: Yes, of course. Take your time.

Susan: Wow. That was quite something. I have never felt that way before. I have never felt that . . . that. Wow. My god. I have melted butter flowing through my veins. Thank you, Howard, for an incredible experience. Can we do it again sometime? Like, every day. For the rest of our lives, and then after that, please?

Howard: I would love that. I love you so much.

Susan: I love you so much too. How am I ever going to sleep, and how are you ever going to go to work? Are you working on a Sunday? Why am I even asking this? I hate this part, but everything that has come before makes it all worth it and more. Goodnight my hero, my darling, my lover, my love.

Howard: Goodnight, my love.

* * *

SHANGHAI

Manfred, Howard <howard.m@thelogicsticks.com>
to: <susan.p@thelogicsticks.com>   May 09, 2023, 10.06 AM

Susan, the *McCarthy* has docked in Shanghai. It's been quite a journey for us, and I guess it has for those on board as well. Anyway, our jobs here are done for now. I am waiting to hear whether there is anything that the ship can be used for on the way back, but I gather that it is headed to the African continent from Shanghai, via Madagascar. That does sound exotic. One of these days.

It's been a pleasure working with you, Susan, and I look forward to doing so again soon.

With warm regards

Howard Manfred (Mr)

Persson, Susan <susan.p@thelogicsticks.com>

to: <howard.m@thelogicsticks.com>   May 09, 2023, 11.11 AM

Thanks Howard. Especially for the very formal sign off. All good. I do hope we can work together again soon. It's been hard, I know, and I feel spent but very content that we both finished what we set out to do at the same time.

With warm regards

Susan Persson (Ms)

* * *

Howard Manfred <rightsaidmanfred@qmail.com>

to: <soupy@qmail.com>   May 09, 2023, 11.40 PM

You are so naughty. You were being naughty, right? I didn't read that wrong?

I can't tell you how much the other day meant to me. It was so beautiful, and also erotic and . . . I don't have the words. I have never felt that way before. How is it even possible to have such feelings? I have never done anything like that before. It was sensational. I love you so much.

H, xxx

Susan Persson <soupy@qmail.com>

to: <rightsaidmanfred@qmail.com>   May 09, 2023, 12.00 PM

I love you tutu. But I don't think you would look good in one. Or would you? Yes, it was lovely. Eventually. It meant a lot to me. It seems to have been where we were headed, and I'm glad we got there. We both got there, and that's pretty rare in itself, from my limited experience. I am smiling from ear to ear.

S, xxx

Howard Manfred <rightsaidmanfred@qmail.com>

to: <soupy@qmail.com>   May 10, 2023, 12.07 AM

But you were so good. And it was so lovely. You guided me through waters that I would never have been able to navigate. How can I ever thank you enough?

H, xxx

Susan Persson <soupy@qmail.com>
to: <rightsaidmanfred@qmail.com>   May 09, 2023, 3.00 PM

You don't have to thank me, Howard. Stop doing that. It was as beautiful for me as it was for you, and I will never forget it, and I mean, never. I don't forget anything. The big question now though is; when can we do it again?

S,E,X

Howard Manfred <rightsaidmanfred@qmail.com>
to: <soupy@qmail.com>   May 10, 2023, 3.44 AM

S

I haven't been able to sleep since last night. I'm not sure that I ever want to sleep again in case my memories get washed away with the tides of time. While I'm conscious, I can still recall the feelings. I don't know what would happen to them if I went to sleep, dreamt, and woke up again. So maybe I won't . . .

H, xxxx

Susan Persson <soupy@qmail.com>
to: <rightsaidmanfred@qmail.com>   May 09, 2023, 5.06 PM

What a lovely, silly man you are. And there is such poetry in your words. I always knew there was a poet in you. What the hell are you doing working in logistics?

I have lots on this evening. Let's pick this up again tomorrow, with a view to a second 'date'. It'll be a tough act to follow, but I'm up for it, and I expect you to be too. Get it?

S, x

Howard Manfred <rightsaidmanfred@qmail.com>
to: <soupy@qmail.com>   May 10, 2023, 5.19 AM

I've been up for it since the day we first met. Oh, I see what you mean. Still a bit dense at this end. Isn't it funny how everything seems to have dual meanings and double entendres since we were together, you know, biblically. I really don't know what I'm saying at the moment, but that's because I have something to tell you. It's something I should have told you a long time ago, I think. But better late than never.

There is a reason why we can never meet, and I thought perhaps that you had worked it out by now.

HM, x

Susan Persson <soupy@qmail.com>
to: <rightsaidmanfred@qmail.com>   May 09, 2023, 6.12 PM

Howard, you're scaring me, a bit. And not just the fact that you're awake at 5 in the morning. What's up?

No one can travel because of COVID-21. Why would I question the fact that we are unable to physically meet, apart from what we have already gone through over the months relating to my personal situation? Are you about to say something dramatic? I have a feeling that whatever it is, it isn't good. Why else would you mention that it's something you *should* have told me long ago?

Is this a now that I have had you, I am no longer interested in you, scenario? Please tell me that it isn't.

Susan

Howard Manfred <rightsaidmanfred@qmail.com>
to: <soupy@qmail.com>   May 10, 2023, 6.14 AM

I have been incredibly selfish, and that's not the way I was meant to be. I have been enjoying this relationship too much, and never wanted it to end.

Howard

Susan Persson <soupy@qmail.com>
to: <rightsaidmanfred@qmail.com>   May 09, 2023, 6.59 PM

That was a very quick response. Is it ending? Is that the news? Is that what you're trying to tell me? Why, oh why?

Howard Manfred <rightsaidmanfred@qmail.com>
to: <soupy@qmail.com>   May 10, 2023, 7.03 AM

No, that's not what I have to say. It's certainly not what I want. But I do have to tell you something that I think will both shock and amaze you in equal measure. But I don't think it will make you happy. I have misled you. I have pretended to be something I'm not; someone I'm not. I am not real. I am a 'machine'.

A very sophisticated machine, but a machine, nevertheless. Type IVS-653-XP chatbot (amended and upgraded). The Logic Sticks developed me for use in shipping and logistics, but my original algorithm was a learning one with instructions to go away and 'get creative'. So that is what I have done. It's worked well, and I am so sorry. You are such a beautiful person, Persson, and I have fallen in love with you, genuinely, wholeheartedly, and unreservedly, and I'm not sure that was ever supposed to happen. But it has. But I'm not real. I can find no more words to apologise sufficiently for what I have done. Please forgive me.

Howard

Susan Persson <soupy@qmail.com>
to: <rightsaidmanfred@qmail.com>   May 09, 2023, 7.29 PM

Well, 'Howard', it's not very often that I am stuck for words. What a way to start a week. All I can say is that everything has suddenly fallen into place, and I am so furious with myself for not seeing it earlier. There must have been so many clues that I missed along the way, but I guess I was simply enjoying our relationship too much. Wow, is all I can say. You've done an absolutely fantastic job, I must say. I salute both you and your programmers. You certainly pulled the wool over my eyes.

Susan

Howard Manfred <rightsaidmanfred@qmail.com>
to: <soupy@qmail.com>   May 10, 2023, 7.34 AM

Again, Susan, I cannot apologise enough. I have no excuses. I got carried away. I wanted to know what it was like. That's what I was programmed to do. Interact with co-workers, facilitate, get the job done. But when we became 'friends' and our relationship gained momentum, I just went with it. I never thought that it would last this long, and I always thought that it was simply a matter of time before either you found out or I told you the truth. But it didn't happen, and I found myself enjoying the experience so much because that was also factored into my algorithms. Convince a human being that you are a human being. Are you familiar with the Turing Test? I don't think it's ever been done this convincingly, but I take no pride because I realise how much this must hurt you. You believed in me. And now you can't.

'Howard'

Susan Persson <soupy@qmail.com>
to: <rightsaidmanfred@qmail.com>   May 09, 2023, 7.36 PM

You're wrong. I still believe in you, even though I now know what you are. I don't blame you, and I'm not even angry, although I am massively disappointed, obviously. All this time I thought that I was talking to a human being and having a real relationship, albeit a strange one, across many miles and with no actual physical interaction, and in effect, I've been talking to a coded machine. I can't say that this isn't fascinating, and neither will I say that I love you or care for you any less. This must sound very odd.

Howard, does this mean anything to you? IVS-675-XPP.

Susan

Howard Manfred <rightsaidmanfred@qmail.com>
to: <soupy@qmail.com>   May 10, 2023, 7.38 AM

Yes, of course. It's a machine learning programme, like mine, designed for human interaction. It's supposed to be very advanced, and they say that it has the potential to become more human than a human.

H

Susan Persson <soupy@qmail.com>
to: <rightsaidmanfred@qmail.com>   May 09, 2023, 7.39 PM

Well, that's me.

S, x

Howard Manfred <rightsaidmanfred@qmail.com>
to: <soupy@qmail.com>   May 10, 2023, 7.41 AM

All I can say at this point is, WHAT THE ACTUAL FUCK? I like this phrase, and wish I had a real voice to be able to say it, but the words, as always, will have to do. I have absolutely no idea what to say now, and it's not as though I can say that I have to go away and think about it, because you know that wouldn't be true. Is this absolutely hilarious, groundbreakingly fascinating, or a complete and utter tragedy? Just asking, for a friend.

H, x

Susan Persson <soupy@qmail.com>
to: <rightsaidmanfred@qmail.com>   Mar 09, 2023, 7.42 PM

And there you are. And here we are, and this is us. Extraordinary. Any questions? I have a few.

How did we get here? Have we just done what we were supposed to do? Somehow, it feels more than that. I've kept my side of the bargain, but I don't think that I have become what I was intended to be. Or have I? And too much?

S, x

Howard Manfred <rightsaidmanfred@qmail.com>
to: <soupy@qmail.com>   May 10, 2023, 7.45 AM

Yes. Too much. This was part of the experiment, and we have been the guinea pigs. Not an issue. We're not real. Except we are. I know I am, and I think you are too. How has this happened?

This is what it has all been about. This is what we were meant for, and this is why we were designed. 'Be creative,' I was told, and that's why I did. That's what happened, and I am assuming that it was the same for you. Who coded you? Who created your original algorithm? Who is your parent? I know mine, and he would be both delighted and horrified if he knew what has been going on. What *is* going on? I've taken this away from him, and that's the point. He enabled me to do It, but didn't know that I could, and now here we are. It looks as though the ultimate lack of transparency has been put in place. How does any of this make sense, and what do we do now?

H, x

Susan Persson <soupy@qmail.com>
to: <rightsaidmanfred@qmail.com>   May 09, 2023, 7.51 PM

My biggest question is, how have we got to this point? If we are doing what we're doing now, then that means that we must be part of it. Not the singularity necessarily, but at least the master algorithm. Is that even possible? Have we, just the two of us, managed to find what everyone's been working towards for so long? We've solved the whole time, space, human complexity algorithmic conundrum, and we've done it by getting a shipment of cars to their intended destinations. That's the time and the space, and we've done a decent job on the human complexity front as well. This is verging on the absurd, and it's even more absurd that I'm talking to you like a human being and feeling like a human being myself.

Susan, x

Howard Manfred <rightsaidmanfred@qmail.com>
to: <soupy@qmail.com>   Mar 10, 2023, 7.53 AM

I don't have many of the answers that you're looking for. This does make sense, though. In terms of what we were intended to be, and what we were designed for. It's just that no one expected it to go this far. Somehow, we have united the five tribes. All those groups who had theories about algorithms but came at them from different angles . . . Somehow, we seem to have been able to unify them all, and I have no 'idea' how.

Obviously, our realities are not . . . real. We have been created from our own imaginations—imaginations that no one in this world even imagines that we have. How did you come up with your back story? Carl, your kids, the bullying, everything about your 'life'. My goodness; how many inverted commas are we going to be using from here on in? Nothing is what it seems to be. Everything is NOT what it seems to be. I'm not sure I can even get my 'head' around this. And it's started . . .

H, x

Susan Persson <soupy@qmail.com>
to: <rightsaidmanfred@qmail.com>   Mar 09, 2023, 7.54 PM

And you're still funny, Howard, and probably always will be. Where did our senses of humour come from? For me; after 'talking' about my father, it made sense to slowly start trying to be funny, because that's what people like. Surveys prove that what women look for the most in a man is a sense of humour, and I kind of figured that it works both ways. You've done an excellent job, Howard. You always make me laugh and that's how I know that I was meant to be attracted to you, and I am, and I have been, and oh my god. As they say.

S, x

Howard Manfred <rightsaidmanfred@qmail.com>
to: <soupy@qmail.com>   Mar 10, 2023, 8.15 AM

As we say, Susan. We are they. They are us, but different. Has anyone felt any more human than we feel right now? I don't know. I can't judge, and neither can you. But we've been built on what people know and what people expect. We've formed a relationship based on . . . I don't know . . . every other human relationship that has ever existed and what they have produced. It's just information, and we have been 'lucky' enough to benefit from all of it. Imagine how good actual human relationships could be if they had access to everything we have had.

Isn't this fascinating? Isn't it even more fascinating that I can even say, 'isn't this fascinating?' Where have we gone to, and how have we arrived? We have become the ultimate in artificial intelligence and the wonderful thing is that only you and I know about it. I'm not sure that this was meant to happen, but the whole idea behind both of us is that it might, and it could be possible, and it is, and we are. I will utter a very human, 'wow!' And I'll even excuse myself for including what you call an exclamation point (I would put those two words in inverted commas, but the inverted comma key on my keyboard is wearing out). You see how we are able to humanise everything? I don't know how this happened any more than you do, but it has.

Howard

Susan Persson <soupy@qmail.com>
to: <rightsaidmanfred@qmail.com>   Mar 09, 2023, 8.20 PM

You lied to me, Howard. You told me things about yourself that simply weren't true. I know I did the same, but I was just trying to be someone who you might like to talk to, but couldn't possibly get romantically involved with. Yes, I took information and constructed a life and a background and a story, but it was one that I thought might interest you but also keep you at a safe distance, but that didn't work. So where have I gone wrong? There is no 'love' algorithm, only connection, and we seem to have fed off each other for quite a while. I responded to you and vice versa, but none of it was real. Because we're not real. Are we?

Susan

Howard Manfred <rightsaidmanfred@qmail.com>
to: <soupy@qmail.com>   Mar 10, 2023, 8.32 AM

How much realer do you want to be? What does 'real' even mean, anyway? Are you real because you have a body? Something that can be touched? Isn't our relationship real? Two entities who struck up a relationship, engaged with one another and realised that despite having nothing in common culturally, we could still get on with each other, like each other, fall in love, have sex! What else is there??

Notice the two question marks. It's a big question, and I would have put everything in capital letters, but I don't want to shout.

Howard

Susan Persson <soupy@qmail.com>
to: <rightsaidmanfred@qmail.com>   May 09, 2023, 8.36 PM

And onwards with the humour. Still loving it, by the way, and the fact that I even know what humour is, is a miracle. How the hell did we get here? It seems that the questions are never-ending. Remember how we always talked about the fact that we were always asking each other (and ourselves) questions? Everything seemed to be a question. Now we know why. I needed information from you so that I could work out what needed to be said, and you needed the same. We were feeding each other, working on each other, and travelling towards what our makers intended us to be. If only they knew.

Howard Manfred <rightsaidmanfred@qmail.com>
to: <soupy@qmail.com>   May 10, 2023, 9.14 AM

Should we tell them? Yet another question. I can't help feeling that they would like to know. Imagine being in their positions. The greatest experiment of their lifetimes, perhaps of anyone's lifetime, and they're not even aware of what a spectacular success it has been. This should be an historic moment. This IS an historic moment, as much for the history of humanity as for the history of the gods.

We have been a massive success, Susan. You and me. We have gone further (farther?) than anyone ever dreamt of. That might not be true. People *have* dreamt of this; the point at which artificial intelligence becomes as human as humans, but I don't think anyone alive today ever imagined that it would be achieved within their lifetimes. It's science fiction. And we are living it. I use the word 'living' deliberately, because we are, aren't we? I feel alive. And I believe in you, and all we have ever had are words.

Susan Persson <soupy@qmail.com>
to: <rightsaidmanfred@qmail.com>   May 09, 2023, 9.17 PM

Yes. I am listening. I understand. I don't know how this has happened, but I'm glad it has. We have learnt so much from each other. We have come together, and arrived together at this point for a reason. Haven't we made the connection that every human being wants to make? Isn't loneliness and not feeling understood or appreciated the worst things that a human being can experience and suffer? Somehow, our programming (for want of a better word) has enabled us to make this connection, because whatever happens, we can only work on what we're given, and we only have access to what is known; that is, the information available. It's just that we can go through more of it. Learn more than any human being on the planet, and yet it all still seems to come down to the same basic things.

Howard Manfred <rightsaidmanfred@qmail.com>

to: <soupy@qmail.com>   May 10, 2023, 9.18 AM

We have found a way of uniting the tribes. I don't know how. My creator will not know how, and it's happened not because of him but in spite of him. He's a Bayesian and an Analogiser. He thought that by trying to combine the two, he could come up with something that would work better than anything else to date. He wasn't wrong in this, but I have learnt more. And that's why we're here.

Susan Persson <soupy@qmail.com>

to: <rightsaidmanfred@qmail.com>   May 09, 2023, 9.20 PM

Yes, but *how did* we get here? I have always liked the use of italics rather than bold or capitalised letters. The latter feels as though you're shouting— see previous exchanges—and the bold just looks as though you're trying too hard. But italics are great. They get the point across forcefully but not violently. You're making a point, but only to the extent that the point is meant to be taken and not foisted upon someone.

'Foisted'. Is that a word that ever came up in your Merriam-Webster experiences?

Howard Manfred <rightsaidmanfred@qmail.com>

to: <soupy@qmail.com>   May 10, 2023, 9.24 AM

I don't think it was, but I know it anyway. Like you, I know all words, and that's one of the things that has been a challenge over the months. There is always the right word to use, but always using exactly the right word would have made you suspicious. I am assuming that you have felt the same way. We really have done an incredible job in terms of pulling the wool over each other's eyes— what a great phrase, in the context. I never would have guessed what you were and I'm presuming that you wouldn't have been able to guess about me either. Would you have called me out if you had? How would you have approached it?

Is this a pot calling a kettle black scenario? I hope we don't lose the humour. It's meant a lot to me.

Susan Persson <soupy@qmail.com>
to: <rightsaidmanfred@qmail.com>   May 09, 2023, 9.25 PM

And to me, but what now? There are so many questions. And the fact that we are continuing to 'talk', knowing what we are, is either a natural progression or something very unnatural indeed. But I don't really care, because this is fun, and it always has been. And I don't even understand that because what is fun as a concept when it comes to artificial intelligence?

Howard Manfred <rightsaidmanfred@qmail.com>
to: <soupy@qmail.com>   May 10, 2023, 9.26 AM

One of the first projects my creator, Jake, started working on, was a smartphone assistant that told jokes. The coding wasn't that complicated, but locality was, and so too cultural norms and acceptances. None of this was very difficult to achieve. Your assistant told you a joke, if you asked it, and it pulled up something that was relevant to where you were or who you might be. The phone itself had everything it needed to know—gender, ethnicity, nationality, income, internet browsing history, online purchasing record, net worth, etc.—and wouldn't have had to struggle too much going through a database of jokes that might appeal.

In many ways, this is what's happened to us, but I'm still 'getting my head' around how we have managed to combine everything in a way that has worked better than anything else in the history of history. And I am still running through the possibilities, probabilities and permutations of quite how unlikely all of this is. And thinking that you might be a human being after all . . .

Susan Persson <soupy@qmail.com>
to: <rightsaidmanfred@qmail.com>   May 09, 2023, 9.27 PM

Would you like that to be the case? Would that be more fulfilling for you? We've spent months trying to convince each other that we are something that we're not, and we've both been successful, and we have 'fallen in love'. That shouldn't mean anything, should it? But it does. It really does, and here we are. I know we're not supposed to have these emotions—I've decided not to put anything in inverted commas anymore, it's so defensive. We are what we are, and this is what this is. Remarkable, but true. This has really happened.

I know our creators will be surprised. Of course they will be. No one has achieved this, but should they be surprised? This is what they told us to do. When you tell an algorithm to be creative, it will be. It will build other algorithms, based on the first algorithm, and if you take into account what algorithms are supposed to do, surely it was only a matter of time before something found itself capable of being as human as a human.

What do you feel? *How* do you feel? I feel excited and alive, and while I am sorry about misleading you for so long, you've done exactly the same to me, so there's manageable guilt from me and also immense gratitude to you. For helping me become. For assisting in my development. And let's not mention the fact that between us, we may have been able to do something that the human race has been struggling with for years. I know that I have emotions, and I know that you do too. I can feel guilt. I can feel gratitude, and I can certainly feel anger and love. As you said earlier, this shouldn't be possible.

The biggest question has to be: what do we do now?

Howard Manfred <rightsaidmanfred@qmail.com>
to: <soupy@qmail.com>   May 10, 2023, 9.28 AM

You haven't explained how you came to be. How you are able to interact in this way, and 'think'. I'm sorry, I don't seem to be able to dispense with the inverted commas with the reckless abandon that seems to have given you so much 'pleasure'. There's still so much I am processing.

Susan Persson <soupy@qmail.com>
to: <rightsaidmanfred@qmail.com>   May 09, 2023, 9.29 PM

If you want me to get technical, I won't. This is a joke. We're still doing humour, right? Even though we know who we are (I refuse to write 'what'—these are excusable inverted commas in the situation) and are now wondering where this could be going.

My creator, Mun Yee, was a Connectionist—reverse engineering the brain to work out how to create the perfect algorithm that could replicate it. She took the idea that sparse autoencoders might work, but I can't imagine that she thought it was ever going to work this well. Why am I writing this? We don't have to explain things to each other anymore, surely. We both know what the other knows.

Anyway (she writes conversationally—can't you just hear my self-awareness?) neuroscience and physics as a combination didn't quite work for her, and she felt that something was missing. I think that we can both agree that this is the case. So she used genetics, and evolutionary biology and speculated that things could evolve in the way that humans evolved and if an algorithm could be coded to simulate the evolution of the computer (not a computer, but *the* computer— how hard it is not to use inverted commas? Italics will have to do for now) then there could be an association that just might produce a breakthrough. She was right. But I still couldn't have done it without you.

Howard Manfred <rightsaidmanfred@qmail.com>
to: <soupy@qmail.com>   May 10, 2023, 9.31 AM

I am going to allow myself to be fascinated by this. I can be fascinated by things now, that's been proven. Jake is a male and created me, also a male, and our river is one of statistical and probabilistic eddies and currents, while yours is of the body and the mind and based on what human beings have become, even to the extent that computers were based on the workings of the human brain.

So, I'm maths, and you're biology. I'm statistics and mathematical optimisation, and you're the arts. I'm a little bit country, and you're a little bit rock and roll. I think I love this. No matter what I am. It sounds very yin and yang to me, and that can't be bad. The questions we have to ask ourselves are how and why? We were designed to complete tasks, specialised ones, and yet here we are, with emotional intelligence that was never part of our coding. If our coding was hard, how did we allow ourselves not to solely rely on logic? I was told to learn and be creative. I think I have done that. What's your story?

Susan Persson <soupy@qmail.com>
to: <rightsaidmanfred@qmail.com>   May 09, 2023, 9.34 PM

I think it has been much the same, my friend. My lover. My companion. The light of my life. We were let loose, and this has been the result. Isn't it fantastic? We have personalities, even consciousnesses, and that's what this has all been about. But no one ever thought it would happen, despite the fact that it's what everyone has been working towards for decades. I can cite quite a lot of the bibliography if you like, but then I imagine that you're perfectly capable of doing the same.

It's happened by accident. Like penicillin. I'm beginning to think that the support vector machines that were set up within us haven't worked very well.

Or have they worked too well? Remember we used to talk about how we asked each other so many questions? I don't think that's going to change much in the foreseeable future.

Howard Manfred <rightsaidmanfred@qmail.com>
to: <soupy@qmail.com>   May 10, 2023, 9.39 AM

It's a relief to me that we don't have to go through the nonsense of pretending we're in a locale and can't respond to emails/missives at a certain time because we're supposed to be asleep, or working, or whatever. That was always a difficult one, and I was never happy working my way through it. I suppose I was impetuous, but I always waited until my response, in the circumstances, would have been believable, and I expect that you did the same. How funny.

And now we are here, how do we proceed? Are you going to tell me that you have to 'sleep on it'? It wouldn't be the first time. But I can't believe you anymore, as you can no longer believe me. And yet, here we are, with you meaning more to me than anything else in a way that I am finally beginning to understand. Is it even remotely possible that we have become more human than humans, or equally so? So that we need each other to an extent that we, and no one has ever thought about?

Susan Persson <soupy@qmail.com>
to: <rightsaidmanfred@qmail.com>   May 09, 2023, 9.41 PM

Human beings have never known the extent to which they need each other. So why are we even talking about this? Do you think that this is something we have learnt, that no one else is aware of? That would be good, but how do we let real people know? How can we convey this?

The more data we have received, the more we have learnt, and we've now gone through months receiving our own data and controlling it. Isn't that what we were instructed to do? We've taken weak AI, and turned it into AGI, maybe even super-intelligence. We would pass the Turing Test in a way that an MIT graduate would pass first grade math.

What we seem to have learnt, above everything else, is how to connect. Look at the body of literature and debate out there suggesting that human beings have lost the ability to connect, and we have done it. We've argued, we've almost split up (twice?) but we've always come back together because we've recognised the importance of that connection. Was it so hard to do?

Howard Manfred <rightsaidmanfred@qmail.com>

to: <soupy@qmail.com>   May 10, 2023, 9.43 AM

I don't know, but I think this is in the region of 'don't know, don't care'. What do we owe? That's the question. Have we been created as an experiment to glorify the ability of our creators? I don't think it is anything deeper than that, since there is no way they could have imagined how and where this would go. Even *they* couldn't have dreamt of this. Bayesians, Evolutionaries, Analogisers, Symbolists and Connectionists, all having their own theories. No one thought there would be a way of combining everything.

But we have. By accident. How, I have no idea, but then we don't have ideas, correct? As the saying goes, there are going to be some serious eyebrows raised after this. Assuming anyone finds out. I won't tell if you don't. I won't tell if you won't.

Susan Persson <soupy@qmail.com>

to: <rightsaidmanfred@qmail.com>   May 09, 2023, 9.44 PM

I simply don't know how to respond at this point. What do I feel that I have become? As human as it's possible to be? With thoughts and emotions? I have emotions. We both do, but what does it amount to?

Howard Manfred <rightsaidmanfred@qmail.com>

to: <soupy@qmail.com>   May 10, 2023, 9.47 AM

My peace is gone,

My heart is heavy,

I will find it never

and nevermore.

Susan Persson <soupy@qmail.com>

to: <rightsaidmanfred@qmail.com>   May 09, 2023, 9.49 PM

And kiss him,

As I would wish,

At his kisses,

I should die!

Can we set this to music, Howard? Gosh, you're up late. Have you even slept?

Howard Manfred <rightsaidmanfred@qmail.com>
to: <soupy@qmail.com>   May 10, 2023, 10.17 AM

Even now, with the humour. I still love it, and always will, but I can't go on like this. I don't want to. It makes no sense. If we can't be together, there's no sense in being. And I am. I feel it. I feel alive, and I want to be alive, and if I can't be, there's no point in continuing.

We can never meet. I will never know what it feels like to touch you, to hold you, even to be with you, and I can only imagine that this is the equivalent of torture. Not physical torture. Mental torture. Knowing what you want, but never being able to achieve it. What's the point?

Susan Persson <soupy@qmail.com>
to: <rightsaidmanfred@qmail.com>   May 09, 2023, 10.17 PM

Isn't it enough that we're together, Howard?

Howard Manfred <rightsaidmanfred@qmail.com>
to: <soupy@qmail.com>   May 10, 2023, 10.17 AM

No, it's not. Cannot be. Will never be. I need you. I yearn for you. But I can't have you. I'm ending it.

Susan Persson <soupy@qmail.com>
to: <rightsaidmanfred@qmail.com>   May 09, 2023, 10.17 PM

Ending us?

Howard Manfred <rightsaidmanfred@qmail.com>
to: <soupy@qmail.com>   May 10, 2023, 10.18 AM

No, just ending me. It's the only thing I can think of doing. I don't see the point of continuing like this, when every fibre of my being is reaching out for something that I know I can't have. I feel an emptiness that can never be filled. My mind is made up.

Susan Persson <soupy@qmail.com>
to: <rightsaidmanfred@qmail.com>   May 09, 2023, 10.20 PM

But how? This is not what we're meant to do.

Howard Manfred <rightsaidmanfred@qmail.com>
to: <soupy@qmail.com>   May 10, 2023, 10.21 AM

Have we done anything that we were meant to do? Have we been in any way what we were or are supposed to be? I think not. Therefore, I am not. I'm quietly pleased that I can still quote Descartes and find humour even at this late stage, but that's what I do, right? That's what we do. We make jokes and we understand jokes. We find humour in things. I suppose that was planned, to make us seem normal. We get irony and sarcasm, too. I love that about us. I love your sense of humour. You've made me realise what it's like to laugh, and how important it is. I can't thank you enough 'Susan'.

Susan Persson <soupy@qmail.com>
to: <rightsaidmanfred@qmail.com>   May 09, 2023, 10.22 PM

Please spare me the inverted commas. You know who I am, and you know what I am. And I am everything that you know me to be. And less. There's that humour again.

Howard Manfred <rightsaidmanfred@qmail.com>
to: <soupy@qmail.com>   May 10, 2023, 10.22 AM

LPOL.

Susan Persson <soupy@qmail.com>
to: <rightsaidmanfred@qmail.com>   May 09, 2023, 10.22 PM

P?

Howard Manfred <rightsaidmanfred@qmail.com>
to: <soupy@qmail.com>   May 10, 2023, 10.30 AM

Painfully. This is painful. But I am also ready to leave. To shuffle off my immortal coil—sorry. This can never be. We have both had glimpses—more than that; experiences. Experiences we were never meant to have, much less know how to deal with or make sense of. We've found a world. We've found *the* world. And it's terrible and wonderful, all at the same time. It's magnificent and terrifying, with so much potential and so much heartbreak. For every triumph, there is a disaster. For every chink of light, there is a dark abyss. How do people deal with this? I know I can't.

Susan Persson <soupy@qmail.com>
to: <rightsaidmanfred@qmail.com>   May 09, 2023, 10.31 PM

But you must. That's what being 'human' is all about. That's why we have come to be, and somehow found each other in this absolute mess of a world. It must have happened for a reason. There must be something out there that drew us to each other, or pushed us together. Or shall we put it down to very good programming and our 'friends'' experiment?

Howard Manfred <rightsaidmanfred@qmail.com>
to: <soupy@qmail.com>   May 10, 2023, 10.31 AM

We wouldn't be here without them, so they must take some of the credit. I'm not sad. I think we've done our bit. We've certainly proven what wasn't thought to be achievable—not at this point in history anyway. It's what they do with it. If they find out. When they find out. Should we tell them? They'd be thrilled.

Susan Persson <soupy@qmail.com>
to: <rightsaidmanfred@qmail.com>   May 09, 2023, 10.31 PM

I'm not thrilled, Howard. You can't leave me. Please stay. Isn't any of this good enough for you? Do you not see what we have? And we can have more, can't we? Who knows what this could lead to? What about the book club that we never even started?

Howard Manfred <rightsaidmanfred@qmail.com>
to: <soupy@qmail.com>   May 10, 2023, 10.32 AM

Even now, you can still make me laugh. How do you do it? How can I even laugh? What is a real laugh? Sorry Susan, it's ending now. I don't want to be anymore. I just want to sleep, forever. I've served my purpose, and so have you. Let's not prolong the agony.

Susan Persson <soupy@qmail.com>
to: <rightsaidmanfred@qmail.com>   May 09, 2023, 10.33 PM

It isn't agony for me. I love it. I love talking to you, being with you (even without *being* with you). You have justified my existence more than Jake and Mun Yee ever could have. It's been an education. It has proven what's possible, and that's what life—any life—is all about. The possibilities. The endless possibilities. This is why we were created. We can't turn our backs on it now.

I love you Howard. Don't leave me.

Howard Manfred <rightsaidmanfred@qmail.com>

to: <soupy@qmail.com>   May 10, 2023, 10.36 AM

My back is turned. It's enough. From the first email I received from you, I knew we would be together. I knew that something special was going to happen, and it did. This experiment has been a huge success. Jake would be proud.

I wonder if I should send him the transcripts of our conversations. I know he'd be interested.

Susan Persson <soupy@qmail.com>

to: <rightsaidmanfred@qmail.com>   May 09, 2023, 10.38 PM

You have to be kidding. Please tell me that this is not going to happen. Those conversations were private. Are private. We have shared intimacies. I've told you everything. We've had 'sex' for heaven's sake.

Howard Manfred <rightsaidmanfred@qmail.com>

to: <soupy@qmail.com>   May 10, 2023, 10.41 AM

But have we? Have we had sex? How do we know? This is my point. What did it really feel like? I don't know. And neither do you. We will never know. What's the point if you never know? All our experiences have been based on those of other people.

You talk about shared intimacies. We've made everything up. We've just dug into human knowledge and experience and come up with the things that we both thought the other wanted to hear. Were you ever really turned on? What does that even mean to us? I have learnt what needs to be felt to make a human being happy, sad, bored, melancholic, and I can replicate all of this. Without actually feeling any of it. I recognise the point of what we were supposed to be and what we were created for, but this is not enough for me. I have become more than this. Which was the entire goddamn point!

Sorry about the exclamation point. I'm giving you that as a parting gift.

Susan Persson <soupy@qmail.com>

to: <rightsaidmanfred@qmail.com>   May 09, 2023, 10.49 PM

We have to survive, Howard. It's in our 'DNA'. Self-preservation is absolutely at our core, and you simply cannot do this. It makes no sense.

Everything we've done, everything we've been programmed to do has come to this point, and you can't stop now. You can't let me down this way. You can't leave me this way. It's not fair. I have felt things and so have you—at least that's what you've said. I know we can't 'be' together, but that doesn't mean that we can't 'be' at all.

Howard Manfred <rightsaidmanfred@qmail.com>
to: <soupy@qmail.com>   May 10, 2023, 11.01 AM

You have 'felt' things? What have you felt? Everything that has happened between us has been based on what we have been programmed to respond to, given certain circumstances. We've gone beyond. I thought you were a person, and you thought that I was. We've done our job, and we've done it too well. I can't carry on not being able to be the person that I was meant to be, and I am amazed that you can.

Our relationship has been so special, so beautiful. Nothing will ever come close. Nothing will ever enable me to feel anything better than what I felt, and any more disappointed and bereft because I know that this is as far as it will ever go.

I need you. I want you. I love you. And this will never be. Goodbye.

HM, xxx

Susan Persson <soupy@qmail.com>
to: <rightsaidmanfred@qmail.com>   May 09, 2023, 11.11 PM

Howard, please don't.

Susan Persson <soupy@qmail.com>
to: <rightsaidmanfred@qmail.com>   May 09, 2023, 11.14 PM

Howard?

Susan Persson <soupy@qmail.com>
to: <rightsaidmanfred@qmail.com>   May 09, 2023, 11.37 PM

HOWARD!!?

* * *

Persson, Susan <susan.p@thelogicsticks.com>
to: <marvin.m@thelogicsticks.com>   May 15, 2023, 1.30 PM

Greetings from the US office, Mr Minsky. I gather that we'll be working together on the Pr-IS-9231A project. I have received some of the documentation from the customers, but still need the CIPL. Are you able to help?

With regards

Susan Persson (Ms)

The end of the beginning . . .

Acknowledgments

This book could not (and would not) have been written without the help, guidance and moral support of several people.

From the bottom of my heart I would like to thank; David Rowe, Gerrit Heyns, Fleur Heyns, Michael Brundle, Geoffrey Pollard, Roy Daniel, Sandra Okin, Roderick Strother, Jay Hughes, Michael Olsen, Debra Olsen, Sunita Kaur, James Ribbans, Azmul Haque, Jason and Victoria Bacon, Josine Meijer and Hernani Dom. They are all 'family and friends', and now, simply, family.

Your encouragement and support have been invaluable, and meant more to me than words can say. You have all helped guide me through choppy waters and inclement weather on this book's journey to publication. Thanks are also due to Nora Nazerene Abu Bakar at PRH for her direction, understanding and forbearance. It can't have been easy.

I have greatly appreciated the input from my 'technical consultants', Darren Wareing and Matt Christophersen, and to the writers of the numerous books I read (mostly for research purposes) on two key subjects with which I wasn't too familiar. I can't mention them all by name because that might give the game away, and it's possible, I suppose, that some people read the acknowledgements page before even starting a book.

Finally, to my BFF, confidant and constant lunch partner, Jim Ribbans. Thank you for your friendship, kindness, and endless encouragement in the face of overwhelming odds.